Praise for Cordelia Kelly

An imaginative take on the teen-vampire trope with plenty of action and romance and a compelling antihero

— Kirkus Reviews on *The Well of Souls*

Atmospheric descriptions, vividly portraying tempestuous weather and the eerie ambiance of Duchesne Island, heighten the suspenseful mood. A gripping read that seamlessly blends adventure and emotion.

— Bookview Review on *The Well of Souls*

Stellar fantasy of a young woman facing a curse and daring to rebel.

— BookLife by Publisher's Weekly on *The Sibyl and the Thief*

Dynamic characters galvanize this entertaining, well-paced magical tale.

— Kirkus Reviews on *The Sibyl and the Thief*

OTHER BOOKS BY CORDELIA KELLY

The Sibyl and the Thief

In the Port of Lost Souls series:

1 The Well of Souls
2 The Carnival of Fools
3 The Seabourne Legacy
4 The Salt Roses

Short story collections and anthologies:

Then She Said Hush
Goblincore
Prairie Witch
Dark&Stormy

The Carnival of Fools

A Port of Lost Souls Novel

Cordelia Kelly

BCP

For Élodie and Alexandre

Duchesne Island

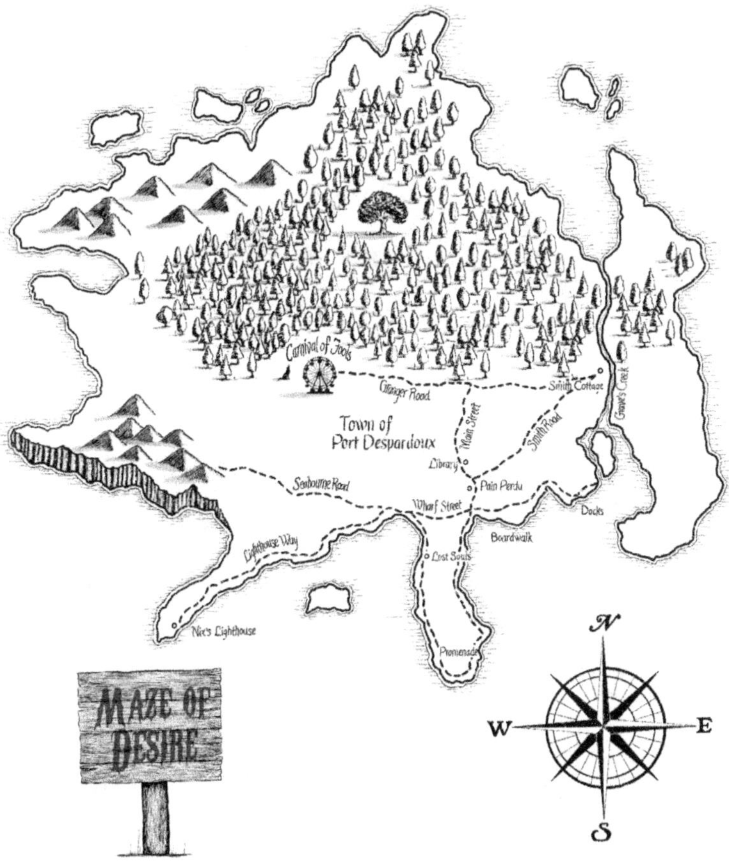

Prologue

Six minutes to midnight. The summer heat was stifling warm and thick with enchantment. Men cursed as they struggled over a dusty patch of earth, and the shrill squealing of a pig broke the hush of the night air.

The abandoned field was lit only by the stars overhead. A man paced a circle, the brittle grass crunching under his heavy foot.

"Hurry up, hurry up." His voice came out a snarl. "If the ritual is late, we'll lose the whole month."

The woman kneeling on the ground glared at him, her shaggy bangs falling into her face. Despite the darkness, her black eyes glittered as though lit from within. "The magic can't be rushed."

"You're well aware we're on a deadline. You've done this enough." He tapped his boot against the ground, sending up puffs of dirt. "Are you sure this is the right place?"

With the scratch of a match, the acrid tang of sulphur floated in the air. A candle guttered then held, forming a weak circle of light.

Her grin stretched wide, teeth flashing like a wolf scenting blood. "This is it." Her outstretched hand formed a claw over the earth, her voice coming out a rasp. "I feel it. It calls to me."

She lifted a butcher's knife from the ground. "The time is ripe. Bring her to me."

The men clustered behind them hesitated. Dressed in shabby workers' clothes, their heavy boots shuffled against the dirt, but no one moved.

The woman's eyes narrowed. The woman hissed, a sibilant curse in a foreign language. The men jolted as though struck by lightning, then lurched forward as one.

With muffled swears, they hauled a massive squealing pig towards the clearing. The woman stood as they approached, staring into the sky at something none of them could see, chanting low and fast, echoes of ancient spells on her lips.

"This place." She let out a long breath. "I've never felt such power."

The man was at her side in an instant. "What do you mean?" They couldn't afford any hiccups in the plan. "Will it slow us down?"

"I mean, there's magic here; it goes down and down, stretching back millennia. There are forces here I've never encountered."

"Is that going to be a problem?" He took out his pocket watch; they had a schedule to keep.

Her eyes opened, locking gazes with him. "Not a problem, darling. An opportunity."

He tilted his head as though examining a new angle, always on the lookout for fortune's favour. He brought a heavy hand to the back of her neck and tilted her head back. "Explain."

"The power in this island could fuel us for centuries. No more scrabbling for our next meal; no more pulling up stakes month after month. We could rule here." She lowered her voice to a whisper. "Immortal."

His hand tightened for a breath. "Immortality? I didn't think it was possible."

Her eyes narrowed. "You doubt me?"

"After all we've been through? Of course not. You've never steered me wrong."

"Then trust me. With enough power, anything is possible."

"Why have we never come here before, then? If all this power has been lying around for centuries, we could have capitalized sooner."

"No." She waved her sharp-taloned finger in his face. "This place was protected, hidden away. But something has changed. No longer guarded, the power seeps from the earth like an oil spill."

"That is why you were so insistent we come out to this God-forsaken island?"

"*All* will be forsaken by the time we're through with it." Her teeth shone in the candlelight. "And we will rule here, our own island kingdom."

He released his grip on her with a low whistle. "I knew you'd be worth the investment." He smirked as her lips curled into a sneer. "Well, get on with it," he said, gesturing to the men huddled around the pig.

The clearing crackled with an electric shock, smelling of ozone before a summer storm. The beast bucked and scrambled to free itself, pulling the ragged cord loose from their hands and scampering from its captors.

The woman sneered at the men. "Can't keep control of a piglet? You're pathetic."

"She's a sow, and she's enormous." One of them lunged for the pig as it dashed out of his reach. The group formed a circle, closing in tight to keep the beast inside. "She's stronger than us, for now."

The woman raised an eyebrow. "Let's do something about that, shall we?" She pointed to the earth with the tip of her blade. "Exactly here."

Bound in on all sides, the sow was shoved to the centre, where it shivered, grunting. The woman raised the knife, and the pig snorted in panic, charging.

The woman only smiled, grabbing the cord at its neck and dragging it towards her. The flickering candlelight flashed off the knife blade, and the pig shrieked, the shrill sound carrying for miles.

In one clean movement, she slashed the beast's throat. Blood gushed over the earth, the knife and the woman's hand. The air filled with the smell of blood and offal as she carved into the tender underbelly. Several of the circle licked their lips, growling as the air vibrated with the hum of magic.

Starlight dimmed as a flash of silver pulsed from the centre of the circle.

The man shook his head. It never ceased to amaze him how she always found the exact spot. As tendrils of light crept over the earth, he felt the crackle of building power. It boiled across the circle, blasting into him like an endless high.

His head fell back in abandon. Nothing rivaled the energy from a sacrifice.

The shivering beast fell still, and he pointed to the patch of dark blood soaking into the dirt. "This will be the epicentre; you know what goes here. We'll set up camp on the edge of the fields. You there, take this carcass to the butcher."

The worker he signalled, barely more than a teenager, shuffled his feet. "It'll upset the others. They'll be restless with the smell."

The man laughed, drunk on the magic and giddy with the power that crashed through him. Nothing could touch him.

"Who cares? Chaos will feed off their energy, and we will feed off the chaos."

He snapped his fingers at the woman, her forearms glistening red in the flickering light. "Is there anything on the island powerful enough to stop us?"

Her eyes glinted. "Not when I'm done with them."

He turned to the others, lifting his arms with a flourish. "It's time to build. I want to see my name in lights. I want a spectacle this pathetic island has never seen before. Something these marks will never forget. Until, of course, they lose their minds."

He stretched out the moment, catching the woman's eye, matching her wild grin with his own. "It's going to be one hell of a show."

ONE

Three young girls, no older than nine, dashed to the ice cream stand in bathing suits, giggling and shoving as they took in all the pastel colours on display.

Behind the counter, Lola leaned forward on her elbows, letting the sunshine fall on her cheeks as she gave them time to discuss every flavour. When they quieted, she grabbed her scoop.

"What'll it be?" she asked. The girls answered in quiet, lisping voices.

Once all the cones had been prepared and grubby fingers had counted out coins, Lola watched them dart down the Port Despardoux Boardwalk, scraping stray wisps of curls off her neck. Sweat trickled down her back, and the skin of her forearms tingled from being out in the sun for too long. The idea made her smile.

"How's life in the trenches?"

Nix approached barefoot, sneakers dangling from her fingers. Skinny legs stuck out from oversized shorts and her fiery red hair was shoved under a battered baseball cap.

"I have a sunburn." Lola brandished her arm for her friend to see.

"Yikes, that's pretty intense. Lola, do you remember what we said about SPF?"

"Anything less than 30 is bullshit."

"That's right. Here," Nix fished a bottle from her bag. "I burn if I even think about the sun."

The cool cream tingled on Lola's overheated skin. "You don't understand. The last time I got a sunburn, it burned all the way through to my bone. It took me weeks to recover. This is nothing." She pressed the rosy skin, admiring the patch of white that bloomed then disappeared. "See? A working circulatory system."

Nix snorted. "Yes, you're very special."

Lola's laugh was bright and girlish—no predatory growl underneath. Sunburns were her greatest worry now, not Otherworldly creatures, vengeful demons or being stalked by ancient exes.

She grabbed a plastic spoon. "Want some? I just tried the hazelnut triple fudge. It's so sweet, I think I'm going to lose most of my teeth." She'd been passing the time sampling every flavour. Sweetness was still so new to her.

A smile tugged at Nix's lips. "We've talked about this. You need to take care of yourself now." She grabbed the sample anyway and stuck it in her mouth. "Holy, that is *sugar*."

"But worth it, right?" Lola smiled at Nix. She'd been practicing her smile in the mirror, her *I-am-a-human-girl* smile. Somehow, it never fit exactly right, like she had picked the wrong mask to wear.

Still, her humanity was not in doubt. Her lungs expanded as she took in a deep breath, surveying the stretch of beach before her. The breeze was fresh and smelled of brine, mingling with the scent of Nix's coconut sunscreen.

Duchesne Island in the summer was nothing like the quiet, haunted place it had been when she'd arrived. Now, it buzzed with life. Striped beach cabanas the colours of French macarons lined the beach and the summer tourists, crammed cheek to jowl, wandered shops that lined the wooden Boardwalk. Over the cries of gulls, people stopped to chat with vendors and peruse the trinkets on display: knick-knacks mainly, made with sea glass or fishing lures.

Children ran full tilt for the waves crashing against the sand. From where she stood, Lola could look out over the broad expanse of the Atlantic Ocean.

"So, this is the famous stand." Nix circled the pink-and-white-striped shack, reading the wooden sign overhead: *The Ice Cream Shoppe*. She popped extra emphasis on the "PE."

Lola shrugged. "Faye wanted a Brighton Pier feel. Tourists love that kind of thing."

"Does that include the outfit?" Nix's eyebrows rose at the flouncy pink dress, complete with starched apron and matching cap.

Lola angled the cap over her brunette curls. "They go crazy for it. Works well on your—" she waggled her fingers as she wrinkled her nose, "—you know. Social media thingies."

"Are people actually taking photos of you?"

"I usually duck out of the way." Her gut tightened; she should be lying low. As a human, she was no longer a threat to her former vampire crew, but she also wasn't supposed to be alive.

If Jacquotte, the vampire who created her, could remain unaware of her continued existence for, say, the next ninety years, that would be fine with Lola.

"We'll drag you into the twenty-first century yet," Nix said. "Even if your outfit is stuck in the sixties."

"Fifties," Lola corrected, tugging at the hem of her skirt.

"You'd know better than me. You were there and all. Now, I hear that you and Faye are cousins?" Nix said this with sarcastic finger quotes.

"Third cousins twice removed." Lola scrunched her nose as she recited the story she and Faye had invented. "She was my au pair for a few months when she lived in Paris before she went to culinary school. Now, due to vague tragedies in my family, I've come to stay with her to finish high school."

It wasn't a particularly strong backstory, but it passed muster if you didn't dig too deep. Unfortunately, some people on Duchesne Island were far too willing to probe into her background.

"Does she know the truth? About…you know." Nix lowered her voice.

"Are you *stunned*?" Lola tried out the island slang and Nix rewarded her with a grin. "How could I possibly tell her? 'By the way, Faye, I used to be a vampire but now I'm human, and I don't think that's ever happened before.' She'd have me committed."

Nix tilted her head from side to side. "I'm not sure. I wouldn't be surprised if she took it well. This is Duchesne Island, after all. Weird things happen here."

"The kinds of things that happened to me are the types of things people only read about in storybooks. And not the cleaned-up Disney ones. We can't tell anyone." Her voice lowered to a whisper. "You never know what might be listening."

A gust of wind rippled over the beach, sending hats and towels scattering across the sand. A flyer tumbled by, catching on Nix's ankle. As she stooped to grab it, Lola got a waft of sweet corn and fried cakes. The delicate tinkling of an organ grinder seemed to whip by in the breeze.

The hairs on her arms raised with a chill that belied the summer sunshine.

"*The Carnival of Fools*," Nix read aloud. "*Midway Rides, Music, Prizes. Fun for the Whole Family.* So that's what's going on at the old Granger Farm. That property's been empty forever, but now there's a bunch of trailers set up."

Lola took the flyer. A large Ferris wheel dominated the design. A tremor took root in her mind. The sketchy lines appeared to shift, the image flickering like an old film reel as the ride turned in its endless loop. Then, a slow wash of scarlet red dripped across the paper, coating everything in syrupy blood.

She dropped the flyer as though burned.

"What is it?" Nix bent to retrieve it. "Not a fan of carnivals?"

"I just...did you see...?"

Nix's blank look told Lola she hadn't seen anything out of place. The flyer looked perfectly normal now.

Visions of blood were never a good sign. It was also extremely *Other* of her; perhaps the hallucination was a side effect of her transformation from vampire to human, her brain scrambled by the process? Or was it simply that her past was so soaked in blood, there would be no escape from it?

Lola wiped her shaking palms off on the skirt of her uniform, trying to get herself under control. Maybe it had been a fluke, a glitch. Whatever caused it, she didn't need an encore.

"You okay?" Nix watched her with concern.

Lola let out a slow breath, regaining control. "I've never been to a carnival. At least, not during the day."

She had witnessed extravagant spectacles over the decades; festivals in Prague, or Bangkok, or Mexico City, rife with humanity and ready for disaster. She remembered countless nights of stalking through the crowds, hunting her prey through electric lights and chaos. Luring unsuspecting victims away from the crowd. The spray of blood and gurgling screams had been her carnival entertainment.

She had seen many spectacular things, but never in the daylight.

Her memories from her life as a vampire seemed to be engraved on her mind, while she had access to none of her life as a human before. She wished it could be the other way around, or even better, that she remembered nothing at all about herself. *Tabula rasa*: a clean slate, a brand-new girl.

Lola shook her head as though to dislodge her bloodstained past. "It opens today," she said. This could be her chance to show how ordinary her life was. "Should we check it out?"

"Absolutely. It's going to be ridiculous, and we'll love it."

"I'm in." Lola clapped her hands together, determined to get into the spirit of things, which made Nix chuckle.

"You've really changed, you know. Used to be all, 'I'm going to rip your spine out.' And now you're losing your mind over a carnival."

Losing her mind was right. But as Lola focused on the poster again, nothing moved, no blood in sight. Maybe she'd just been in the sun too long. "I want to try everything. And do it right this time."

"I'm happy you're up for it. For a while there, you were the most boring new human I've ever met."

Lola had slept for weeks after her transformation. Faye worried about her, wondering if she should get blood tests done while Lola's friends had called it "the human flu."

However, she hadn't shared with them how awkward and slow she felt, as though her skin didn't fit quite right. The light was too bright sometimes, or her reactions delayed. She had given up so much for her humanity, and now she was finding it had its drawbacks.

"What about the boys?" Nix said, gesturing at the flyer.

"Boys?"

"We already have plans. Like with Gael? Remember him?"

Lola's stomach performed a loop at the thought of Gael Smith. As if she could ever forget him. "Name rings a bell."

"As if you haven't been spending every day since you woke up attached at the hip."

Lola's cheeks heated. "There's lost time to make up for."

"Yes, you've been good at making time," Nix said in a deadpan tone. "He wanted to go to Lost Souls."

"Perhaps we can change his mind."

"Change my mind about what?"

Lola brightened at the sound of his voice. She drank in the sight of Gael as he approached, still not used to how tall he was.

She wasn't sure if she had become smaller or if he'd grown. He seemed to get larger and broader every time she saw him. He wore only board shorts, showing off the warm brown of his chest, and Lola's thoughts stuttered.

"Hey there," she managed as he leaned over the ice cream counter.

He pulled himself forward to skim his lips across her cheek. She closed her eyes as the warmth of his skin brushed over hers. He smelled of salt and sunshine.

"Hey there right back." His smile was as wide as ever. Nothing of the horrors of the spring had changed the warmth in his gold-brown eyes.

"How's business?" Walt Seabourne came strolling up behind Gael, wearing a collared shirt rolled at the sleeves and leather boat shoes. Every inch of him shouted wealth and privilege, and if Lola didn't know him, she would have thought he fit in perfectly with the beautiful, popular people who lived on the island. But his furrowed brows gave away his anxiety at how much he struggled to connect with others. "I thought we were headed to Lost Souls? Nix put it in my calendar."

"You're organizing his calendar?" Lola laughed as Nix put her arm around Walt's waist.

"I didn't want him to forget." Under Nix's attention, Walt relaxed. "But the big news is there's a carnival in town. So, we're going to go there instead."

"A carnival? Like, with little kid rides? You'd want to do that?" Gael's smile turned somewhat shy as he looked at Lola, his gaze running over her face as though she was a riddle he couldn't figure out.

"Why not?"

"I guess I thought it might be a bit...childish for you?" His gaze met hers, giving that dazed look that sometimes came over him when they were together. "I mean, you've lived forever. Why would you want to go on some stupid kid rides?"

"I was *undead* forever. I'm very new at being human."

"Besides, Lola needs more fun in her life." Nix stepped in. "Rides and games and music and food. Honestly, what's not to like?"

Lola straightened. "I've never had carnival food before."

Seeing that she meant it, Gael warmed to the idea. "You've got to try everything, then: corndogs, kettle corn, candy apples…"

"Candy apples are gross," Nix said.

"Says you." Gael elbowed her. "Candy apples are delicious. Walt, weigh in."

"Candy apples are good as a novelty, nothing more. Doesn't matter; Lola will eat it."

"What does that mean?" Lola tried to pretend to be offended but couldn't help but laugh.

"You'll try anything. I've seen you."

"Hey, I was on a restricted diet until now. I want to try all the things."

Gael leaned forward to whisper in her ear. Her skin splayed with goosebumps as his lips brushed the curve of her ear. "Going on the Ferris wheel with me is a new experience."

She imagined being caught with Gael high above the fairgrounds as the sun was setting over the ocean, warm in his arms. The light caught the curve of his cheekbones, and her heart gave a thump; she felt the same tug towards him she'd been feeling since they met.

"Oh my God, get a room!" Nix called.

Lola gave a guilty grin to Nix and Walt who stood to the side, though both were laughing. She glanced at her watch. "It's pretty late and the beach is emptying. I'll just close up the shop."

Her friends continued chatting about the carnival novelties as Lola changed out of her ridiculous uniform. She had nearly put the bloody vision behind her. She'd figure out this life thing by living it.

All the potential energy of being alive seemed to surge through her. "I'm ready."

"Do you mean it? Sure you don't need to take a nap?" Gael's voice was both teasing and tender.

"Absolutely." She raised her arms to the sun. "I want to feel *everything*."

"Excellent." Gael grabbed her around the waist and started hauling her away from the beach. "Come on, let's get her there before she goes back to sleep."

Two

The old Granger Farm had sat abandoned for years, but now it had been utterly transformed. The dusty fields on the outskirts of town pulsed with flashing lights and spinning rides. Pipe organ music and shrieks of laughter filled the air—the whirling kaleidoscope like a dream come to life.

Half the island, along with what felt like all the tourists in town, waited to be let in. Lola and her friends stood transfixed at the entrance. An elaborate archway had been constructed, *The Carnival of Fools* written in electric bulbs. It looked like a portal into a fantasy world. Beyond the threshold, everything was washed in crimson light.

She pressed against the metal fencing like a child, taking in a deep breath. The air carried the dizzying scents of things buttery or sugary or fried—all indulgences she'd yet to try.

"There was nothing here a week ago," Nix said. "How'd they manage this?"

Gael pointed. "Check out that monster Ferris wheel."

It loomed above the rest of the carnival, its black frame stretching against the twilight sky like the skeletal legs of a spider.

The seats rocked precariously as children leaned over the edges, their laughter carried away by the wind.

"What do you want to try?" Gael asked, his eyes reflecting the carnival's brilliant hues.

Lola grinned. "Everything."

He squeezed her hand, and at that moment it felt like they were talking about so much more than rides.

At the entry, a man in a faded red uniform barely acknowledged them. "Free entry," he repeated in a flat, mechanical tone, as if he'd already said it a thousand times that night.

"Free?" Lola asked as they passed him.

"I'm not complaining," Nix said, her gaze shifting to Walt. Lola assumed she'd have had to ask him to spot her.

"But how do they make money?"

Walt scoffed. "A thousand ways they'll bleed us dry. They lure you in, then take you for all you're worth."

"That's cynical." Lola looped her arm through his, and he smiled down at her.

"Realistic. You need to learn how humans work."

"What? They're as bloodsucking as vampires?"

"Exactly. Knew you'd figure it out."

The path led to a crossroads where a painted sign pointed in dozens of directions. Stalls lined the zigzagging paths, painted with crimson stripes. Electric lights draped between them like vines.

A single sign stood out, larger than the rest: *Maze of Desire*, its lettering in red dripping paint. It made Lola think of her vision— blood dripping everywhere.

"I wonder what that's all about," she said, a chill skittering down her spine.

Nix studied the signs. "Rides are near the back. Games over here, and this way is—"

"Food stands," Gael finished, his eyes lighting up. "Let's make Lola's carnival foodie dreams come true."

Walt, Nix and Gael took it as their personal mission; Lola

watched them fondly as they prowled the stalls for the best treats. Walt returned first, holding a corn dog like an offering. "You have to have it with mustard. It's the law."

Lola took a bite of the snack on a stick, still hot from the fryer, and hummed in delight. "Why do people even use cutlery?"

"It's efficient," he said, taking a bite out of his own. The smile tracing his lips, so often missing, made him seem a younger, more light-hearted version of himself.

Nix returned with a half-eaten bag of pastel pink cotton candy. "I don't understand it," she said through a mouthful. "But I can't get enough of this."

Lola pursed her lips at the sweetness. "Ugh, it makes your teeth all gritty."

Nix grabbed the bag back and stuffed more into her mouth. "Your loss."

Gael approached last, holding out a candy apple. "To settle the debate."

The green apple was covered with buttery caramel, old-fashioned and evoking another time. "Delicious," Lola pronounced, catching a drip of tart juice trickling down her chin.

"Whatever, Grandma," Nix said. "This is a sign you and Gael are meant to be since you both like old people food. Ah!"

She jumped as a carnival worker dressed like a harlequin cartwheeled past her. His white-painted face was adorned with black diamonds along the cheeks and eyes, his lips stretched into a grotesque grin.

"Clowns?" Lola laughed as Nix flinched. "Seriously? You're not afraid of anything, except for...heavy makeup?"

"They give me the creeps." Nix let out a shudder. "Don't tell me you like them—that's a sure sign you're still a demon."

"They don't bother me, but I get it. I think it's the fact that they conceal reality with fantasy. Genuine emotion is covered by the mask of the real thing."

"Okay, I didn't need a psychological thesis on clowns, Lola. Yes or no next time." Nix rolled her eyes, stuffing more cotton candy into her mouth.

"I like your theses," Gael said, putting his arm around Lola. "Never change. I'm going to grab some lemonade, okay? I saw a stand back there where they were like ten bucks; that means they have to be good."

Gael and Walt strolled away down the midway. "I still can't believe you like that thing," Nix said, swatting at the apple while giggling.

"Says the girl eating candied air." Lola grinned, nudging her back.

"What are you losers doing here?"

The familiar, contemptuous voice cut through the din, and Lola's stomach dropped. She and Nix exchanged a look before turning.

Violet Wynn strolled down the dirt path flanked by her besties, Sam and Cassidy. Their dresses were barely there, their skin sun-kissed and glowing. The three girls looked like an ad for everything summer was supposed to be—effortless, golden, untouchable.

A pang reverberated in Lola's chest; she would never belong the way they did.

Violet's blonde hair was pulled back in Dutch braids, her perfect face dwarfed by oversized sunglasses. She sighed, tapping her lavender-tipped nails along her metal cup. "Nobody wants you freaks here."

Lola gave her a gigantic fake smile. "Have you tried the candy apples? They're *delicious*."

Violet levelled an icy glare at her. "Are you going to throw it at me? That's kinda your thing, isn't it?"

A few months ago, Violet had taunted Nix at Lost Souls, and Lola had lost her temper and poured a drink over Violet's head. A riot had followed. They'd nearly gotten arrested, but the memory was still *so* satisfying.

"Only if you want me to, Violet."

Violet stalked forward, and Lola fought the instinct to flee.

"You seem to have things all backwards, you little upstart. I run things around here. And you? You're totally going to pay for what happened last spring."

"Can't we put that behind us? It was a crazy night."

"It was crazy, alright. Ethan still won't shut up about it. But here's what I know—" Violet leaned in, her voice sickly sweet. "No way do you pull a stunt like that and pretend you're, like, normal. You're a freak and always will be."

Nix scowled at Violet. "Just leave us alone."

Violet looked the tiny girl up and down with contempt. "Like I want *anything* to do with you."

Sam giggled and coughed the word "queer."

Nix's face darkened. "Get out of our space, Violet."

Violet's lips puckered as though she tasted something sour. "Come talk to me when you've hit puberty. Until then, maybe you do belong at the carnival. There must be a freakshow around here somewhere."

Nix took a step forward, eyes narrowing. "At least I'm not a —"

A shadow fell over them.

"What's going on?"

Gael approached, holding iced drinks and cutting Nix off before she said something even she might regret. His presence shifted the energy, breaking the hostility. Violet's lips parted as she took him in.

Lola couldn't hide her smirk as she accepted her lemonade, standing on tiptoe to brush her lips across his. Her nose bumped into his cheek; she was clumsy in a way that was new to her.

"Please." Violet rolled her eyes. "You two are so sugar I'm going to puke, like, actually."

"Always nice to see you, too, Violet." Gael continued to smile at Lola.

"Hey, Gael," Cassidy said, her voice sweet and soprano.

Gael looked up in surprise. Both Cassidy and Sam ogled him as though he were a pair of designer shoes on sale.

"Oh, hey, Cassidy. How's it going?" His brows knit together.

"I saw you pitching the other day. We were cheering you on."

"Yeah, I saw you. Thanks for that."

Cassidy's tan darkened with her blush. Her apricot sundress perfectly suited her olive skin and auburn ponytail.

Lola's throat tightened, and before she could stop herself, a low growl slipped out—quickly disguised as a cough. Sometimes she forgot she wasn't a vampire anymore, especially when pretty girls swarmed her boyfriend.

"Walt!" Sam called out suddenly. Walt, strolling to join them, slowed as he took in the scene. He handed over Nix's drink but kept his gaze down as Sam leaned in, her fingers trailing over his arm. "So, when's your next pool party? Last summer, your raves were killer. I'm waiting for my invite."

Walt shrugged, unmoved. "Pool's closed for good."

Sam pulled back with a huff. "Fine. This scene is so done." She linked arms with Cassidy, tugging her away. Cassidy shot one last hungry glance at Gael over her shoulder, and Lola fought the urge to growl again.

Violet lingered. "No more pool parties?"

Walt's gaze flicked to hers and he set his jaw. "Don't think so."

"Why not? Everyone knows you throw the best ones. Your parents basically bankroll them."

"Maybe you should hang with them, then."

Her manicured brows pinched together. "Your house was *the* social scene last year."

"I've found a new scene, Vi."

She studied him for a long moment. "So, last spring wasn't temporary insanity. You've gone and joined the freaks."

He let out a scoffing laugh. "You've always made it clear you think I am one."

Violet's mouth pressed into a thin line. When she finally spoke, her voice was quieter, almost measured. "You'll regret it, you know. Before us, you were the nerd who co-chaired the science club. We befriended you despite all that."

Walt's expression didn't waver. "You didn't befriend me, you used me. My house. My money. My parties. The only thing I regret is that I didn't do this sooner."

Her eyes narrowed behind her glasses. "Do what?"

Instead of answering, Walt turned his back on her and walked away. Nix followed, a delighted smirk playing on her lips. His voice carried to them as he spoke to Nix. "Should we bring back science club?"

Violet's glossy lips fell open. She turned to Lola, then to Gael, her gaze locking onto their joined hands. Her mouth curled into something that wasn't quite a smirk, wasn't quite a sneer.

"Aren't you two just the sweetest? Be careful; it looks like you're trying way too hard. Don't want anyone to notice the cracks."

She spun on her heel, her honey-blonde tresses sliding down her back as she stalked away.

Lola glanced at her hand in Gael's. Their fingers didn't seem to fit quite right anymore. A slow-moving cloud passed in front of the sun, casting them in shadows.

Gael watched her with careful eyes. "That Violet. Really knows how to win people over."

She released his hand and wiped her sweaty palm over her thigh. "She's something, alright."

The stringed lights flickered overhead, and the first notes of a song curled through the air. Somewhere in the distance, a band was warming up.

The music thrummed low and electric, a pulse Lola could feel against her skin. It whispered through her veins like static before a storm.

Whatever this show was, it sounded like it was going to be electric.

THREE

Workers in their harlequin makeup lined the paths, directing the crowd. Like lambs, Lola and her friends followed the flow of bodies until they reached a clearing in front of a raised outdoor stage.

Overhead, a wrought metal sign fastened to the archway read: *The Gardens*. Heavy red curtains hid the backstage area. The setup was far from amateur—lights and sound equipment gleamed with professional precision.

The stage was empty, but transcendent piano music filled the air, each note deliberate, masterful. Something classical, in a minor key—Schumann, maybe. But before Lola could place it, an electric guitar crashed through the melody, twisting it into something raw and primal.

The place was packed. At the front, people were jammed together, shoulder to shoulder. Nix took the lead, wiggling through the crowd, Walt trailing reluctantly behind her. When he hesitated, she grabbed his wrist, tugging him along like a fish on the line.

"We'll get a better view from over here," she insisted. "It's been ages since we've had a proper—" She stopped mid-sentence. Walt and Lola both crashed into her.

"What's with you?" Gael asked, steadying Lola.

"Nothing." Nix voice was strangled, her face a mottled flaming red.

"That's not a nothing face." Lola followed her gaze, then smirked. A few groups over from them in the crowd stood a slim girl about their age—Asian with sleek black hair tipped in platinum blonde.

"Ohhh, I see. Checking out the tourists?"

Nix blushed all the way to her roots. "She's adorable."

Lola grinned. "She really is. You should go talk to her."

"I couldn't."

Lola took her friend's hand. "When you're ready. You're a catch, and don't forget it."

Nix inhaled sharply like she wanted to say something, then her shoulders slumped. "I might not be ready until I'm off this stupid island."

Lola gave her hand a squeeze. "That's fair. I've got your back, no matter what."

The music built to a crescendo, and the crowd hushed, turning to the empty stage. The song swelled to a blaring climax—then cut off abruptly. Lola's ears rang in the sudden silence.

A deafening boom shattered the stillness. At centre stage, an explosion of crimson smoke erupted, billowing towards the fading sky. The crowd gasped and ducked away from the blast.

Spotlights snapped on, illuminating the figure conjured before them.

A man, tall and statuesque, emerged from the smoke, his presence cutting through the chaos. He was old-Hollywood handsome, all sharp angles and charming smiles. As he strode out of the drifting fog, the dramatic lighting cast shadows across his face like he was some kind of vengeful demon.

His tuxedo was vintage—pinstriped with tails, a perfectly tied bow tie, and a top hat polished to a high shine. A mane of dark hair brushed his shoulders, and his skin shimmered with silver makeup that twinkled under the lights. When he smiled, his teeth flashed white as moonlight.

He spread his arms wide. "Welcome, one and all."

Though he held no microphone, his voice boomed to the farthest corners of the carnival, overwhelming the rides, the laughter and the chatter of festival goers. The sound wrapped around the crowd, pulling them in, demanding attention.

"I am Duke Louis, your patron for the next few weeks while The Carnival of Fools spins your every desire into existence." His voice dropped into something silky, conspiratorial. "I've heard all about your famous island, the haunted isle of Duchesne."

A ripple of nervous laughter spread through the audience.

"Unusual things happen here, don't they?" His grin widened. "Well, I wouldn't want to break tradition. While you are here, *all* your wishes will be granted. No want shall go unheeded."

He reached into his coat and pulled out an enormous lollipop, one that couldn't possibly have been hidden there a moment ago. He placed it into the reaching hands of an eager toddler at the front of the stage, an indulgent smile on his lips. "We only wish to make you happy. To give you what you *want*."

A sly look stole over his face as though he had other secrets hidden all over his person. Lola couldn't look away. As if sensing her scrutiny, his gaze found hers.

His white smile grew, and he winked.

Repulsion surged through her.

She didn't know why, but something inside screamed *wrong*. Clenching her fists, she forced back the impulse to rush the stage and slap the candy out of the child's hands.

Duke Louis straightened his jacket. "Every night, our house band, The Bayous, will perform for you, right here in The Gardens, led by the incandescent Otsana Volkov. Believe me when I tell you, it is a spectacle not to be missed.

"There are other pleasures to discover here as well. Try your hand at winning a prize, perhaps for your lovely lady friend." He gave a dark chuckle, and his voice lowered. "Or perhaps you will have the courage to enter the Maze of Desire. Not everyone is ready to face their deepest cravings. But if you have the guts to meet your truest self, we'll see you there." On that last word, Duke Louis threw his arms into the air as another bang sounded in an explosion of coloured lights.

When Lola blinked the spots out of her vision, the enigmatic ringmaster was gone.

In his place, a full band had materialized.

Walt stiffened beside her, cracking his knuckles—a habit he had when something didn't add up.

A woman stepped forward, cradling a deep indigo guitar painted with silver moons and stars. She looked like she'd stepped out of another era—shaggy-haired, wrapped in leather and lace, arms inked with swirling tattoos. Dark liner framed her sharp eyes, which shone under the stage lights.

She struck a chord. The sound rolled over the crowd, electric and hypnotic. A rhythmic beat started as the rest of the band joined in. The drummer's kit bore a sketch of a moon and the band name: *The Bayous*.

Then, she began to sing.

Her voice was both a whisper and a growl, trilling up the melody, then dropping into her bottom register without falter. The melody slithered through Lola's veins. Something restless stirred inside: an undeniable want, though she wasn't sure what for.

The drumbeat quickened and the air shifted. Lola's pulse staggered as the world became flux around her.

It seemed as though she was back in the treasure hole, drilling to the Well of Souls, pressed against the wall by Gael. His lips were on hers, his hands lifting, claiming—

A memory? A vision? No, it felt real. She could feel him, taste him.

Here in the crowd, Gael's hands found her hips. His touch was heavier than usual, possessive. When she met his gaze, there was something knowing there—something older.

She looped her arms around his neck, swaying with the music, letting the sensation consume her.

On stage, the singer's grin stretched wide—too wide, showing more teeth than she should have. The stars on the guitar sparkled as though lit up by their own energy.

She changed keys.

A shockwave ripped through the crowd like a cresting wave.

Lola dragged in a deep breath, all her focus on the feeling of Gael's skin beneath her fingertips. His pulse beat at his neck where the scar of a bite mark had healed. Lola wanted to lick that spot. A part of her wished she was still a vampire so she could taste him that way again.

He trailed his fingers along Lola's arm, sending excruciating ripples over her skin.

"You're incredible." Gael's voice was rough with want. He hadn't been this intense with her, not since she'd become human. He'd been acting as though she was fragile, about to shatter, but she liked how he was treating her now. She wasn't about to break.

She tilted her head up and kissed him deeply. His hands went around her waist, pulling her into him until she could hardly tell where she ended and he began. The depth of her desire for him could swallow her whole.

The song grew louder and louder until the sound spun to the deepening sky above them. Lola wanted to lose herself to it completely, stay where she was forever.

But as she pressed herself even closer to Gael, a dissonance sounded from somewhere deep inside her. Something shifted in the world, like everything spun and righted itself.

Lola gasped, yanked out of her trance. Around her people weren't just dancing—they were losing themselves. Couples clung to each other, some kissing feverishly, others sobbing like their hearts were breaking. Hands roamed over bodies with reckless abandon. Even adults were tangled together like drunken teenagers.

Gael ran his hands over her body, but Lola found she'd been knocked out of her overwhelming lust, now dizzy and sticky with sweat. She tried to tug away from Gael, but he held tight.

Firmly, she disentangled herself from his grasp, as utter devastation flashed across his face. Her friends swayed to the music, eyes glazed. They seemed entranced

Then Lola saw her.

The tourist girl Nix had pointed out. Unaffected by the music, she stood stock-still amidst the sea of writhing bodies. As if sensing someone watching her, she turned to Lola, her grey gaze cold like a northern storm.

A fight broke out near the stage, distracting her. Lola blinked and looked back, but the tourist girl was gone.

Onstage, the singer barked a single triumphant laugh, getting Lola's attention. She locked eyes with her as though singing for her alone, and Lola's head spun as if something was trying to get inside.

"No," she said, though it came out in a whisper.

With a silver flash of the guitar, a pulse of energy exploded from the stage.

Tendrils of silver light reached out towards the crowd of festival goers like a tangle of luminous vines. The web of light touched everyone who stood in that crowd.

Lola jerked back.

Then, the singer cut off the song.

After a stunned pause, the floor erupted in a roar of approval. Even those who'd been crying moments before cheered in wild applause.

Lola's stomach twisted. Something had just happened, something terribly wrong. And no one had noticed but her.

Perhaps Violet was right; she would always be a freak, standing outside of everyone else.

"Hello, Port Despardoux!" The singer yelled into the mic, her voice rough and raspy, the product of whiskey and cigarettes. Her accent was foreign and hard to pin down, somewhere from Eastern Europe. "I love being here with all you beautiful people, and I hope you like being here with me."

The whistles and cheers left no room for discussion. Her grin showed far too much canine, her eyes glittering behind dark makeup.

"That's what I like to hear." Satisfaction laced her voice. "The Bayous will be playing here nightly, so come back often to see me. Let's see what kind of trouble we can get into." Her voice dropped to a purr, the raw triumph in her voice setting Lola's teeth on edge. The singer played another riff, and everyone in the crowd moved with the beat.

Lola was the only one standing still, staring up at the singer, who frowned at her.

She finished her song with an angry squeal, then the singer stomped away from the microphone, leaving the audience reeling.

Four

"That was incredible." Gael used the same tone he had used to describe her, giving her a momentary pang of loss. Had he actually meant it when he said it to her?

Lola's friends all shared a glowing look, cheeks flushed and dreamy smiles plastered over their faces.

"No, not incredible. Something weird just happened." Lola stumbled over her words, not sure what to say. "Some kind of lights, like a spell was cast."

"Yeah, the spell of good music." Nix shoved her and giggled. "This is what we were talking about, this thing called fun. You don't even know what it feels like anymore. What we need to do is find some people." Her eyes flicked over the crowd, and Lola suspected she sought the grey-eyed girl. Lola would have liked to find her, too, since she seemed immune to the spell The Bayous had cast.

"Maybe we should leave." Lola tried to convince her friends as they basically carried her onto the fairgrounds. "That was a great show. Let's leave on a high."

"No way! Boo!" Nix said. "You promised you were going to

have fun tonight. And things are just getting started. We have the whole evening ahead of us.”

“Do you really want to leave?” Gael asked her, gripping her waist. His hands seemed to be all over her, as though he was still under the influence of the music. Normally Lola wouldn’t mind, but it seemed as though the impulse wasn’t coming from him. She stepped out of his grasp and took his hand instead.

“I’m serious; I feel like something strange just happened.”

“Does it have something to do with being one of your first times out...as a human? I can’t imagine how it feels, but it seems like strangeness might go hand in hand with coming back from the undead.”

Her breath left her like wind emptying from sails. That was exactly what she had wondered before—was it just her?

“I...don’t know. Nobody felt anything unusual? Or saw weird lights?” She felt as though she’d grown an extra head the way they were looking at her.

“Nothing like that.” Gael’s eyebrows were creased as he watched her. She didn’t want to be the person that caused him worry; she wanted to be the person who experienced the joys of this world with him.

“I guess I don’t really know what humanity feels like.”

“Oh, yeah, humans feel all kinds of weird things,” Nix said, her tone airy. “Half the time, I have no idea what’s going on.”

Lola squeezed Gael’s hand. She’d try to enjoy herself, for his sake.

A crowd had formed ahead of them, and they stopped in front of a towering, red-striped tent. It was round, with a peaked roof and billowing curtains at the entrance. Shouts and hoots came from the unruly crowd as a stream of couples entered the tent, hands slipping into each other’s pockets.

“The Maze of Desire,” Gael said. “Looks kind of cool. Want to go in?”

"Oh God," Nix rolled her eyes. "Of course you two want to go in. Walt and I have much better things to do."

"We do?"

"Yes. It involves standing here making fun of all the people who are happily coupled parading around in front of us."

Walt watched the crowd of couples with a pensive expression. "Maybe we should get more corn dogs."

Beyond the entry curtains came shouts and echoing laughter. The longer Lola stared at the tent, though, the more it felt wrong. The building seemed to be glowing, but not by any electric lights.

The more she concentrated, the more it radiated dark energy. She could see a halo of shadows around it.

"It's like it's full of darkness."

Gael's grin disappeared.

A howl came from inside, and everyone near the front jumped, then burst into laughter.

"It's just a cheesy attraction," he said. "It's probably all dark and things jump out at you, and you get freaked out. It's part of the fun."

Lola used to be the thing that jumped out from the darkness, but nobody ever had fun other than her. "I don't know." She took a few steps towards the entrance and stopped, as though something inside was warning her to go no further.

Gael was watching her carefully. "Know what? This whole thing looks lame, anyway. Let's find something else to do."

Nix had convinced Walt to buy more cotton candy and was thrusting it under his nose while he laughed and tried to push her away. Lola threaded her arm through Gael's and forced a smile.

They meandered through a snarl of booths and games, each one playing a different jarring tune. The sounds mashed together like something out of a nightmare, and she longed to press her hands to her ears like a child.

Then she turned a corner, and the cacophony receded. In front of her was a booth displaying art prints.

An extraordinary hand had painted them: bright colours swirling over midnight backgrounds. Within the images, fantastical creatures seemed to hunt one another, emerging then fading into darkness. Wolves edged with gilt reflected electric lights.

"It's gorgeous," Lola said, looking at the one nearest her. Masks and predatory animals swirled out from the green and purple paint.

Nix stopped in front of a large painting, her head tilted to the side. "I don't think I get it. It kinda gives me the creeps."

"It's masterful," Lola said with a decided nod. "Whoever painted this is a true artist."

"Thank you." A shape separated from the shadows, and a hunched-over man shuffled forward into the light. His whispery voice hissed like a broom scraping a dusty floor.

As the flashing lights of the carnival caught his figure, Lola forced herself not to gasp. Next to her, Gael tensed. The man's face was ravaged with criss-crossing scars, causing his mouth to droop to one side and his one visible eye to twist with scar tissue. He wore an intricate half-mask, a golden panel where his other eye should be.

His gaze flickered over them like a bird that couldn't find a perch.

"Are you the artist?" Lola asked.

"I am many things." The man's lipless mouth tightened as though he was in some pain. "My name is Conri. Perhaps you have heard of me?" At Lola's mute shake of the head, he deflated, letting out a self-deprecating laugh. "I have made many things, many works of art, jewelry too. Perhaps I could tempt you with something even more elaborate. Something that would match your exquisite beauty."

The man held out one gnarled hand as though to touch her face. Gael's arm tightened around Lola's shoulder. "Thanks, we're good."

"Are you sure you don't want to see *everything* the carnival has to offer?" The artist's mask glinted in the lights. "I could show you so much more. Come with me." The man shuffled into the shadows of the back.

Lola hesitated before finally giving in to Gael's insistent tugging on her arm. Something about the art spoke to her.

"Don't you want to see what else he has?" Lola asked.

"Lola, are you stunned?" Nix stopped and stared at her. "That guy is not someone you go into a back room with."

"I don't know, he seemed..."

"Deranged?" Gael suggested.

"Absolutely wondering how you would taste in soup?" Nix added.

Lola gave them both a playful shove. "I was going to say sad. I don't think he's dangerous."

"Maybe your instincts are off," Nix said. "You don't remember what it is to be human and to have to figure out who's a threat. Trust me, anyone who painted those things is probably unstable."

Lola glanced back to the booth as they continued on. Maybe they were right, and she wasn't a good judge of character. The man had returned and watched her leave, surrounded by the firework colours in his paintings, his single eye dark and sorrowful.

FIVE

Walt stopped at a strongman game, paying the harlequin-painted worker before hefting an oversized hammer. Nix wrapped a strand of cotton candy around her finger and laughed as he could barely lift it. No matter how hard he swung, the slider never climbed past 3.

"Next," the game master called, his scowl cracking his thick makeup.

Gael stretched his arms over his head with a grin and stepped forward. He paid, grabbed the giant hammer, and heaved it overhead. With a grunt, he smashed it down.

The slider hit 4, and his smile wavered. "One more."

"Three tries," the harlequin said, barely looking up.

Gael wiped his palms on his shorts and swung again. Another 4. Jaw tightening, he took a deep breath, flexed his forearms, and slammed the hammer down with all his strength.

The slider wobbled to 5.

"Ha." He turned to Lola, grinning, and she pressed her lips together, fighting a laugh.

"Very impressive," she teased, grabbing his shirt and pulling him forward, having enjoyed the show immensely.

"Step aside, princesses. Let me show you how it's done."

A voice cut through the chatter, cocky and smooth. A young man swaggered up, nodding at the harlequin, who rolled his eyes but let him pass. The newcomer took his time cracking his knuckles, shooting them all a sharp grin.

He didn't wear full face paint, but his eyes were edged in glitter and black. A carnival worker. His dark hair fell into his face, and he flicked it to the side before gripping the hammer.

Shorter than Gael but solid with heavy muscle, he moved with an odd shimmer like heat rising from the pavement. Lola squinted. The harder she focused, the more her temples throbbed. Was it a trick of the lights—or something more?

In one smooth motion, he swung the hammer and sent the slider flying to 10. The bell rang out with a sharp peal.

"And that's how it's done. Do I get a prize?" he asked the game master, tossing the hammer aside like it weighed no more than a pillow.

One painted eyebrow rose. "You didn't pay to play."

"Ah, well." The young man clapped a hand on Walt's and Gael's shoulders. "Better luck next time, mates."

Gael jerked away. "Hey, man."

As the worker turned to leave, his hand ghosted over Walt's back pocket. Nobody else noticed—except Lola.

"No harm meant." He raised both hands, empty, flashing an easy smile before sauntering off. "Just wanted to show the girls what real strength looked like."

"What a dick," Gael muttered, rubbing the back of his head. "The game's probably rigged."

"Walt, your wallet," Lola said.

"What?" Walt's hand flew to his pocket and his eyes widened. "Shit. He stole it. I didn't feel a thing."

"I'll get it."

Lola took off through the crowded carnival without waiting for the others.

She wasn't supernatural anymore, but she was still fast. Winding through strollers and couples, past the scent of fried sugar and the blur of neon lights, she kept her eyes on the thief.

He sauntered along, scanning the crowd, probably searching for his next mark. Clearly a small-time criminal, taking advantage of the chaos to make some extra cash. Then he glanced back—and spotted Lola.

His brows lifted. Grinning, he ducked between an elderly couple and a man handing a little boy an ice cream. Lola picked up her pace, matching him for speed.

Through the maze of booths, she kept track of him. If she turned her head just right, faint silver light trailed from him.

They rounded the bumper cars, filled with squeals and wails as little kids on too much sugar smashed into one another, before he darted behind the spinning carousel.

Painted mythological creatures blurred together in a never-ending hunt, the colours swirling together like a dream. For a heartbeat, Lola was mesmerized. When she snapped out of it, she'd lost the pickpocket.

Damn.

The ride was so brilliant that everything else was midnight dark around her.

She followed the curve of the ride, scanning the shadows. If she could just catch that silver light—

A solid figure planted himself in front of her path. She crashed into him, nearly knocking them both over. His drink sloshed onto the ground.

"Shit," he snapped. "What the hell is wrong with you?"

Lola recognized his voice and winced. *Merde.*

Ethan Vaughan. Head alpha asshole in Port Despardoux. And one of the few people she showed her true demon face. Last spring, during the Lost Souls riot, he'd attacked her, and Lola, as a vampire, didn't hold herself back. He came out of the fight babbling about monsters, something people still laughed about.

And she suspected the humiliation wasn't the kind of thing a boy like him would easily forgive. Or forget.

Ethan straightened, tossing his blond hair back. Lola backtracked, hoping he wouldn't recognize her. "Sorry, didn't see you." She turned to leave.

It didn't work.

"Looking for someone else to jump?" Ethan's hand shot out and clamped around her wrist like a vise. "Not so fast. You and I have unfinished business."

The sour bite of alcohol clung to his breath. In the flickering lights, his handsome face was loose, his usual sneer dulled at the edges—drunk. Double *merde*.

"I don't think that's a good idea." She twisted, yanking against his grip, but he tightened his hold until his fingers dug into her flesh.

"But we have lots to talk about." He dragged her into the shadows behind the carousel, away from prying eyes. "Like what the hell you did to me that night? You made me see things."

"You only have yourself to blame. Let me go." Lola wrenched her arm, but he only smiled, lazy and mean.

She lifted her chin, trying to summon the cold confidence she once had as a vampire. But her body betrayed her—heart pounding, breath tight, muscles weak. She was on her own and no one knew where she was.

"I don't like being made a fool of." He threw his drink to the ground and grabbed her other wrist, pinning them above her head against the wooden back of the carousel. "And I definitely don't like it when people tell me I'm crazy."

"Then stop acting like you are." Lola lunged, shoving against him, but he barely budged.

A low, malevolent laugh escaped his lips. "Not so scary now, are you?"

She remembered Gael's warning—Ethan wasn't someone to cross. That he was capable of hurting her. She'd laughed it off at the time because teenage boys were no more than flies to be swatted back then.

Now, she fought against the rising panic in her chest. "I'll scream."

"Yeah?" His grip tightened. "And who'd hear you?"

Beyond the carousel, children shrieked with glee. Lola thrashed, but Ethan only grinned. This was fun for him; he was the type of boy who liked her fear.

Just like Beau, her ex, who could never allow her to walk away. He enjoyed being more powerful than others; he got off on making people squirm. The difference was this time, Lola had no way of fighting back.

Ethan stared as though considering her. "Now, how can you make this up to me?"

A growl sounded from deep under the carousel.

Low and guttural, it vibrated through the wooden beams. Every hair on Lola's arms lifted.

Ethan stiffened. "What the hell was that?" Alcohol slowed his reflexes as he blinked into the dark space.

In the darkness beneath the ride, two eyes gleamed silver.

His grip loosened. Lola tore free and stomped on his ankle.

"Dammit!" Ethan stumbled. She barreled into him, sending him sprawling in the dirt.

Then she ran—away from Ethan, and from whatever lurked beneath the carousel.

Six

Only once she had covered the entire length of the carnival did Lola dare to stop. Near the back of the grounds, the noise faded into a hush. Beyond the flash and lights of the carnival, tents stood in rows like soldiers in formation; utilitarian, drab, built for function over spectacle. This must be where the carnival workers lived.

She spun, scanning for pursuers, then sagged against a fence post, breath ragged.

During her long years, she'd occasionally come by humans with excessive cruelty. But they bled red like everybody else. She never had to worry about them because *she* had been the predator.

Now, she was the prey. By surrendering her demonic power, she'd made herself vulnerable. What had she done, landing herself in this strange world, in this helpless body? She couldn't even fend off a drunken bully.

Her jackrabbit heartbeat slowed. She watched the passing crowds, smiling, carefree. These humans navigated the world without crumbling in fear.

But they didn't *know* the world the way she did. Unaware of all manner of beasts and demons that stalked them through the shadows, they lived in blissful ignorance.

Lola had no such luxury.

She remembered everything, like all the horrible ways people could die. She remembered inflicting pain. She had been the monster. Now, she feared the monsters would come for her.

Even her friends, who had seen what lay beneath the world's surface, moved forward. Despite the horrors they'd survived in their hellish descent into the Well of Souls—Walt poisoned, Nix crushed and Gael's throat torn open—they still dreamed of their futures. Maybe that was the gift of humanity: hope, or ignorance. Either way, she envied them.

Across the path, a row of free-standing sinks gleamed under fluorescent bulbs, mirrors mounted above. Lola approached, hesitating before looking up. The myth that a vampire had no reflection was false. But since she'd regained her soul, it seemed as though something different gazed back at her.

If she was going to face the world as a human, she had to be able to face herself. She forced her gaze up. Solemn brown eyes stared back.

In the garish carnival lights, her freckles looked darker, splotchy. She leaned closer, realizing they weren't freckles at all. Blood spattered her face.

She flinched. When she looked again, heart in her throat, the spots were gone.

"*Merde*," she whispered.

An echoing growl rumbled behind her; the same sound that had saved her from Ethan.

She froze.

Then she heard the swish and click of a lighter.

"I won't hurt you," a raspy voice said.

From the shadows between the tents, a familiar figure emerged, her face lit orange by the glow of her cigarette.

The lead singer of The Bayous, Otsana, swaggered towards her, hand on her hip as she took a deep drag, then let out a long stream of smoke. Her heavy makeup was smeared, and she looked both sensual and punk as she approached, cornering Lola.

"Look at you, little rabbit," Otsana murmured. "You know the big bad wolf can smell you, even when you're hiding?"

Lola swallowed. "I was just—"

"It's a shame," she continued, ignoring Lola's stammering. "Without strength, you can only cower." Her gaze was knowing, cutting deeper than it should.

"Was that you behind the carousel?" Lola hated how fragile her voice sounded as the woman gave a curt nod. "Why'd you do it? Help me?"

Another drag, another slow exhale. "Maybe it was fun. I like watching the big ones shake; it always makes me laugh. Want one?" She held out the cigarette pack. Her nails were long, glossy black.

"I shouldn't." Lola had been trying to quit. She'd smoked for so long and missed it desperately, but as Nix pointed out, she had human lungs now. "They could kill me."

Otsana arched a brow. "Lots of things can kill you."

Lola's hand darted out before her mind caught up. "Thanks," she said as the woman lit it for her. She took a deep drag, welcoming the curling smoke in her lungs.

The singer studied her from head to toe, smirking. "Now, what do we have here? Not quite a rabbit, are you?"

"What do you mean?" Lola got the sense that Otsana was looking at something beyond normal sight and took a step back.

She didn't like the sense of invasion, but an instinct warned her not to flee. Running would spark something in Otsana, and the chase would be on.

It wasn't any fun being on this side of the hunt.

Otsana waved her cigarette lazily, smoke tracing the air around Lola. "Your spirit is fractured. Like a prism. Something was put back together, but not exactly right. Now, what could have done that?"

The memory of her transformation from demon to human flashed back to her. She had been shattered. She was no longer a vampire, but she also wondered if she was still Lola.

Perhaps something essential had been lost in the change. Put back together wrong was exactly how she'd been feeling these past weeks.

"I don't know what you're talking about."

Out of the corner of her eye, she caught a flicker of light glimmering around Otsana like a faint aura. Or was it only the glow of the cigarette? Silence stretched as smoke curled between them.

"Memories cling to you like faded photographs. You used to be *something* before you became a rabbit. Now you're neither here nor there. It's not safe, not knowing which world you stand in."

An owl hooted in the distance, a lonely cry. Otsana's face lit up. "Maybe you should be an owl instead. They are wise. They know about transformations." Her voice dropped to a throaty whisper. "But they are still hunters."

"Who are you?" Lola asked, her voice strangled and tight. She wanted to ask Otsana *what* she was but wasn't sure she wanted the answer.

Otherworld creatures weren't invited to Duchesne Island— they were cursed if they stepped foot on the land, and immortals would only risk that if they were desperate or insane. If Otsana was some kind of demon, she shouldn't be here.

Otsana tilted her head to the side, eyes gleaming as though she could read Lola's mind. "It is amazing what sneaks in when the gate has been left open."

"What gate? What are you talking about?"

"Otsana!"

A sharp voice shattered the stillness. Otsana's expression darkened, and her eyes narrowed to slits. She jerked her chin, the meaning instantly clear: *hide*.

Lola backed into the shadows until she was wedged behind the row of mirrors, reluctantly crushing her cigarette under her sandal. She could see a sliver of Otsana's face from her hiding place.

Duke Louis, the carnival owner, strode towards Otsana. Though the expression on her face spelled murder, he outstretched his arms to embrace her. Any man who approached the prickly lead singer that way could only have a death wish. But Otsana threw her cigarette to one side and let him take her, let him grab her by the back of her neck and kiss her deep.

His hand still fisted in her hair, he broke away.

"You were exquisite, *ma petite loup*. The trap seems well and truly set."

"And you told me you never doubted me."

"Never. I trust you in all things. These poor saps never had a chance."

Otsana was still for a long moment, her eyes boring into his. "I will need more power if I'm to achieve what we discussed."

He pulled back, a frown creasing his face. "Not another one. You know how I hate the mess. We need to keep a low profile."

"If everything goes according to plan, we'll never need to keep a low profile again. Besides, I think I've found the perfect candidate."

Her smile unspooled, slow and sinister, and she kissed Louis back. Her eyes stayed wide open, and her gaze flicked to Lola, watching her, sensual and knowing.

SEVEN

Feeling like a voyeur, Lola backed away from the tangled couple, circling around the empty workers' tents. The carnival grounds stretched behind her, but beyond the makeshift fencing lay the forest that swallowed much of the island. The air back here was heavy, the carnival din muffled by the dense canopy. The silence coiled around her, tightening her nerves. She crept along the path, every step deliberate, unwilling to draw any more predators to her.

The treeline guided her to the foot of the Ferris wheel. She'd ended on the wrong side of the ride, dwarfed by the massive metal structure braced by thick iron posts driven deep into the earth. The grinding gears and hissing hydraulics swallowed all other sound.

Above her, the carts whirled by in hypnotic rhythm, faces flickering in and out like a broken film reel—laughing, kissing, shouting. Glimpses into other lives, untouched by what had just happened to her.

The wheel groaned as it slowed and came to a stop. Lola darted between the unmoving seats.

"Hey! You can't—!" A worker's shout barely registered before she plunged back into the carnival world.

Everything came alive, music and sound slamming into her. The flashing lights and whirling games and chatter of the crowd, it all wrapped around her, making her feel less like a target. But the tension in her shoulders didn't ease. She couldn't stop darting glances over her shoulder.

The base of her neck prickled as though eyes bored into her. She spun, gaze raking over the people milling around her, trying to see what was pulling at her subconscious because something inside her was desperately telling her to beware.

And then she spotted a face she did recognize: the grey-eyed girl.

She stood just beyond the crowed, platinum-tipped hair catching the light. Her posture was controlled, like she was approaching a deer with a bow hidden behind her back.

Everything about her screamed at Lola to be wary.

Lola swallowed, throat suddenly dry. The girl's eyebrows were straight black slashes, a hoop of silver hooked into one. From under the collar of her band tee, a hint of ink curled at her collarbone. A symbol, but not one Lola recognized.

Lola hesitated. Should she say something? Ask if the girl had seen the same flickering lights? If she felt something was...wrong, too?

Or would that just make her sound insane?

Before she could decide, the girl's frosty gaze flicked up over her shoulder and her eyes widened.

Lola turned just as Gael pushed through the crowd. Relief crashed through her, a fleeting jolt of happiness in all the confusion. She lifted a hand, waving him over.

When she turned back, the girl had disappeared into the crowd.

Gael reached her, his expression tight. "Where did you go?" He put his arms around her, pulling her into his chest. "I was worried. I can't believe you took off after that thief."

Lola's head swam; she'd had far too many strange encounters over the past few minutes. The Carnival of Fools was rife with strange people, and she had a sinking feeling the Otherworld was involved.

Something Otsana had said, that the gate had been left open, nagged at her.

What did that mean?

She brushed off the thought. Now wasn't the time. "I'm fine. I didn't catch him, but I did have a run-in with Ethan."

"Something's shaken you up. What did that jackass do?" Gael's voice hardened. His jaw tensed and his eyes went flinty like a brewing storm.

He was more combative than normal; she searched his face, trying to find the easygoing boy she'd met in the spring. She couldn't tell him how threatening Ethan had been; it would only make things worse.

"Nothing," she said, trying to pull off an airy tone. "He's a jerk, is all. He promised to make my life hell."

Nix materialized beside them, eyes wide and movements jittery. She let out a sharp, staccato laugh. "Ethan was being a jerk? Welcome to the club; you'll get used to it."

She slung an arm around Lola's neck, bouncing on her toes.

Lola huffed a laugh despite herself. "How much sugar have you had?" Her friend was practically vibrating.

"So much. It's everywhere." Nix pulled a crumpled bag of gummy worms from her pocket and offered them to her.

"I'm good. Maybe Walt wants some."

Walt grimaced at the offered worms. "Seriously, Nix, you're going to give yourself ADHD."

Lola turned to him. "Sorry I couldn't get your wallet back."

Walt cracked his knuckles; unconcerned. "I don't get how he did it. I didn't feel a thing."

"Good pickpockets are like that. They use distraction and misdirection to make you look the other way. It's an art form."

"You seem to know a lot about pickpocketing," Gael said with a teasing smile. "Is this another hidden talent?"

"It's not something I ever had to practice."

Silence. The weight of her words settled between them. She assumed they realized what she meant. Lola had been more likely to rip out a victim's throat than steal their wallet.

She cleared her throat. "I hope you didn't lose anything valuable, Walt."

"Just money." He shrugged, then laughed at Nix's disgruntled squawk.

Gael grabbed Lola, wrapping an arm around her as he tugged her down the path. "Come on, we're wasting time. We have so much to do. Rides to go on, games to play..."

"Candy to eat..." Nix's eyes were dilated despite the lights.

"Seriously, are you okay?" Lola asked.

Nix's grin was frenetic. "What do you mean?"

Lola put a hand on her shoulder and could practically feel the energy buzzing off her. "This level of sugar is excessive, even for you."

"It tastes so good here. Like, better than anything else."

The screech of an amp tore through the night sky. The Bayous, kicking off another set.

The deep pulsing chords thrummed through her bones. The sound tugged at Lola's chest, wrapping around her like the current in a live wire.

She stiffened. They should leave. Something about Otsana, the lead singer was all wrong, and they needed to get away from her.

Her friends, however, had already turned towards the music, drawn in as if the notes had hooked under their ribs and pulled.

"Gael Smith?"

A nasal voice cut through the noise like a blade. A slight, gawky young man with thick black glasses stood before them. His buttoned shirt was too formal, his slicked-back hair too polished for a carnival. Standing still in the sea of moving bodies, he was jarring like an off-key note in the melody.

"Yeah?" Gael's head tilted to the side. "Do I know you?"

"Richie Dawgsby." He thrust out a hand, which Gael took but didn't shake.

"Wait, Richie Dawgsby, the editor of the *Duchesne Daily*?" Lola piped up. She read the island paper every day.

Richie turned to her, keen interest in his gaze. A notebook materialized in his hand like a magician's trick. "I'm working on a piece about The Carnival of Fools. Odd name, don't you think? And you are?"

"Lola."

Richie jotted something in his notebook. More than just her name.

Gael bristled. "I recognize you, I've seen you around the cottage. Taking pictures."

"Town photographer as well. The *Duchesne Daily* is kind of a one-man show. But I'm really here for you, Gael. Duchesne Island's very own treasure hunter."

Gael's jaw tightened. "You've called my mum a dozen times. She's not interested in talking to you."

Richie pressed the tip of his pen on his notebook. "And do you let your mother speak for you in all things?"

Lola's fingers curled around Gael's wrist in warning.

Richie's smile didn't meet his eyes. "The island treasure— some say there's more to it. That your family got *very* lucky. That you—"

"Everything we found was on our land. We followed all the proper protocols."

"And yet," Richie mused. "Some of us need more answers. For years, many have attempted the dig, only to be driven off by terrible luck or the threat of a curse that some believe your family invented. Then *you* seem to be able to dig it up over the weekend with the help of a group of high school students."

Richie waved at Nix and Walt, who were both edging away from him.

Lola let out a frustrated huff and stepped in front of Gael. "Listen, we're not interested in speaking with you."

Richie's gaze shifted. To her.

"Lola Monteux." Richie's voice lingered over her name as though he knew a juicy secret about her. "Recent arrival to the island and now under the care of Faye Ducharme? You're her cousin, is that right? Only when you arrived here you were living on the streets. Unusual, don't you think?"

Lola's mouth opened but nothing came out. It was a dance he seemed primed to win—she hadn't been expecting an ambush. She supposed that was the point.

He moved in closer, and Lola winced back. "You showed up right at the same time as the vampire serial killer, correct?"

Lola's breath caught. *What?*

Gael thrust forward and shoved Richie. "Stay away from her." His voice was deep and aggressive; the muscles on his neck corded as he advanced on the reporter.

Richie stumbled back, though a sly smile stole over his face. Strangers gathered around, sensing a fight. Encircled by the crowd drawn in by the promise of bloodletting, the air seemed dense and crushing. Lola struggled to tug Gael away.

Richie's eyes gleamed as though he had won a game the rest of them didn't know they were playing. "Lola, can you comment on the fact your personal effects were found in the home of the first murder victim?"

Lola shuddered away from the reporter. He knew too much; he was going to be trouble.

Gael lunged.

His fist connected with Richie's face with a sharp crack. The crowd gasped, then cheered, roaring in approval at the assault.

Richie's hands flew to his face as he fell on the ground, his notebook flying. He scrambled after it with frantic fingers. His nose was bleeding, and as he stood, he straightened his glasses. There was something in the speculative look he shot at them Lola didn't like, before he staggered away through the crowd.

A group of girls moved closer to Gael, giggling. Cassidy was at the front of the crowd, her hands clasped in front of her as she bounced on her toes.

Lola grabbed his arm, unsure if she wanted to get him away from Richie or his fans. "Let's get out of here." She had to shout over the din of the crowd.

Gael stared at his hand as though he wasn't sure it belonged to him, his voice wooden and detached. "I was so angry, I didn't even think." He looked to Lola as though she might have answers.

The air sucked out of her lungs as she stared back at him. His eyes shone silver, as Otherworldly as could be.

EIGHT

"What?"

Lola grabbed Gael's face in her hands, tilting his head one way then the other to catch the light. His eyes were normal—a warm brown with veins of gold. No trace of silver. He recovered quickly, enduring her scrutiny with a half-smile.

"What's what?"

"Your eyes, they were…" But there was nothing unusual about them now. The light must have caught them at a weird angle. She let go, shoving him hard in the chest. He barely moved.

"What were you thinking?"

"What do you mean?" he asked.

"Going all barbarian on that reporter."

"He was being a pest. To you, Lola. He pissed me off."

"You can't just…" she trailed off, knowing she had no moral high ground. A few weeks ago, she might have snapped the intrusive newspaper man's wrist without a second thought.

"Are you completely stunned?" Nix asked Gael, offering him some cotton candy, which he shook his head at it, giving her a sheepish smile. "Since when do you punch people? That was awesome!"

Even Walt gave him a subtle nod—his version of high praise.

Lola sighed. "Come on, we need to talk."

She hustled them away from the crowds, not stopping until they reached the gates of the carnival. The entrance no longer seemed like an enchanting portal but an open maw, waiting to swallow them whole.

"We all need to go home," she said, eyeing Gael. He wasn't himself. And after that strange encounter with Otsana, Lola's gut screamed to get them all away from the fairgrounds until she knew what was happening.

The music pulsed behind her, pulling at her. A longing curled in her chest, urging her to stay, to give in, to let the sound crash over her.

"Why exactly are we leaving?" Nix asked, her feet trailed in the dirt as she looked back at the festival grounds like a little girl being dragged away from the party. Red lights flickered over her face.

"I think the band cast a spell over you."

The three of them stared at her. Walt's brows knit together. "Like a magic spell?"

"Exactly like. I keep on seeing these lights everywhere, and I think Otsana is a witch—"

Both Gael and Nix snickered.

"What?"

"The lead singer?" Nix asked. "I mean, she totally looks like a witch, but that's just her look."

"Well, you were all dancing like drunken fools with your eyes glazed over, and it was creepy." Even as she said it, Lola realized how lame it sounded. "But I've been seeing lights! And the whole place gives me a weird feeling, and I *know* the Otherworld."

She rubbed her knuckles over her brow, and when she spoke, her words were sharp and clipped. "I can't believe you guys are gaslighting me on this."

"Lola, we're not trying to gaslight you." Gael slung an arm around her. "If you're seeing weird things, I believe you. But maybe you're seeing this stuff because you're looking for it? Like, maybe it's normal weird, not Otherworld weird, but you're conditioned to see magical things."

"I mean, the carnival's a trippy place, magic or not," Nix said.

Walt folded his arms over his chest. "Why do you think you're seeing these things?"

Maybe because she'd been put back together wrong, like Otsana said.

Lola squared her shoulders. Whether or not something was wrong with her, deep inside, she knew they needed to get away. "We should still leave. Gael could get into trouble for hitting that reporter."

She jerked her head to the RCMP cruiser parked near the entrance. She wondered if Sergeant Greyson was there; he always seemed to be in the least convenient place at all times.

The others followed her gaze, and the reality sank in. "We better hope Richie doesn't press charges," she said.

"That guy was a creep. Do you think he will?" Nix twisted her hair around her fist and tugged, her sugar high finally seeming to break.

Lola hesitated, remembering the look on Richie's face. "I'm not convinced he will. It's almost as if he wanted that reaction from us. But we shouldn't hang around, just in case."

Her friends paused for a beat too long, defiant. But as the song ended, releasing them from the pressure of the continuous beat, they deflated.

Walt shrugged. "Probably a good idea."

The others followed him as he led the way down the dirt path. The carnival's glow faded behind them, but people still streamed in, drawn towards its open gates.

Nix and Walt veered off towards their side of town, but Gael walked Lola to the front door of The Pain Perdu.

Faye's café had been a shelter when she'd first arrived on Duchesne Island, and it had become her actual home when Faye had offered for her to stay. Chocolate and buttery pastry perfumed the air, as close to paradise as Lola could imagine. Against all odds, she had found a safe place to land.

"So about tonight." Gael leaned against the doorframe. "It was kinda crazy."

"I would say downright weird. I didn't know you had that anger in you."

"I don't know what came over me." Gael flexed his fingers as if still feeling the impact. "I've never hit anyone before."

"You pack a solid punch for a newbie."

His smile was small, distracted. "But I was talking about before, though. When we were dancing? It was intense."

Though his tone was light, he watched her unwavering, gauging her reaction.

When she first heard the music play, she'd wanted to lose herself in him—not caring about the world or her future or her messed up past. Nothing but his arms around her.

"It *was* intense." She couldn't match his teasing tone. "I'm not sure what came over me."

"It's going around." His fingers twined around hers. "I wanted to say I liked it, but if you're not ready for that, I get it. It seemed to freak you out."

Speechless, Lola brushed the lock of hair that had fallen over his eyebrow. She had only ever been with men who took and took, who never asked what was too much.

Running her thumb along his jaw, she felt him swallow. "I appreciate that." She rose onto her tiptoes and pressed her lips to his, before letting out a slow exhale. "When I was with Beau..." she started, her heart hammering as she tried to put their relationship into words. She had been immortal, but he had made her feel so small.

Gael brushed his thumb over her lips. "We seriously don't have to talk about it. Or him, ever again."

She pulled back. "Right."

Obviously, he wouldn't want to be reminded of her ex—the one who had ripped out Gael's throat with his teeth. Still, a part of her wanted to. To talk about that part of her life with someone who might understand.

"Are you okay?" He spoke quietly, as though he didn't want to disturb the delicate balance that floated between them.

Things between them were already off kilter. She was seeing things nobody else was; hearing things no one else did. But Gael thought she was normal now, just a human girl.

She needed a therapist who specialized in the Otherworld.

"I've got a lot going on up here." She tapped her forehead. "See you later?"

"Yeah." Gael bit his lip as though he wanted to say more but only rapped his knuckles against the wooden doorframe. "Later."

NINE

The lights inside the café glowed, but there were no customers. Probably everyone was at the carnival, stuffing themselves with funnel cakes. They didn't know what they were missing, though; carnival food had nothing on Faye's pain au chocolat.

But tonight, the café didn't feel like the haven she had come to count on. Despite the lingering smells of coffee and chocolate, tension crackled in the air.

The café should have been closed an hour ago, but Faye still bustled around the shop, scrubbing tables. She scowled as though trying to scare the crumbs away. Her curves were wrapped in a cashmere sweater and fair isle patterned tights, her long dark hair tied back in a scarf.

Faye's head whipped up at the ding of the bell. "Thank goodness, there you are."

"Here I am." Lola paused in the doorway, caught off guard by the worry in Faye's voice. "What's wrong?"

"I was worried." Faye cleared her throat, her lips tightening. "I realized how late it was, and I hadn't heard from you."

"I was out with Gael and some friends and didn't notice the time. There's this carnival—"

"You should have called." Faye's face was lined with concern, her expression harder than usual. "It puts me on edge, not knowing if you'll…"

Lola knew what Faye was thinking: not knowing if she'd come back. She still thought of Lola as a runaway, convinced that, sooner or later, Lola would take off again.

"Sorry Faye. I'm not used to checking in with somebody."

She was used to a different kind of family. The last time she had seen Jacquotte—the woman she had considered a mother— she'd been ordering Lola's ex-boyfriend to kill her.

"What were you doing at the carnival?"

The deep voice startled her. Lola jumped, not realizing someone else was in the café. The fact bothered her more than she could say. There had been a time when she could sense every living creature in her vicinity, catalogue them by the sound of their heartbeat and the whoosh of their blood in their veins.

Now, apparently, a corner booth was beyond her powers of perception.

She scowled at the man sipping his coffee, guessing he was the real reason behind Faye's unusual worry. Sergeant Greyson. He'd arrived on the island around the same time as Lola. He'd fallen for Faye's charms and developed a deep distrust towards Lola, with roughly the same intensity. He had an infuriating ability to command attention and authority and Faye, unfortunately, listened to what the man had to say.

Sergeant Greyson was a compact man with dark brown skin and a penetrating gaze that seemed to observe eighteen extra layers of detail more than everybody else. He'd been an irritant since she'd set foot on Duchesne Island, and he hadn't become any more friendly since she'd become human.

It didn't help that he still suspected her of murder. It helped even less that he was correct.

"What are you doing here?" she asked.

Behind her, Faye hissed, "Be polite."

"I stopped by for a coffee," he said. "No harm in that. You didn't answer my question."

And I'm not going to, she wanted to answer, but she didn't want to stir things up with Faye, who clearly respected the man. "It was a carnival," she answered. "Rides, food. This thing called fun?"

"I've heard there've been some fights out there." He raised his eyebrows and Lola's gaze slid away. Did he know about Gael and the reporter?

She shrugged. "Seemed pretty normal to me."

He either didn't know or let it slide. "Some questionable people are running things."

"What do you mean, questionable people?" Faye squeezed the rag in her hand until water dribbled out. Her gaze flicked to Lola, clearly concerned. "What kind of things are they into?"

Lola's jaw tightened. Greyson's presence was an unwanted intrusion, like a burr in her shoe. She wanted to shake him out of their lives.

True, every single person she had met at the carnival seemed more than questionable and closer to downright dangerous, but she never wanted to concede a single point when it came to Greyson. "What are you worried about? Deranged clowns?"

Greyson harrumphed. "I don't think it's wise for a teenage girl to be wandering the island at all hours of the night."

Lola's lips twisted into a dry smile. She could only imagine what he would say if he knew what she used to get up to.

She raised her eyebrow at him. "What do you suggest? Lock me up?"

His gesture was wide, almost disbelieving, as though the answer was obvious. "How about a curfew? Is that so strange for a sixteen-year-old girl?"

Lola bristled. She had prowled the world like it was her playground before arriving on Duchesne Island, and now this man wanted to impose something so mundane as a curfew? A flare of heat passed over her, and she pictured having fangs again, of vaulting over the tables and tearing into him for daring to cage her.

"I'm not some naïve child," she said, her voice low but shaking with suppressed anger.

Faye patted her arm. She'd brought over a cup of herbal tea Lola loved—rosehips and lavender, a calming blend that usually soothed Lola's nerves. She took in a deep breath of the aromatic steam, resisting the urge to snap. Ripping Greyson's throat out wouldn't solve anything.

"Greyson, thanks for keeping me company," Faye said, her voice sterner than usual. "I've got it from here. It's time for me to close shop."

Greyson hesitated, as if he might argue, but finally finished his coffee and brought his dishes to the counter. "Anytime." He tipped his head to Lola as he left. "Miss Monteux."

"Sergeant Greyson." She poured all her resentment into those syllables.

She was sure he saw Lola as a manipulative runaway taking advantage of Faye's generosity.

Though it was clear the sergeant was smitten with her, Faye hadn't given any real sign as to how she felt about him. She was certainly flirtatious around him, but that was true of most men.

Lola didn't know how she would react if Faye gave a sign that she wanted to be with him. The man was far too observant for his own good. It was the kind of quality that would get somebody into trouble someday, and Lola didn't need that kind of trouble in her life.

Faye locked the door behind him and turned off the lights, so they were illuminated by the glow of the patisserie display. She leaned against the display case beside Lola, the tension in the air easing.

"Lola," Faye began, her voice gentle. "I don't see you as a child, and I don't want to make you think I don't trust you. What I do see is someone who hasn't had a lot of stability in her life, and I...I thought I could give that to you." Faye took a deep breath. "It might be hard to imagine, but my own childhood looked very different from this. I understand people not being there for you."

Though she gestured at her beloved café, her gaze turned inward as though she was lost in memories. "I got into a lot of trouble when I was a kid. And it would have been good for me to have a safe place to go to, but I didn't. It made things so much worse. So, I was hoping to give you what I didn't have when I was your age."

Lola studied Faye's striking face. She was only in her early thirties, but at that moment, her eyes held deep wisdom earned through painful experience.

"I'm not used to people worrying about me," Lola admitted.

"I know." Faye carefully brushed a stray hair from Lola's face. "But I do worry. I don't want you to make the mistakes I did when I was young or suffer the consequences. I want to see you thrive. You deserve that."

Her tender words hit something deep in Lola, a part of her that had longed for this kind of connection. On her more optimistic days, she could almost imagine Faye was the family she'd never got to have, but she was scared she wasn't built for it.

"I'll try harder." Her voice was rough and scratchy. She cleared her throat, unable to meet Faye's eyes.

Faye gave a soft smile. "So will I."

She pushed off from the counter, stifling a yawn. "Now I need to get a few hours of sleep before I need to be up for the bread tomorrow. You good to lock up?"

Lola nodded, watching as Faye headed upstairs. The lump in her throat grew, the weight of everything Faye was offering settling on her chest. She wanted to believe she could make this work— that she could stay, have a life here.

But all Lola could think about was all the ways she could mess this up.

Ten

"Are you guys ready for the beach?" Lola squinted against the bright summer sun, standing on the stoop of The Pain Perdu, her beach bag slung over her shoulder. Walt and Nix waited at the bottom step, both looking equally prepared for a day in the sand.

It had been far too long since she'd gone for a swim. Most days, she only got to stare longingly at the water from her shack.

Lola finally had a day off from the Ice Cream Shoppe, and she was going to use it well—by basking in the sea until she was fully marinated.

"Are you sure you don't want to go to the carnival?" Nix asked, draining an enormous Slurpee in the most unnatural shade of blue. Walt chuckled, sipping a coffee from a stainless-steel mug as he watched their sugar-fiend friend with amusement.

"Yes, I'm sure," Lola said. She wrinkled her nose. "Ugh, Nix, is that your breakfast?"

"No, I had some Pixy Stix." Nix paused. "That's probably not great. I can't seem to get enough sugar lately. And why not the carnival? You never want to go."

"And you've been there every day since it opened, so I think you can take a break." Lola shifted her bag higher on her shoulder. "All I want to do is take a delightful dip in the ocean. We can get some fresh air. Maybe eat a vegetable," she added, side-eyeing Nix.

Before Nix could retort, she stiffened, eyes rounding.

"What?" Lola asked. "Did mentioning produce go too far?"

But Nix wasn't looking at her. Her gaze had gone over Lola's shoulder, and Walt's expression had taken on that careful, unreadable quality he got when people made him uncomfortable.

Lola turned—and instantly tensed.

A girl was making her way towards them. Lola recognized her immediately: the cute Asian tourist Nix had pointed out. The only other person who hadn't seemed affected by The Bayous when they played. And right now, she was staring directly at Lola with her serious, storm-grey eyes.

Her hair had been tied back into two space buns, showing the contrast between black and icy blonde. She was dressed in black shorts and a T-shirt and wore heavy boots out of season for the summer heat wave.

"Hey," the girl said, giving them a nod and slowing as she neared them. "Do you guys live here?"

"What?" Lola asked.

"Sorry, that sounded weird." The girl gave a self-deprecating smile. "I didn't mean, *do you live at this café*? I mean, do you live in Port Despardoux?"

"But Lola does live here," Nix said, pointing at The Pain Perdu as her cheeks blossomed with stains of colour.

The girl's lips quirked. "Lola lives in a café?" Her assessing gaze flicked to Lola, but they weren't giving anything away. There was something calculating about her. Lola had no idea why she'd approached them or how she was connected to what she had seen at the carnival the other day, but all her senses were on red alert.

"Why the interest?" Lola resisted the urge to cross her arms over her chest. She had the strong impression that the girl already knew she lived in the café and had been waiting for her to come out.

"Right, still weird. I'm new here, actually. Just moved in. And it's hard to figure out who's a local, what with all the tourists, but I basically just wanted to say hi."

"You're *not* a tourist?" Nix's voice cracked, and she flushed even deeper magenta.

The girl took in Nix, and a smile spread over her face. Lola didn't like the look of it, sly and stealthy, like a fox who'd found her way into the henhouse.

"Not a tourist. I'm going to be starting at the high school this fall. I'm Reiko Frost. Moved from Tokyo."

"Oh my God, that is so cool," Nix said. "You are going to be so disappointed with our insanely small island."

Reiko shrugged. "Tokyo's as cool as the next place, but I move around a lot. And Duchesne Island seems pretty interesting."

Once again, that look. Her grey eyes flicked to Lola, settling a second too long, her eyebrow raising with a flash of a silver hoop.

"I'm Nix, and this is Walt," Nix introduced eagerly.

"And you are Lola from the café," Reiko said.

Lola clenched her jaw. Her instincts told her never turn her back on this girl. "I live in the apartment upstairs," she said. "But we're just on our way out, so—"

"Are you going to the carnival?"

"No," Lola said at the same time as Nix blurted, "Yes."

Reiko's smile crept back again, tucking up on one side of her face. *Cunning* was the word that popped into Lola's mind. "Well, that's where I'm heading today. If you end up there, come find me. It's nice to meet new people." With a wave, she turned and continued up the hill.

The three of them watched her in silence until she had turned the corner before Nix whirled on Lola. "We are totally going to the carnival."

"Nix..." Lola wanted to argue but also knew how much Nix

was crushing on Reiko. She'd spoken of little else since she'd first spotted her, and an invitation to join her was hard to turn down. "Why does everyone like that place so much?"

Nix folded her arms. "Are you completely stunned? It's fun, and everyone is there. You're literally the only person on the island who doesn't like it."

Which made Lola all the more suspicious.

"It is odd how obsessed everyone seems about the place," Walt said. "It's for kids. So why the appeal?"

"But you've been there every day as well," Lola pointed out.

Walt shrugged, frowning. "It's odd," he repeated, cracking his knuckles.

"So, you're in on this plan too?"

He took a sip of coffee and gave a shy smile. "I just follow the redhead. It makes everything easier."

"There, I've already texted Gael," Nix said, her fingers flying over her phone. "He'll meet us there. Now you have no reason not to go."

Lola could think of several, but she couldn't accuse Reiko of anything. All she had was a hunch that something was off about her. And Nix would absolutely not want to hear that.

Maybe she would go to the carnival and find that everything was normal, and she'd been stressed for no reason. All of her weird suspicions were nothing more than the aftershocks of becoming human, and she was making monsters out of shadows.

"...Fine," she muttered. "We'll go to the carnival."

"Yay!" Nix did a skip and grabbed Walt's hand, dragging him up the road in the opposite direction of the Atlantic Ocean. Lola trudged behind them.

The Carnival of Fools was different in bright sunlight.

Without the flashing nighttime lights, it seemed normal. Wholesome. A place where parents could safely bring their kids for the day.

So why did staring at the grounds make her skin crawl?

As she walked along the fencing to get to the entry, she tried not to look at it, not wanting to see glittering lights she wasn't supposed to see.

Gael waited for them at the front archway, his normal, easygoing self.

It had been several days since Gael had punched Richie. No charges had been laid, and Lola breathed a bit easier. Surely the reporter would have made a complaint by now? Everything could just go back to normal.

Except she'd been on edge around Gael since they made out the other night, as though something was straining against a leash inside of her. From the way he was being extra careful around her, she suspected he noticed. It was as if both were dancing around the same space but neither knew exactly how to approach it.

"Hi," he said, pulling her into a hug.

She let herself sink into his warmth. Stop overthinking things, she told herself. Just be here.

"Hi." She tilted her chin up, pressing a brief kiss to his lips. It was like lighting a sparkler of heat inside of her.

"So?" he asked. "See anything...weird?" Weird being the code word for supernatural.

Something inside her chest seemed to shutter closed. Would she always be the weird one? The outsider?

She refused to look anywhere other than his eyes, searching for a flicker of silver—and finding none.

"Nope," she said, forcing a bright smile. "Everything normal."

As they stepped onto the carnival grounds, the laughter and music swept over her. Nothing seemed unusual or different; there was no elaborate sign of the Otherworld.

Maybe she *was* looking for something that wasn't there—seeing the Otherworld in every corner just because her past was drenched in blood.

The sunshine was lovely and warm on her shoulders, and she turned her face up to it. She wore a lacy sundress she'd found in the vintage shop run by Nix's mom. It made her feel pretty and carefree. Had she worn dresses like this when she had originally been human? Considering it had been the 1940s, she was certain she wouldn't have worn something so revealing and strappy. But she wondered if she had liked pretty things; she always had as a vampire.

The air smelled of fried food and popcorn and coconut sunscreen. She slipped her hand into Gael's; his warm palm enveloped hers. Nix's head swivelled back and forth as she pulled Walt down the paths through the stands; obviously, she was looking for the new girl.

"We did it last night." A teenage girl was giggling to her friend next to them. Her hands covered her cheeks as she spoke. "Dane asked me to go through the maze with him. It was amazing."

"Really?" The girl at her side stopped to peer at her, intent on the answer. "What happened?"

The first girl blushed and stammered. "I...I don't remember, exactly? My head was kind of fuzzy. But I know it was great," she said, with a certain nod. "It must have been. I mean, we were alone and..." She trailed off as though she didn't know what to say.

Her friend narrowed her eyes. "Weird. I went through with Greg, and it got kind of freaky. I don't know how it started, but when we came out, he was yelling at me. It wasn't cute. I told him to get lost."

"What did he do?"

The girl shrugged and looked away. "He went to The Gardens and hooked up with somebody else. He's a jerk anyways." She sniffed.

"Sounds like everyone has a different experience in the maze," Lola said, nodding to the girls.

"I've been hearing people talk about it. It sounds cool." Gael didn't look at her, though the tips of his ears reddened. "Should we...check it out?"

A slow smile spread across Lola's face. "You'd like that?"

She loved how his ears grew more and more red. "Is that a trick question?" His grin seemed to be an invitation.

She bit her lip. Maybe it was time to stop holding herself back.

"Let's do it," she said.

"Awesome." He spun and tugged her along, nearly running. He turned back, his face lit with a brilliant smile, and Lola tried to catch her breath through laughter, caught up in a whirlwind of want.

Eleven

They arrived at the Maze of Desire, slowing as they approached. For the moment, they were the only ones there. All was dark behind the tent entrance, hushed. Lola hesitated at the threshold, a pulse of dread thrumming through her, but she shook it off.

It was just a cheesy carnival attraction. There was no way it was going to scare her.

"Are you sure you're ready for this?" A voice cut through the quiet.

Lola jumped. The ringmaster, Duke Louis, had appeared out of nowhere, blocking their way forward. His tuxedo jacket looked freshly pressed, his top hat perched at a jaunty angle. Silver makeup lined his face, gleaming in the dim light.

His smile seemed directed at her alone. "Are you truly willing to see your heart's desire?"

Gael moved slightly in front of Lola, his hand out as if to fend him off. "Yeah, man, we're good. We can probably handle this on our own."

Louis's eyes lingered on Lola's face, his interest far too intrusive. "Many have lost their hearts inside these walls," he said softly, "but not always in the way they expect."

Lola fought the impulse to shrink away from his penetrating gaze; instead, she tossed her hair back and lifted her chin. "I guess it depends on who you enter with."

Louis didn't blink. "That confident, are you?" His eyes were a pale grey that matched his silver eyeliner.

She held his gaze, defiant. "I know exactly what I want."

His smile faded into something more unreadable. "Everyone thinks they know what they want. Few people are truly ready to see their deepest desires."

With an ominous chuckle, he turned and sauntered away, leaving Lola and Gael in uneasy silence, their joyful moment soured. The air between them was heavier now, almost suffocating.

She shifted as she peered into the darkness of the maze. "It's like he's trying to scare us away."

"He's just messing with us," Gael said. "Now we're primed to freak out if something spooky happens." He gave her the smile that always made her a little melty. "Let's show him we got this."

"Together." Lola nodded, clutching his hand. In tandem, they passed beyond the curtains, stepping into the unknown.

Inside, the air was warm and hazy, scented like a cloying herb. After a few steps, dizziness hit Lola—but not in an unpleasant way, more as though her head was floating above her shoulders. It was intoxicating. After weeks of confusion, of questions she couldn't answer, it felt like a strange kind of escape from the weight that sat on her shoulders.

They shuffled into a hall of mirrors, the reflections stretching out in every direction, repeating into infinity. The corridor seemed to expand far beyond the limits of the tent. She exchanged a look with Gael in the mirror, stifling a nervous laugh.

The space was darker than she would have expected, as though the walls absorbed the light. The air hung heavy with a thick silence she didn't want to disturb. Even the sounds of the carnival

—the faint hum of music, the distant laughter—faded to nothingness. All Lola could hear was the rush of her heartbeat and the quiet shuffle of their feet.

"Ow." Gael banged into a mirror. "I don't know why I didn't see that."

He gazed at his reflection, which sagged and morphed unnaturally, his expression warping. "What the hell?" he muttered, rubbing his eyes. His face returned to normal after a beat, but it left an unsettling chill in the air.

Lola tightened her grip on Gael's hand, his palm slick. "Probably a trick of the light," she said, but her voice sounded hollow even to her own ears.

"Weird trick." Gael rubbed his forehead where he'd hit it. "I guess we go this way."

As she turned to follow him, her reflection lingered a half-beat too long, like it wasn't in sync with her movements. Her stomach bottomed out.

"What?" she whispered, pressing her fingers to the glass. Her reflection mirrored the motion, a fraction of a second too slow. "It's a trick," she said, struggling against the growing unease creeping into her chest.

"Trick, trick, trick." An echoed whisper bounced across the glass surfaces, and Lola sucked in her breath.

"Are you scared?" Gael asked.

"A little."

"Me too." His gaze flickered nervously around them. "Want to go back?"

She frowned and shook her head. "I'm not going to be scared away by some guy named Duke Louis. I'm curious to see what the big deal is, why nobody can stop talking about it."

Gael's lips quirked into a half-smile. "Let's keep going, then."

His voice echoed through the hall. As they moved deeper, mirrors popped out of nowhere, reflections appearing where there had been none moments before. Lola's head spun, and she found herself caught in a maze of endless glass, unsure which way was the right one.

Suddenly, she came face-to-face with herself. Her reflection smiled, showing all of Lola's pearly teeth.

The real, unsmiling Lola stumbled back. "What the hell?"

Her grinning reflection followed, tilting her head, watching her dispassionately as though observing something in a zoo.

A jolt of adrenaline flickered through her, making her queasy. "*Merde*," she gasped.

Gael turned, putting an arm around her as though to shield her. "Are you okay?"

"These mirrors, they're…" Lola broke off, horror-struck, as the reflected Gael didn't stop where the real Gael did.

Their reflections, his and hers, moved together with a slow, deliberate hunger. The mirrored Gael's hand slid possessively around the waist of her reflection, pulling her towards him with fluid grace. His other snaked up under her hair, holding her in place as his mouth took hers, with an intensity that was a far cry from the light, teasing kisses they'd shared lately in the real world.

Lola's breath hitched as she watched this unfold like a movie playing in front of her. The moment Gael's mouth met her reflection's, desire stabbed through her, low and sharp.

"Gael?" Her whisper echoed back to them.

"Yeah." His lips parted in shock, but the reflection of him—of them—continued their unrelenting, passionate kiss. Every nerve in Lola's body sparked like an electric shock.

"Are you seeing this?"

He gave only a guttural grunt in response.

"We need to get out of here." Her voice cracked as she pulled back from the mirror. "The mirrors—they're messing with us."

"Definitely. We have to get out of here." But instead of turning to run, he turned to her, taking her in his arms.

As their reflections continued to move with a life of their own, an insatiable hunger in their eyes, Lola felt her body betraying her.

Her hands reached for Gael before she could stop them, pulling him closer with raw urgency.

When they came together, their kiss was consuming. Every nerve in her body was lit up, and she gasped at the trail of fire left by his fingers as they grazed the hemline of her dress, over the tops of her thighs. Her head fell back as his mouth trailed down her neck, his tongue swirling into the hollow at the base of her throat.

Surrounding them, their reflections were locked together, pressed against mirrors, all intent on their fervent purpose. The nearest reflection caught Lola's eye, holding her gaze as she bit Gael's earlobe. Lola couldn't tear her gaze away from the knowing look on her image's face.

The face transformed into something fearsome, with crystalline eyes. Needle-like teeth descended, and Lola's reflection winked.

Even as the real Lola screamed, the reflection plunged her teeth into the crook of Gael's neck. Gael-reflection's eyes shut in ecstasy as his head lolled back.

The memory of her former self, her deep desire to drain Gael dry, welled up inside of her.

Lola broke away with a horrified gasp. "No."

Her Gael, the real Gael, had swollen lips and eyes clouded with concern. Did he see what she saw? He reached for her. "Something isn't right," he said, his voice hoarse.

Lola nodded against his lips. "We have to escape." His hand found her wrist and pressed it back against the mirror, holding her in place while pressing his body against hers as she arched against him.

"Escape. Yes." He spoke into her hair, against her skin.

A voice chuckled. The sound was a rolling echo that bounced off the mirrors, building on itself louder and louder. It was male and deep and familiar.

Duke Louis was in there, spying on them.

The desire was doused by revulsion. She pushed away from

Gael, breaking contact. "We have to go." She banged against the mirrors, spinning, trying to find the way out. Her reflections turned on her, frowning. As though they hadn't gotten what they wanted yet.

Finally, she found an open space and nearly fell through. "Gael, here." She grabbed his hand. As soon as skin met skin, the lust flared through her again like a rekindled bonfire, and she was tangled around Gael. The reflections redoubled their efforts, happy to be attached again.

The laughing built to a crescendo, vibrating the mirrors until she thought the ceiling would crash down on them. But still, she couldn't break away.

A new voice sounded under the booming laughter right next to them on the other side of the mirror.

"What is the point of humanity when we all long to break free from it?"

Lola turned, eyes wide, and froze.

This voice mumbled like someone talking to themselves. "Desire is a cage; humanity is a cage. We are all but prisoners. We are the creatures that know and know too much."

One of the mirrors faded, the image within shifting. She recognized the man bracing himself on the glass, watching them, his fingers drawing idle pictures on the glass: Conri, the artist with the gilded eye patch.

Lola screamed and her voice magnified around them as her reflections joined in. They screamed even as they leered at her, their voices joined in the cacophony.

Gael's grip tightened on her wrist, and together they ran—racing through the maze of mirrors, desperate to escape the prison of desire that threatened to consume them whole.

TWELVE

Lola barrelled forward, hands to her ears, bouncing off mirrors as she went. The maze's oppressive grip started to loosen, the air around her feeling less suffocating. Cautiously she cracked open one eyelid. The sight of blue sky beyond the exit ahead filled her with a rush of relief.

"There!" She tugged Gael's hand. The hold of the maze seemed to fade; the dizzying intrusive desires losing their hold.

They stumbled into the sunlight, blinking in the brightness. Lola panted; her breath jagged from the adrenaline rush still coursing through her veins.

"What happened to the two of you?" came Nix's voice, laced with amusement.

Lola turned to find Nix standing with Walt at the entrance of the maze, a smile teasing at her lips as she popped a piece of candy into her mouth. "Oh, I see. You guys couldn't control yourselves in the Maze of Desire." She wiggled her fingers at them. "You two couldn't resist? Look at the 'get-a-room-iness' of you right now."

Gael's hair was dishevelled, and his cheeks glowed with high colour; Lola's dress was rumpled.

Lola flushed. "No, it wasn't like that. It was...strange." The words tumbled out in a clumsy jumble. As the fresh air cleared away the cloying scent of the maze, her memory of what had just happened faded as well.

What had it been like? Lights and reflections everywhere, and laughter that made her want to cover her ears, but she couldn't resolve the actual details. It was like waking up to a dream that fled the moment you tried to capture it.

They'd been kissing, she knew that much. She remembered the pressure of Gael's hands on her hips and her lips at his neck, and she blushed. "It was kind of intense," she said after a pause.

Gael's earlier panic had morphed into a lazy smile, and he shrugged. "Definitely something."

Nix hooted with laughter, her eyes gleaming. "You guys are ridiculous."

Lola laughed with the rest of them. But when she glanced at the maze's entrance, it filled her with dread that didn't make sense.

"Gael!"

A voice rang out from behind them. Lola turned to see Cassidy, Violet and Sam walking towards them, their arms linked. Cassidy waved, her auburn ponytail swaying. "What are you guys doing?"

Violet raised an eyebrow, her expression smug as she caught sight of Lola. "Isn't it obvious? They're taking advantage of the rankest place in town. The Maze of Desire is so low budget." She gave a derisive smirk. "Like, at least find yourselves a proper backseat and save the rest of us from it."

Lola's cheeks flamed with heat at the jab.

Gael, looking slightly amused, shook his head. "It wasn't like that. Seriously."

"Maybe you haven't gone in because nobody's asked you yet," Nix said to Violet, crossing her arms.

Violet sneered, turning her weaponized glare on Nix. "Was that a proposition?"

Nix squared her shoulders. "Sorry, Violet, you're not my type."

Her tone was casual, but her eyes narrowed. "But maybe you're not Ethan's either."

Sam snorted, then sucked hard on the lollipop she was holding, avoiding Violet's glare.

"If you think you know a single thing about me..." Violet said, her voice a low hiss.

"Where you girls at?" A voice called out.

Lola stiffened. Ethan's smooth deep voice was instantly recognizable. He approached, shining with that it-factor dust that kept everyone enthralled in his wake.

But seeing him again made Lola's stomach churn. His charisma, his wealth, the way he moved so easily in a crowd, hid the darker elements that clung to him.

Several girls passed by, giggling to each other as they ogled him, but Ethan seemed oblivious to their attention. His focus was fixed squarely on Lola, a calculated smirk spreading over his face.

The memory of being trapped by him behind the carousel replayed in her head, and she looked away. She couldn't say anything; she didn't want to make a fuss, and she didn't want a repeat of Gael's overly aggressive show from the other night.

One of the other boys—shaved head and an eyebrow ring—approached Gael. He took a swig from a red plastic cup, already a little tipsy. "Crazy place, right? Fun times at The Gardens, though."

He nodded at Lola. "Hey, I'm Ross. Seen you around."

"I remember." The last time Lola had seen him, he'd been standing behind Ethan, seething with mob violence. He was more mellow now, though it might have to do with whatever was in his cup. It was barely noon and fumes of vodka wafted off the boys. They were already laughing too loud.

As the boys launched into a conversation about baseball, Gael's attention shifted, easing into the familiar banter. The tension in his shoulders relaxed, but as he turned to speak with them, he released Lola's hand and she immediately felt the absence.

She watched as Gael laughed with the same people who used to ridicule him. He didn't seem to care; he greeted them with ease, a smile on his face. But Lola couldn't shake the uneasy feeling it stirred in her. Did he forgive them so easily? Or was he just eager to belong, so much that it didn't matter?

Ethan hadn't taken his eyes off her, even as he casually draped an arm over Violet's shoulder. Violet winced. It happened so quickly, Lola might have imagined it...except she didn't.

She knew the look of someone trying to get away from a touch that made them feel trapped. Ethan's behaviour reminded her of Beau—possessive, controlling, suffocating.

Violet shifted, playing the role of flirt. "So we were talking about the Maze of Desire. Low rent, or the place to be? I hear things get crazy in there." Her voice dropped lower as she placed a hand on his chest. "Want to try it sometime?"

Ethan glanced down as if he was only half paying attention, finishing his drink with a quick gulp. "Yeah, sure," he muttered, his gaze flicking to the rest of the group. "But there's a carnival worker near the back of The Gardens not checking ID and serving up drinks as fast as we can order them. Let's get trashed."

Nix snorted, clearly amused, and Violet shot pure poison at the redhead. The other boys whooped and finished their drinks, leaving their empties scattered on the ground.

Cassidy turned to Gael, her doe eyes hopeful. "Want to come? Tons of people are there."

Lola's throat went dry. The urge to lunge in front of Gael, to shield him from other girls who clearly had no boundaries, nearly overwhelmed her. She felt wrong-footed, still rumpled and confused by the maze, and unable to stop a girl from flirting with her boyfriend right in front of her.

Gael looked to Lola. "What do you think?"

Her instincts were telling her to run the other way. She didn't want to face more of this group—the drinking, the games—but there was something in his eyes that made him seem so hopeful.

Like they could be a normal couple hanging out with friends from school.

"I'm in," she said, her voice grimmer than it should have been.

Violet smirked, tossing her hair over her shoulder. "What about you, Walt? Still too good for parties, refusing to drink like a good little boy?"

Walt's face went stony. "I've seen nothing to change my mind." With barely disguised scorn, his raised eyebrow took in the boys who were braying with laughter.

"Glad you see it that way." Gael hooked his arm around Walt's neck as though he had decided everything and dragged him along.

Nix's face was alight with excitement, her blue eyes sparkling as she grabbed Lola's arm. "Tons of people, right?"

"Like maybe a blonde-tipped newbie?" Lola nudged her. In truth, she was also curious to see what the new girl was getting up to. "But is it worth spending time with people you hate?"

Nix let out a puff of air. "Listen, it could be nice to go through a few years of high school without being dumped on all the time." Her voice lowered. "If they decide Gael is popular, then I say we ride with it."

"Gael is not some prize."

"Are you jealous? You don't have to worry, you know. Anyone who saw the way Gael was looking at you coming out of the maze would know the truth. You have that boy on his knees."

"I just don't like this group. Don't you remember in the spring? They were ready to tear us apart. And now they're all at some level of day-drinking I don't trust."

Nix rolled her eyes. "Okay, mum, thanks for that. God, Lola, you're such a hypocrite. You've been to tons of parties, and I'm sure you've had harder things than some sketchy beer."

Lola clenched her jaw, unwilling to say more. If Nix only knew about the banquets she attended—hosted by queens and actual dukes, where blood flowed as freely as the champagne—she wouldn't be so cavalier about it. Powders and potions were traded along with bodies. She remembered what it was to be caught in the euphoria of drugs and magic.

But now she could see the other side of indulgence, the desperation and the sadness in the people she consumed, the small and large cruelties that littered her past.

"It's not that great," she whispered.

Nix paused, but her voice was stubborn. "Just 'cause you're over that scene doesn't mean I am. You're not the only one who wants to try new things." She marched ahead, leaving Lola behind.

Before Lola could respond, Richie Dawgsby, the reporter from the *Duchesne Daily*, passed by, fighting against the crowd as though he was trying to get to a train that had already left. He wore a long trench coat despite the summer heat, his swollen face a silent reminder of the violence Gael had inflicted.

Her curiosity piqued, Lola hung back. Where was the nosy reporter heading?

"Where are you going?" Gael frowned as he noticed she wasn't following.

Lola gave him a distracted wave, her eyes locked on Richie's retreating form. "I need to use the ladies. Go on ahead, I'll be there in a second."

She shadowed him as he moved quietly through the carnival to the back of the grounds, past the laughter and creaking of aging rides.

Keeping to the side of the path, she trailed Richie until he came to the off-limits area where the workers' tents were arranged in rows. This was where she had spoken with Otsana the other night.

In the daylight, the contrast between the carnival and the utilitarian tents was even more obvious. This didn't seem like a place where laughter was often heard. Instead of sweet sugar and popcorn, the odour of sausages hung greasy in the air.

With a glance behind him, Richie snuck into the tent city. The workers' living quarters were quiet in the middle of the day, the stillness palpable.

A sudden crack sounded behind her, making her jump, and she swivelled to look over her shoulder, but no one was there.

She counted to ten before moving again, wondering what exactly she thought she was doing, as she hid between two tents.

Richie seemed oblivious, intent on his own mysterious purposes. He hesitated at one of the tents, then flipped back the flap and slipped inside.

Was he meeting someone there, romantically? Lola didn't think so; the scrawny writer had the look of someone who was up to something. Was he on to a story? Perhaps something that had to do with the strangeness of the carnival—something Lola would certainly like to get to the bottom of herself.

Before she could sneak across and see what it was Richie was looking for, Duke Louis appeared—swaggering along the rows of tents, spinning a cane in his hands. He had the look of a man who owned the whole world.

Lola froze, heart pounding in her chest. His sharp eyes scanned the area, then he stopped mid-stride, going completely still. He took a deep breath. His nostrils flared and he sniffed several times.

A smile spread across his face, and he twisted to look at the tent the reporter had snuck into.

Did he *smell* Richie? Goosebumps flared over Lola's arms and her leg muscles tightened as she prepared to run. Should she yell and warn Richie? But she didn't want to be discovered by the strange ringmaster, skulking around where she shouldn't be either.

Cowering behind the tent, she felt vulnerable like the little rabbit Otsana accused her of being. She eased back and her arm brushed against the side of the tent with a whisper. Louis's head shifted ever so slightly.

He reminded her of a creature in the forest—vigilant and ever-aware of his surroundings. If he could smell Richie, then he could smell Lola too.

Frozen in panicked indecision, Lola could only watch as Louis slowly turned. But instead of coming after her, he let out a chuckle. He strolled back to the carnival grounds, swinging his cane back and forth. His movements were slow and calculated, as though he had control of everything and everyone in his carnival.

As soon as he'd disappeared around the line of tents, Lola exhaled, her muscles aching from the tension. She eased out of her hiding position, wiping her sweating hands on her dress. Should she let Richie know? He wasn't an ally of hers, not if he was set on discovering her secrets.

Secrets were woven through the carnival as well, though, and she would stake her mortal life that the Otherworld was involved.

She should leave. Leave the carnival and spend the rest of the summer slinging ice cream as though she knew nothing other than the heat of sunshine, her only worry a sunburn.

But what if something bad was happening here? Her friends could be in danger, and whether or not she wanted to be reminded of it, Lola's knowledge of the paranormal could help.

Besides, a flare of curiosity had sparked inside her. She had travelled the globe for decades searching for lost treasure and braving mystical legends, and a part of her longed for the rush that came with the discovery. She may be mortal now, but she still wanted to uncover the arcane mysteries of the world.

Despite how much the carnival in general, and Duke Louis in particular, gave her the creeps, she wanted to get to the bottom of what was going on here.

She hesitated, considering going into the tent where Richie was hidden after all, when a young man with dark hair wandering the carnival grounds caught Lola's eye.

Walt's pickpocket.

If she left now, she might not know what Richie was getting himself into. But she couldn't risk losing the pickpocket now that she had a track on him. She hesitated for only a moment before shifting course, her footsteps quiet as she moved into the crowd.

Thirteen

The pickpocket strode along the path, his eyes scanning every mark. His fingers, too, probably. Lola slid up beside him, her stride matching his own.

"Find anything you like?"

The pickpocket nearly jumped a foot off the ground. Lola's smug satisfaction at outfoxing the fox evaporated as he took off at full speed into the milling crowd.

Without thinking, Lola lunged after him. Her blood heated as she remembered the hunt: the thrill and the urgency to win awakening something primal inside her. Getting closer, knowing you weren't going to let your prey slip away from you. Not this time.

The man shot a glance over his shoulder, his gaze incredulous when he saw Lola still on his tail. He veered sharply, abandoning the crowds and making for a towering barn away from the rides.

The structure wasn't a part of the carnival. The decrepit barn had sat on the Granger Farm property for decades, warped and wind-whipped until it leaned at an impossible angle. Its roof sagged, gaping holes revealing the hollowed-out ribs of the frame.

Lola put on a burst of speed and caught up with the pickpocket. Her fingers brushed his sleeve, and she lunged—

He twisted at the last second, as though expecting her. His abrupt turn threw her off balance, and she stumbled, nearly pitching over the fence into a pen.

A startled cry escaped her as she found herself nose-to-snout with an enormous sow.

Warm hands caught her, pulling her back to solid ground and setting her right. The smell hit her then, and she wrinkled her nose.

"Pigs."

"Pigs," the young man agreed, amusement curling at the edges of his voice. Up close, his face was well-crafted, all sharp angles and smirking confidence. A prominent scar slashed over one of the eyebrows, leaving one side permanently arched, as though he were skeptical of the world.

Or maybe he was just that cocksure; he didn't seem shy as he flashed her a grin. "Come here often?"

She shouldn't be standing here, bantering with the thief. But there was something about him that made her feel sharp, like she was stepping into a role she'd forgotten she could play.

She arched a brow back. "Steal anything good lately?"

"Hmm." The boy bit his lip, pretending to concentrate as he patted his pockets. "Now that you mention it, I did come across this the other day." He pulled out a wallet and tossed it to her. The Seabourne name was embossed across the leather.

Lola flipped it open. "It's empty," she said.

"Found it like that." His dark eyes widened with feigned wonder. "It's amazing that I found you so you could return it to the rightful owner."

Lola couldn't help laughing at his shamelessness. "*I* chased *you*."

"And you are very fast."

The indulgence in his tone made her pause. "You let me catch you."

He tilted his head, considering. "Maybe I wanted to have a conversation with you. Somewhere away from the pigs."

Lola gave a pointed look at the swine milling in their pen. He shrugged. "You know what I mean. The real pigs." He nodded his head to the carnival, where people stuffed their faces with food, their laughter obnoxious.

"Why'd you let yourself get caught?" She braced her hands on the fence. "I could turn you in to the authorities."

"What, call the sheriff or whatever you have in this nowhere town? Nah, you're not going to do that."

Lola imagined going to Greyson with a complaint and puffed out a breath at the thought. "No, I'm not."

"Didn't think so. You're different from most townspeople." He watched her out of the corner of his eye.

She shifted, unsure what his probing gaze sought. "What do you mean?"

"I can't explain it." The boy scrunched his face. "There's an aura around you; it's like you go so much deeper. Like you've gone further than most."

Lola stilled. "I go deeper than most?" She let out a scornful laugh. "Is that your best line?"

He winced, finally looking abashed. "Unfortunately, yes. You probably deserve better. I'm Chann, by the way." As he spoke, his accent broadened into a light brogue. Irish, probably.

"Lola." She placed her hand into his offered one. It was hardened with calluses. He had the face of a boy her age, but his hands told another story—a life of work or labour. Of struggle.

She took in the breadth of his shoulders and found herself blushing. "So, is it your job to steal from customers?"

"Nah, I work the crowd and rile up the guests, taunt them into spending more money at the games. The stealing? That's for my own pleasure." He glanced up. "Does that bother you?"

In her long years as a vampire, she had committed atrocities that made a lifted wallet seem like a child's game. "Not really. But stay away from my friends."

"Does that include you?" His gaze flicked over her, and something in his expression made her skin warm, a tug of attraction pulling her towards the brazen thief. She looked away. What was she even doing here?

Still, she made no move to leave. "Especially me."

Chann smirked. "I'll consider it. It's no hardship to avoid your friends; there's money to burn on this island. It's unusual for a small town. Usually we're setting up in places full of people with harder luck than us."

"Duchesne Island is an unusual place. It's full of treasure, you know." Lola lifted her face to the sun. "You move around a lot, then?"

"Every month." Chann looked wistfully into the forest.

"Sounds lonely. Never setting down roots."

He shrugged. "We've all been with the carnival a long time. These people are like my family."

"I know what that's like." Jacquotte's crew had been brutal and homicidal, but when they set up camp planning their next heist, it brought them together on another level. You couldn't break into a booby-trapped treasure room if you didn't trust your partners.

"Besides, there are other benefits to travelling to a new place every month." Chann tilted his head, and a flash of silver light glinted in his eye.

Lola leaned forward. Was the light real, or was it all in her head?

"Like being able to steal people's wallets with abandon?"

His smile spooled out in a way that caused her cheeks to flush. "Among other things." A look in his dark eyes reminded her of the wild days of her past.

She shoved away from the fence. This was getting way off track; she had no idea who this boy was, but she was certain she shouldn't want anything to do with him.

"So, what is this?" She gestured at the pigs. "A petting zoo?"

Chann frowned as he followed her pointing finger. "The

pigs aren't for the public. One of the workers here used to be this expert sausage maker back in the old country. Munich." Chann's accent grew thicker, and his gaze took on a faraway sheen.

She laughed, disbelieving. "What, you travel around with a herd of swine to make artisanal Munich sausages? Must be something special. Where do I find one?"

His lips pressed tight. "No, it's only for workers. You wouldn't like them."

Lola made a noncommittal noise. "And you keep them in this old barn?"

Chann scowled at the old building. "Not my first choice; this place should be condemned. It's not safe for anyone, including the pigs. But Louis insisted they're kept close."

"Duke Louis? The ringmaster guy?"

Chann snorted, his face hardening. "Louis isn't a Duke. He's a no-name swindler. Or he was once, anyway. He's good at finding and keeping talent. You might call him a collector."

"A collector of performers? How do you collect people?"

Chann's frown deepened, and there was no doubt his eyes burned silver. *Other.* Just like Otsana.

She stepped right up to him, catching his face in her hands. "What are you?" She breathed the question.

Chann stared, his fists clenching and unclenching. She wasn't afraid of him, although something deep inside her told her she probably should be.

"Damn." His mouth twisted. Gently he pried her hands from his face. He tugged her away from the barn, back to the pathway that wound through the carnival. "I shouldn't have brought you here; you need to get back to your people. Don't go around asking any questions, yeah? Things don't turn out great for people who ask questions."

"Should I be a pig instead?" Lola gestured at the people around her.

Chann half-smiled. "You could never be a pig. Just go back to The Gardens, find your friends, and forget you ever met me."

The strains of a guitar began to play in the background. The music did funny things to her head, and she shook it hard, trying to focus on Chann. She wanted to lose herself in the music, but a part of her resisted.

Something important was going on but it kept twisting away from her.

"How do you know where my friends are?"

"Because The Bayous are playing, and nobody can resist Otsana."

"Why—" she started to ask, but he held a finger over her lips, the heat scorching the soft flesh.

"No questions, remember? Go enjoy the party, then go home." He turned her towards The Gardens, where crowds of people were drifting as though not entirely of their own volition.

His lips brushed against her ear. "The carnival plays tricks on you. Don't believe everything you see."

FOURTEEN

Lola turned back, but Chann had already vanished.

As she entered the dancing crowds in The Gardens, she prayed the carnival was playing tricks on her—because there was Gael with Cassidy's arms hooked around his neck. One of his hands rested lightly on her hip, the other holding a half-full beer aloft.

With measured steps, Lola approached, a storm brewing in her chest. Cassidy spotted her first. A slow, knowing smile unfurled across her lips, triumph rippling over her face.

But when Gael turned towards Lola, his face broke into an easy smile.

"There you are." He moved towards her, but Cassidy wouldn't let go, so the two of them lurched. His drink sloshed over her shoulder, and she screeched.

"Sorry, let me just—" Gael had to pry Cassidy's hands off him to jog towards Lola. He went to wrap his arms around her, but she lifted a hand to stop him cold.

"What was that?"

"What was what? You've been gone, like, an hour. We've been having fun."

"Yes, I can see that." Lola's blood would have boiled if that was humanly possible. It wasn't, though; she'd only seen it once in a demon. "Should I leave you to go back to your fun?"

Gael blinked. "You mean Cassidy?"

"Are there other girls who've been hanging off you like a limpet?"

"She's just friendly. Everyone's friendly." Gael gestured to the group of kids. Most of them were entirely too friendly for a public space. "Where did you go?"

"I got Walt's wallet back." She held up the empty leather case.

His smile slipped. "You shouldn't go off on your own. Not after people like that."

"What do you mean, people like that?" Lola's anger was still right on the surface. "People who are—" She was about to say *Other* and stopped herself. Gael didn't know the carnival was enchanted, and he didn't seem to want to hear about it.

"He's a thief, Lola. Who knows what he's capable of?"

"Right. Meanwhile, your friends here are paragons of class." She pointed at the crowd, where several of the guys he was hanging out with were having a chugging contest, foamy liquid dripping down their faces. Violet was recording it all. "Chann was fine."

"Lola, you shouldn't have approached him. You're not...you know, *you* anymore."

And never had she felt it more. Gael couldn't even bring himself to say it outright—what she had been. But the only clear thought she'd had these last few weeks was she wasn't who she used to be, and she had no idea who she *should* be. At times like this, she missed the clarity of being a vampire. Things had gotten so muddled since she'd come to the island. Since the Tree of Life. Since Gael.

"Well, what am I supposed to do?" she snapped. "Cower under my bed? Spend every waking moment with you to ensure my delicate self is always safe?"

"I wish you would." Gael reached for her again, and in his eyes, silver stars sparkled. For a moment she wanted to lose herself in them—to forget everything in her past and to start over as a brand-new girl, the way Gael would like.

But she couldn't forget, not now that something was influencing everybody at the carnival. She pinched the skin on the back of her hand, coming back to herself. It wasn't normal that his eyes were sparkling, was it? Her thoughts were thick and sluggish, like honey.

"Listen, Gael, I think we need to get out of here. Something's happening, something weird."

"Weird?"

He looked like he was going to argue with her, but just then, the beat of the music picked up. His expression smoothed; his face wiped clean of emotion as if their building argument had never happened. "I got you a present," he said.

Lola struggled to hold on to her unease, to stay upset, but the music curled around her, soothing. She peeked up at him despite herself. "What kind of present?"

Gael grinned and nestled something tiny in Lola's palm. A three-banded silver ring shone under the carnival lights like treasure.

"Gael, it's beautiful." She turned it over in her fingers. It was more intricate than at first glance. The three strands braided and looped around one another, hiding within their folds a metal heart. "I love it."

"I went back to that artist's stand you liked." Gael wrinkled his nose. "Still not sure about his paintings, but he makes jewelry too. And this piece made me think of you."

Her stomach swooped and she felt like she was floating. Nobody had ever given her anything this beautiful. Whenever Beau had brought her a present, it was either strictly practical—like high-end wire cutters—or gruesome, like a still-steaming heart.

Gael slipped the ring over her finger. As he did so, it gave a flash of heat so hot it seemed to freeze her skin. She gasped, but the sensation faded immediately. It must have been warm from Gael's hands. "It's perfect."

But as she glanced up something had changed. The easy, soothing haze lifted, and the carnival was no longer charming.

The clearing of The Gardens was grimy, littered with garbage, and the people standing in it even filthier. Many people were chugging back drinks, sloshing all over themselves with no thought to dignity. It was chaos, and nobody seemed to notice.

"Oh." Lola blinked, wanting to put things back to the fun festival it had seemed only moments ago. But somehow, the world had shifted, as though she was looking at it through new eyes.

"Can we put everything past us and move on?" Gael's voice pulled her back.

Lola's gaze flicked towards Cassidy, who stood at the edge of the crowd. Fury twisted her delicate features, her hands balled into fists.

Lola didn't think everything was past them. Not even close.

Cassidy spun around, furious tears in her eyes. Violet and Sam approached her, whispering something low and urgent. With malicious looks, her friends beckoned for her to leave The Gardens. Sneering at the crowd behind her, Cassidy followed them, their arms around her waist.

A premonition that had nothing to do with the Otherworld prickled along Lola's spine, and she motioned for Gael to follow her. She snagged Walt as she passed, putting a finger to her lips. His eyebrows raised, but he nodded and followed them without question.

Lola couldn't hear what the trio of girls ahead of them was saying until they were far away from the band and the dancing crowd. Violet stopped at a food stand, and Lola pulled the boys behind it. Lola had spent far too much time at the carnival sneaking around and spying. That needed to change.

From their hiding spot, Violet's voice carried to them. "That low-budget ginger thinks she's so smart, but I can take her down any day of the week."

Lola exchanged a look with Gael and Walt. "Where's Nix?" she whispered. Gael shook his head, and Walt pressed his lips together.

"Why would she listen to you?" Cassidy said. "She's not that dense."

"That's the best part." Violet practically purred with satisfaction. Lola peeked around the side of the stand, catching the spill of triumph over Violet's face. "I asked the new girl to give her the message. Nix never saw it coming."

"The new girl?" Sam asked. "You mean Gael's girl?"

Violet's hiss cut in. "No, the other new girl. Asian, funky hair? She had mentioned Lola was at the barn flirting with some skeezy worker and wondering if we should tell someone. I only suggested she tell Nix that Lola might need help."

Gael stiffened behind her, and Lola could feel the weight of his gaze between her shoulders, but she didn't turn around. She hadn't done anything wrong with Chann, though a pit in her stomach told her that wasn't entirely right.

"Ew, the old Granger barn? It's like a million years old."

"You should have seen Nix's face. She dashed off like a total loser." Violet's lovely face twisted, and her eyes reflected silver. "Ethan's going to lock her in with the pigs."

FIFTEEN

Lola, Gael and Walt took off at the same time, sprinting towards the decrepit barn at the back of the carnival. Lola knew the way and twisted through the crowd with an urgency that left the boys trailing behind. She reached the barn first.

A jostling crowd had already gathered outside the barn door, their faces gleaming with dark excitement. Though she was no longer a vampire, Lola could still sense the capacity of the crowd to shift into a mob. Underlying violence hummed through the air, ready to be unleashed.

Reiko stood apart from the rest, her frosty grey eyes expressionless as she scanned the scene. In her hands she held an antique device, something like a compass but with strange knobs and dials she kept tinkering with. Her gaze flickered between the crowd and the instrument.

Calculating was the word that popped into Lola's head. She wanted to know what the new girl's angle was, but it would have to wait. Right now, Nix needed her.

Lola shoved past the onlookers, jamming an elbow into

someone who tried to grab her. She made it to the front, flustered and red-faced.

Ethan stood at the door, holding it closed. His grin was knowing, a predator savouring the moment. Seeing him with his eager cruelty on display was like a fist to the gut, and Lola came to a halting stop.

His smile widened when he saw her. "I knew you'd be back for more."

"*Pardonnez-moi* while I vomit." Adrenaline had her shaking as she faced him, and she let out a slow breath. "Move."

Ethan leaned against the doorframe, studying her with deliberate laziness, stretching the moment as the crowd fell silent, sensing drama.

Lola rolled her eyes. "You've proved what an enormous asshole you are. Congratulations. Now let me pass."

His face was slack and ruddy with alcohol, but worse than that, his eyes held the silver gleam overlay that was becoming far too familiar—the influence of the Otherworld at the carnival. The thought of Ethan under the sway of dark magic made her want to run in the other direction, but she refused to let fear take hold. She wasn't leaving until Nix was out of there.

Ethan's grin didn't falter. "If that's what you want."

He swung the barn door wide, stepping aside with exaggerated flourish. Lola hesitated at the edge of the dark space, knowing a trap when she saw one, but she had no choice. She stepped into the barn.

The crowd shifted, restless. Gael broke through the wall of people just as Ethan let the door swing shut behind her. She caught a silver gleam in Gael's eyes as he went after Ethan, before the door slammed closed with a resounding thud, leaving her reeling in the musty old barn by herself.

A roar erupted from the spectators. A scuffle broke out outside the door. A body slammed against the wood, rattling the entire structure.

She tried the door but it wouldn't budge. The dimly lit space showed little more than weathered wood, dust swirling in the faint light that streamed through the cracks in the weathered planks. The air reeked of hay and mould and the ever-present odour of pigs.

"Nix, where are you?" she called.

The voice drifted from above. "Lola?"

Merde, of course Nix would have already made her way to the loft.

"Listen, it's not safe up there. Can you make your way back down?"

"Hang on, I need to get around this—" A sharp crack ripped across the barn and Nix yelped. "Lola, help!"

Lola darted to the ladder. The wood was soft in some places, swaying with every rung as she scrambled to the upper level. "Don't move," she called, pulling herself over the lip of the loft.

Chann hadn't lied; the barn needed to be condemned. She breathed in decades' worth of rotting manure and mouse droppings. The floorboards were rotted through in places, gaping holes revealing the dirt below. And Nix—

Nix was pinned at the far end, gripping the wall with her fingernails.

"I'm stuck," she said, voice tight with panic. "I can't get my foot out."

Lola moved instinctively along the thick centre beam. Large gaps flanked either side, but she focused only on reaching Nix.

Another cheer rose from the crowd, followed by a heavy impact against the barn. The frame trembled.

Lola wavered and fell to a crouch as the floor swayed, gripping the wood. She no longer had her vampire grace—or invulnerability. If she fell, she would feel the bone-shattering impact.

"*Mon Dieu*, Gael, hold it together," Lola muttered to herself through gritted teeth. "You're going to bring the whole place down." She stood, making it the rest of the way across the loft.

Nix's face was pale, her fingers clutching the wall as though sheer willpower could keep her from falling. "I can't find the right angle to get my foot out."

Her leg disappeared up to the calf into the floorboards. Lola left the relative safety of the centre beam and crept on hands and knees over the mildewed floorboards. The wood here was treacherous, every inch a gamble.

She could sense the tension in Nix's body as she tried to keep her weight off her feet.

The wood she had fallen through was splintered and riddled with rusted nails at odd angles. They crowded around Nix's flesh like a bear trap.

"Don't move," Lola said. "It's going to be okay."

Steadying one hand against the wall, she wrapped the other arm around Nix's waist and lifted.

If she were only as strong as she used to be, it would have been simple. As it was, she strained to lift Nix straight so her ankle wouldn't be mangled.

Nix clung to her as she eased her foot through the maze of sharp edges. Her foot came out, sneaker and all.

For a moment, the two girls rested against each other, breathless with relief.

"You did it," Nix whispered.

"We both did." Lola spared a smile for her friend. "But we still need to get out of here."

Nix trembled and her eyelids brimmed with tears. It wasn't fear that caused her to shake. "They set this up, right? They're all outside, aren't they? Waiting to laugh at me for being such an idiot."

"Nix, you're not an idiot. You were being a good friend."

"Why is it always so hard?" Nix breathed out through her nose, as though trying to hold back her emotions. "It's like I was born with a target on my back. And just when I think things might be getting a little bit better, someone shoves me back to remind me of my place."

"Your place is wherever you want it to be, and those islanders don't come close to matching what you have." Lola's voice was tight to control her fury. "Trust me, I've met a lot of people in my life. Some people shine brighter than others, and there's always some bottom-dweller who tries to put out their light because they can't stand to know how lesser they are. But you will always rise above."

Nix sniffled and nodded. "Okay. Let's get out of here—"

A deafening bang reverberated through the barn. The walls quaked.

Nix's foot slipped. She fell to the side, stumbling onto a blackened board.

"No—" Lola lunged and caught Nix's hand as the floor cracked under her feet. She pulled back so hard they both went tumbling backwards, straight through the barn wall. The wood disintegrated around them, and they fell into open air.

They plummeted in a dizzying drop, the ground rushing up to meet them.

Lola braced for the impact and the burst of pain—

Instead, they landed with a soft squelch. A thick, nauseating stench rolled over her.

Merde.

She opened her eyes, squinting in the bright sun. Nix lay beside her, expression frozen in horror.

They had fallen into the pigpen outside of the barn. More specifically, into the slop pile, where the filth was shoveled from the barn.

A stunned silence hung heavy in the air.

"This...this..." Nix tried to pull herself out. Underneath streaks of brown, her skin flamed as red as her hair.

"Oh. My. God." The mob had caught on to what had happened. The crowd jostled to get close to them as Lola and Nix pulled themselves up, coated with the foul stench. Jeers and squeals of laughter filled the air; phones crowded around them. Soon they'd be trending on social media.

The heckling swelled, monstrous and gleeful, wrapping around them like a chokehold.

Nix's breath hitched, her entire body trembling.

Lola clenched her jaw, forcing herself to move. She reached for Nix's arm, pulling her upright. "Are you hurt?"

Nix's chin quivered, but she shook her head. Ignoring their filthy state, Lola pulled her into a hug.

Mean cheers rose from the swarm of people. The crowd was a faceless entity, and their laughs echoed and built until they sounded like animals.

Like hyenas, Lola decided, that mean, scary laugh. Together, they seemed to have lost their humanity.

"Make out!" Lola thought that voice might be Ethan. She swallowed back the fury boiling inside her, wishing for her old strength, her power, something to wipe the sneers from their faces. But all she had now was her voice.

"You're okay, understand?" Her grip was firm on Nix. "They're never going to break you."

Nix took in a shaky breath, looking as though she might prefer jumping back into the foul pile than facing the crowd.

She met her gaze, and something in Nix's face shifted. Her eyes no longer burned with tears but with rage. Rage was good. Rage would get her through this.

They skidded to the edge of the pen. A few of the pigs wandered over to investigate the intruders but only nosed at them with their soft pink snouts. Their snuffling sounded like pleading. Lola nudged them aside.

The crowd pressed in close to the wooden fence, but Gael and Walt shoved people out of the way to make space for them. Lola handed Nix over to Gael.

Nix held her head high and Lola's heart flared in admiration for her courage.

"Pigs or girls, Nix. What do you prefer?"

Nix whirled on the giggling boy who'd spoken. Her gaze promised such vengeance that he blanched and hurried back into the crowd. Gael tracked him as though memorizing his face for later.

The jeers died away as Nix jumped onto the ground, and Walt immediately put an arm around her, no matter how filthy she was. For all Walt seemed awkward and distant, there was no truer friend.

One by one, the mob began to move away, apparently no longer entertained by the events. Reiko hung back until nearly the end, and Lola caught her contemplative look as she turned away, fading into the thinning crowd.

Gael caught Lola as she slipped her way over the fence, putting his hands around her waist and lowering her safely to the ground. "You okay?" His eyes were wide with concern, scanning her for injuries. She was doing the same to him.

"How about you?" He seemed to be in one piece, but his cheek was red and swollen. His eyes were golden brown again, but she knew she'd seen that flash of silver. The carnival had gotten inside him.

She shoved at him, furious and terrified about what that meant. "What was that? Were you trying to bring down the whole barn?"

"No, just one complete piece of shit. I *had* to go after Ethan."

"Since when, Gael? That's not like you."

His eyes narrowed. "You both could have been hurt. I lost it."

Shaken as she was, she couldn't argue with him since only moments before she'd taken vicious pleasure in imagining ripping everyone's throats out. When he pulled her in for a tight hug, she struggled to get away so she didn't ruin his clothes.

"No, I smell terrible," she said. "This is probably the worst I've ever smelled, and I once spent a week living in the sewers of Venice."

"That's a story I'd like to hear." He pulled her closer.

Lola flashed on a memory of hunting a sobbing young man among the rats. "You probably don't. Right now, all I want is to get the hell out of here."

"Where do we go?"

"The ocean." The cool salty waves would cleanse the filth from her.

"Should I call my driver?" Walt pulled out his phone.

"You have a driver?" Nix's humour recovered enough to poke at him. "Like an actual person whose job it is to drive you around this tiny island? How did I not know this?"

"Well, he's the family driver," Walt said, a flush of colour staining his pale cheeks. "And he doesn't have much to do. My dad likes the visual, mostly."

"He wouldn't like the visual we'd leave in his fancy car," Lola said. "Let's walk. We'll take the woods so we don't have to walk through the crowd."

Sixteen

The fencing around the carnival grounds was flimsy, barely holding itself together. Slipping out from behind the barn, they plunged into the cool embrace of the forest. The shift from the hot, dust-choked fairgrounds was instant relief.

Lola exhaled, tension melting from her shoulders. More than anywhere else on the island, the oak forest gave her a sense of peace. Like she'd found something she'd been searching for after all these years.

It had been far too long since she'd visited the ancient oak at the centre of the forest—the Tree of Life.

They stuck to back roads, heading for the beach. Every step made Lola cringe as her sandals squelched, releasing fresh wafts of manure.

"That was truly disgusting."

"I can't believe I fell for it." Nix's neck was corded with tension and her nostrils flared. "I can't believe she played me like that."

"Who?" Walt asked.

"Reiko! She came up to me, all pretty eyes, and said my friend needed help in the barn. I should have known better. But, I mean, she doesn't even know me. What does she have against me? I thought, maybe..."

"Violet set it up; we overheard her," Gael said. "I don't think Reiko was in on it."

Lola didn't comment. She didn't know much about Reiko or what she was capable of, but the girl made her wary. And she would love to get her hands on the device Reiko had been playing with. She'd bet it had something to do with what was going on at the carnival.

"I am such an idiot." Nix's hands clenched into fists, her whole body vibrating with fury. "I'm never trusting anyone again."

"Don't say that," Gael said, but Lola didn't blame her. If anything, she agreed. Trust was a gamble best not taken.

The forest thinned, giving way to a sandy beach. This side of the shore was quieter; fewer families set up where the waves were rougher and more rocks lined the sandbar.

Nix didn't hesitate. She marched straight into the ocean, striding deeper until the water swallowed her whole. A few kids playing nearby ran away screaming as she scraped the filth off her skin and clothes.

The Atlantic crashing towards her loosened something in Lola's chest. She'd be getting her dip in the ocean after all. Despite the horrific day, she ran forward, meeting the waves with a burst of childish delight.

Losing her connection to the ocean had been one of her greatest losses in becoming human. All vampires shared an affinity with an element, and water had been hers.

As a human, she no longer felt the pull of the tide like she used to, but her love of the sea remained. She dove into the waves, savouring the sparkle of salt water over her skin.

Laughter bubbled from her as Walt and Gael waded in, still fully dressed. Gael stripped off his filthy T-shirt, shaking out his hair as he joined them.

When she felt less like a monster from the depths, Lola joined

Nix at the sandbar, far enough from the riptide to be safe. They used handfuls of sand to scrape away any lingering muck. Lola's skin tingled and chafed, but at least she felt clean.

"Better?" Lola asked.

Nix sighed; her anger seemed to have been soothed by the beating waves. "Like, maybe twenty-five percent better." Her gaze drifted across the water, landing on the lighthouse in the distance. "Look at that. My family's legacy. Just standing there like it has forever."

The whitewashed walls shimmered in the sun on the opposite end of the harbour.

"It's charming," Lola said. "I bet loads of people would want to live somewhere that pretty."

"Only because they never had to." Nix snorted. "It's leaky and drafty and always filled with people." She puffed out a breath. "The eldest has always been the lighthouse keeper, every generation. Which means that after my dad, I'm it. You're looking at my destiny. I don't know what I was thinking, dreaming that things could be different."

"You can change your destiny," Lola said, nudging her friend. "I'm living proof, emphasis on living. Nobody is going to force you to stay on the island if you don't want to."

"I don't know..." Nix's eyes stayed on the lighthouse, watching the waves crash against the rocks. "I just wonder if my life will ever get better. Or if I'll always be the poor misfit kid everyone picks on."

Lola put her hand on her friend's shoulder. "Definitely not. I meant what I said to you; you are better than them. You can have whatever you want out of life, and I'll do everything in my power to make sure of it. But you can't let them break you, those..." She wracked her brain for a fitting word. "Hyenas," she settled on, thinking of their disturbing laughter.

"Hyenas." Nix started to laugh.

"They sound like a pack of them and are about as bright."

Nix's laugh rippled over her, transforming her face back to her bright pixie self. "You're ridiculous."

"Meanwhile, you are destined for great things," Lola grinned. "I don't even have to be a witch to know that."

Nix's smile faltered. "Wait, there are witches?" she asked after a beat.

Lola laughed. "You have no idea how much is out there. Listen, I'm going to take a shower in the cabana. I have a change of clothes if you'd like?"

They made their way to the Ice Cream Shoppe. The local girl working the stand glanced up at Lola over the steady line of customers, wrinkling her nose as she took in Lola's state.

"Don't mind me. I'm just grabbing my stuff." Lola slipped her bag off the hook from the tiny back room.

At the cabanas, she handed the shampoo to Nix, as well as a pretty spare dress that would fit her thin frame. "You first." As Nix jumped under the not-very-warm water with a yelp, Lola ducked outside to see Gael and Walt standing at the doors of the cabana like sentries, arms crossed and stony looks.

"Guys, it's okay."

Gael shook his head. "It's not okay, Lola. You fell a full storey out of a building. If you hadn't landed in—" He grimaced. "It would have been a lot worse."

Walt nodded. "One look at that barn and you'd know it was dangerous. Either Violet didn't know or didn't care, but she's responsible for what could have happened."

"Violet went too far this time." Nix stepped out of the showers, wearing a navy-blue dress of Lola's, with tiny straps and bronze waves glittering over it. Since Nix's typical outfit was jeans and baggy T-shirts, she was showing far more skin than normal. Her hand crept up to cover her freckled shoulders.

Lola smiled at her friend's glow-up. "You look lovely, but you need to follow your own advice," she said, tossing a bottle of sunscreen at Nix.

Lola jumped into the shower and kicked her dress into a corner, unsure if it could be saved. Unwanted memories and manure both clung to it. She heaved a long sigh as clean water pounded over her skin, feeling her composure fall away. The fall had been terrifying, but far worse was the crowd. She shuddered at the memory of faceless people, sneering in contempt.

Plunging her face under the water, she stayed there until the unwanted feelings flowed away. Towelling off brusquely, she threw on the last of her spare clothes, shorts and a long-sleeved shirt for when the nights got cool. Her wet hair bunched around her shoulders.

Gael waited for her as she stepped out of the cabana. He wrapped her up in a tender hug. "You okay?"

She rested her cheek against his chest, his presence grounding. "I no longer smell like pig shit, so it's a win." She sniffed herself. "I hope."

Gael laughed. He lifted her hand, where the ring he gave her sparkled. "It looks good on you."

"It means something to me that you went back to the artist, even though you didn't like him."

"It's not that I don't like him. It's that I find him...odd. He told me he'd make me an offer I couldn't refuse." He fiddled with the ring, not meeting her eye. "This design has protective elements, he said. That as long as you're in my heart, you'll be impervious."

He leaned forward and kissed her forehead. Lola's knees got a little trembly.

"Impervious to what?"

"Not sure exactly. Didn't help with falling out of buildings. But I know there are scary things in the world, and I want to be the one to keep you safe."

Lola made a fist, curling her fingers around the ring. "Maybe I should get you a ring too."

"Forget about protection," Nix said, coming up beside them. "I want revenge. Let's plot Violet's downfall."

"Can I help?"

Reiko approached them unsteadily over the sand. She wore a tight band T-shirt and ripped jeans, and her eyes were lined with heavy black makeup. Her face was set as though facing a firing squad.

Lola tensed, readying for a fight. She didn't trust the girl and wanted to be very clear about her involvement in the prank.

But Nix gave her a curt nod. "I got this," she said to Lola. She met Reiko, arms crossed in front of her chest. Tendrils of wet curls clung to her shoulders and neck, almost like a henna pattern. "Did you come to rub it in?"

Reiko cringed, covering her face with her hands. "I want to apologize." Her voice was a shaky whisper. "I had no idea..." She looked away, blinking. "This girl came up to me and was friendly, right? And I'm new here, and I've been through this a thousand times before, and I know how it sucks to not have any friends, so I thought, cool. She asked me to let you know your friend needed you at the barn...well, you know, you were there. I didn't think it was to do...that." She looked down. "I thought I was helping. But I am so sorry for my part in this."

"That's not what Violet said," Lola cut in. "She said you had brought up the barn."

Reiko's gaze flew to Lola's, her eyes icy cool with resentment for a moment, but then she let out a breathy gasp. "That's not true." Her fingers clutched at the collar of her shirt, showing the edge of her tattoo. Wooden beaded bracelets stacked on her left wrist clinked together. "Violet made that up to protect herself after things went wrong, I'm sure of it."

"We know Violet can be cruel," Walt said, his face expressionless.

But we don't know this girl at all, Lola wanted to say, but it was too late.

"Did you really not know?" Nix asked in a hopeful whisper.

Reiko shook her head, making her space buns bobble. "I

would never. Why would I do something like that? I thought you seemed nice. I thought it would be a good reason to come and talk to you." She looked down as though embarrassed.

"It was definitely memorable." Nix's smile was wide and gracious. As if a magic spell had been cast, everyone but Lola relaxed.

Reiko raised an eyebrow, her silver hoop sparkling as she gave a fox-like smile. "You mentioned revenge?"

"Oh, heads will roll. Make no mistake about it. But are you sure you want to hang with us? In case the manure wasn't enough of a visual, you should know we're not exactly the most sought-after social scene."

Reiko's smile showed nearly all her teeth. "This is where I want to be. Listen, do you want to grab an iced coffee somewhere? As a way for me to say sorry."

Her eyes were only for Nix, who flushed magenta. "Yeah, that'd be cool. We could go to Lost Souls. The rest of the idiots will still be off their faces at the carnival. We'll have the place to ourselves."

Lola was about to invite herself along, but Gael put an arm around her, catching her eye with a knowing nod. He wanted this for Nix, to have a win today. He didn't seem to share any of Lola's misgivings about the new girl. "I think we're just going to watch some movies tonight," he said. "You guys have fun."

"Nix?" Lola said before the two left. "Just...don't go back to the carnival, okay? I'm not sure it's safe."

Reiko smiled over her shoulder, with that crafty smile Lola didn't like. "Don't worry—I'll take good care of her."

Walt cracked his knuckles as the two girls wandered down the Boardwalk together. "Are you sure she's okay? I don't want her to get hurt again."

Lola grimaced. "You and me both. But I think we have to let them be." *For now*, she added silently. "They're just going for a drink."

"Are you guys crazy?" Gael stepped in as they started walking towards the town centre. "Stop acting like you're Nix's overprotective parents; she has enough of that. It seems obvious something is there, and it would be awesome for Nix. Now what about us? Does anyone actually want to watch some movies?"

Lola made a face. "I was thinking more of soaking in a bathtub with a million different soaps until my skin is all wrinkly."

"Walt, you in for movies?"

"We could." His tone clearly suggested he'd rather not.

"Oh, got other plans?" Lola asked. "A hot date?"

Walt's face reddened. "Definitely not. I've just been watching videos on how to pickpocket, and I finally received the lock-pick set I ordered. I want to try it out."

"You're learning petty theft?" Lola blinked as she tried to reconcile this with what she knew of him. "You, Walter Seabourne the Third, are full of surprises."

"I don't want to steal anything. It's about the challenge."

"Are you any good?"

"Getting there." He held up Lola's keys.

Surprised, she patted the pocket where they'd been and let out a roar of laughter. "*Mon Dieu*, Walt, I had no idea. How'd you do it?"

"With distraction and sleight of hand." Walt's voice remained perfectly even, and Lola laughed even harder.

"Well done. Now give them back."

Gael patted Walt's shoulder. "I guess we're breaking into places tonight."

"Don't get into any trouble," Lola said.

Movement behind Gael caught her eye. A figure who was becoming awfully familiar to her was creeping up the stairs to the Port Despardoux Library.

Richie the reporter seemed to be everywhere today. Was he researching his latest story? His expression struck Lola as a man on the run. Why was he throwing wild looks over his shoulder as though being hunted, and did it have anything to do with the carnival?

She glanced at Gael, wondering if she should tell him. But he would only tell her to drop it. And right now, she didn't want to play it safe. She wanted to know what was going on.

Ever since she'd first landed on the island, Lola had been reading the *Duchesne Daily*. As editor, Richie loved to bring up the island's mysterious history every chance he could, always working the supernatural angle. Did he actually know about the Otherworld, or was he just one of the many humans who suspected the world ran far deeper than most perceived?

She nodded to the library. "You know, I think I'll make a stop. Grab a little reading material."

Gael reeled her towards him, giving her a teasing kiss. "How exciting. Don't you get into too much trouble, either."

"Please, how much trouble could I find in a library?"

Seventeen

The doors of the Port Despardoux Public Library were carved with intricate details: books and vines wrapped around each other, with owls etched along the frame. Lola's gaze lingered on the birds of prey; Otsana had told her to be an owl, a wise hunter.

Lola had visited libraries around the world—some of the grandest and most famous in history. Throughout the decades, she'd read originals of the world's most celebrated texts and peeked at the least-known scrolls. She had stolen many as well.

She knew libraries, and this was a good one. Stepping inside felt like entering a sanctuary wrapped in a cloak of hushed magic. The air was thick with the smell of old paper and dusty book covers. Leather chairs circled oak tables, and sunshine filtered through the windows, casting mellow golden light over the shelves.

Her footsteps were silent as she glided across the wooden floors, not wanting to alert Richie to her presence. She could be sneaky too, and she wanted to know what he was investigating. She hoped it wasn't her.

As she crept through the aisles, a massive thump echoed from the second floor, as if a body had fallen. Dust was shaken loose from the rafters. Two more thumps followed.

Startled, Lola peered up at the ceiling. Before she could process what had happened, a girl marched out of the office behind the front desk, her sensible shoes tapping along the floor with brittle steps. Large round glasses framed her wide-eyed face, and her mousy hair was pulled back in a loose braid. A lumpy cardigan draped over a knee-length skirt.

The librarian sniffed once, just barely, as her gaze landed on Lola.

Lola stiffened. Did she still smell like pigs?

The librarian put her hands on her hips. "Can I help you?"

"I'm...looking for a book."

"What book?" The librarian's voice was as crisp as an apple. She was likely only a couple of years older than Lola's sixteen but held herself with great gravity.

Lola shrugged. The girl's hostility put her back up. "Just something to enjoy."

The librarian frowned as though trying to find a reason to turn Lola away. Customer service had clearly not been a part of her training. "Escapism is on the main level. The checkout is automated, so you don't need me."

Another thump sounded upstairs. Both Lola and the girl glanced up in unison. The librarian tugged on the end of her braid and sighed.

"What's on the second floor?" Lola asked.

"Hmm? Oh, that's nonfiction, microfiches, old journals... research stuff. Fiction is over here." She pointed towards the stacks of books towering over them. "If that's everything, I'm very busy."

The librarian clacked away, her footsteps echoing through the stillness. Curious, Lola followed, trailing her fingers over the books to appear inconspicuous.

At the back of the library, Richie was hunched over a desk,

absorbed with the books spread out in front of him. Beads of sweat formed at his hairline.

The librarian went to his side, greeting him as though they were friends. She gestured as she spoke as though pleading with him, but he shook her off. He was poring over his notebook, chewing on a fingernail.

Two shelves over from Lola, a book began to wiggle. Nobody was touching it; nobody else was in the library. As the hairs on her arms lifted of their own accord, the thin volume worked its way free and fell to the floor with a clatter.

Lola slapped a hand over her mouth to keep from crying out. The book moved on its own. Had it been a ghost? On an island like Duchesne, was it really a surprise the library was haunted?

The librarian's head snapped up at the noise. Lola ducked behind the stacks. From the bright-coloured spines she hid behind, she could tell she was in the children's section. Peeking through the shelves, she watched the librarian approach and pick up the offending book.

From behind her massive glasses, the librarian's eyes narrowed. "Means nothing to me," she said in an undertone. She reshelved the book and returned to Richie.

She appeared unfazed that a book would jump off the shelf by itself. Was she aware of the library ghost? Is that why she was so prickly?

Lola waited until the librarian's attention was elsewhere, then approached the book. Her knuckles whitened as she read the cover, and she took in a raspy breath.

A children's book, slim and green: *The Giving Tree.*

Perhaps the book didn't mean anything to the librarian, but it meant something to her. She had so many questions about Duchesne Island and the Otherworld.

It was time to return to the place where it all began for her.

She hadn't realized the librarian had returned. The girl's eyes widened as she saw the book Lola held and snatched it out of her hand. "What are you doing?"

Lola frowned. "Looking at books. I thought it was kind of the point of this place."

"Why this book?" The girl's look was guarded, but there was a keen glint of curiosity.

Lola shrugged. "It caught my eye."

Above them, another thump sounded, and the librarian let out a frustrated sigh. "Fine. Take your book and go."

Lola was about to do exactly that when a voice stopped her.

"Wait, is that Lola Monteux?"

Richie had come out from behind his desk. His despondence had disappeared, and now he strutted towards her, notebook in hand. "Could I ask you a few questions?"

Lola left *The Giving Tree* on the shelf. She wanted to find out what Richie was up to, not become the subject of his investigation.

"No comment," she said, making her way out of the library.

She didn't look back until the owl-carved doors were shut behind her.

Whether it was a ghost or other powers at work, Lola had received the message loud and clear: return to the oak tree that had guarded the Well of Souls for centuries.

The bakery was around the corner from the library, so she stopped to grab her bike before heading into the forest. Her legs pumped hard as she pedaled, feeling the wind against her skin and the sweat that built up along her neck.

The effort made her feel more alive than ever. Though it was the heart of summer, the forest was cool, the canopy providing welcome shade from the blistering sun. The tangled branches of the ancient forest cast deep shadows, and the filtered sunlight danced in dappled patterns along the mossy floor. The earthy scent of decaying leaves and the sweet notes of wildflowers surrounded her as she breathed in deep.

She slowed as she neared the Tree of Life. She'd been avoiding this place, perhaps because of the dark memory of everything that had taken place. Or perhaps she feared it had all been a colossal mistake and she had never been meant to dig as deep into the secrets of this land as she had.

But as she came into view of the sprawling oak, awe jolted through her once again. The hum of energy in the air was unmistakable, like the faint echo of laughter just out of hearing. The branches rose in a near-perfect half-moon, stretching many storeys tall. Unlike in the spring, where the leaves had been tiny and sapling green, the tree now bore a magnificent crown of heavy greenery.

The bark, weathered and worn, seemed etched with secrets. If only she could crack the code to the language. She knew how deep the roots went—all the way to the cavern at the heart of the Well of Souls. There, the Elixir of Life bubbled, capable of healing all wounds—even a demonic infestation of the soul.

Lola had been healed there. Transformed into the human girl she had once been.

As her hand grazed the rough bark, the heartbeat that flowed within the sap of the tree pulsed against her palm. It was alive, connected to everything in the forest. She suspected the tree was sentient, at least on some level. Even when she was a vampire, this tree had called to her. Now, she could feel its heartbeat within her own veins, like it had provided the lifeblood running through them. She was connected as well.

Clearing her throat, she spoke, feeling somewhat ridiculous.

"Hi," she started. "Um, when I saw that book today, *The Giving Tree*, I thought of you. You gave me so much: the chance to live a real life. I didn't even know I wanted that until it was offered to me. So...thank you."

Emotion swelled in her throat. "But being human isn't what I thought it would be. It's *hard*. Beau would mock me for this."

She paused, knowing Beau would never do any such thing again. His bones lay deep below her feet.

"I didn't realize how confusing it would be. Sometimes I miss being a vampire," she admitted, her voice a whisper. "There, I said it, and I'm sorry if that's not what you wanted to hear, but there was something easy about it. I would hunt, and I would kill, and that was the end of it. But everything is complicated...and now I'm talking to a tree."

The tree swayed, its branches creaking as though in response.

Lola half-laughed. "I did ask for this, in the end. But *merde*, I have no idea what I'm doing."

The tree pulsed under Lola's palm, comforting. She strolled to the centre of the clearing, where the hole to the Well of Souls once sat. It had been filled in, now wrapped with ugly orange construction tape, a glaring warning.

Lola yanked the plastic away until the area was clear. "There, that's much better. All that did was bring more attention to a place that, I'm sure you can agree, we need to keep quiet about." She glanced up at the branches above her. "I'm worried that something strange is happening on the island. A woman, who may or may not be a witch, said that a gate had been left open."

A gust of wind rattled through the canopy then, sudden and fierce like a premonition of something sinister being unleashed. It whispered through the branches as though desperate to warn her of something.

Lola's hair lifted at the back of her neck, and she leaned forward, trying to understand. But the wind whipped into a fury and the cadence increased, branches rasping against each other. The spectral chatter spoke of horrors to come.

She backed away from the tree and left the clearing, spooked and more confused than ever.

Eighteen

Gael leapt into the air and grabbed the Frisbee with the tips of his fingers, letting out a shout of triumph. Though the sunshine grazed perfect afternoon waves, the beach was nearly empty. Gael and Walt had been playing for some time, their chaotic footprints the only smudges on the smooth, wet sand. Their shouts mingled with the lonesome seagull cries.

Lola was uncomfortably hot in her ice cream outfit, and it seemed cruel to have to suffer in it when there was no one to sell ice cream to. Walt had already gallantly bought three cones, but he wasn't eating them, so she refused to give him more.

Since the Carnival of Fools came to town, business had dried up. Shops on the Boardwalk were as shut up as during the winter slump.

Lola drummed her fingers against the counter, distracted by the shimmer of her ring, and splayed out her hand to admire it. She never took it off. It seemed like a promise of better things to come, something to hold onto.

Peals of laughter caused her to look up. Nix and Reiko strode through the sand, caught up in a joke. Today, Nix wore a striped halter top that showed off her toned arms.

As they walked side by side, Nix stole a glance at the girl next to her, her cheeks blushing rosy-pink.

Lola shaded her face from the sun with her hand. Nix and Reiko had been inseparable over the past few days. It was hard not to notice how happy Nix was—no complaints about her family, the work she did at her mom's shop, or even the general state of living on Duchesne. She'd giggled, even, one time. If that didn't spell serious crush territory, she didn't know what did.

Lola didn't like it.

Reiko had been nothing but charming the whole time. When she was with Walt, Gael and Lola, she was smiling and cheerful, keeping them entertained with stories of her adventures around the world, as she'd been nearly everywhere. It seemed Gael and Walt were completely taken in while Nix had fallen heels up.

It might have been her eyes, the way her smile never seemed to reach them, but Lola couldn't warm to Reiko. She asked pressing questions about Lola's past, especially after finding out she wasn't from the island.

She'd mentioned it once, casually, but Nix had laughed it off. "Can you blame her? You guys are the two new kids, and both have lived all over the world. You have so much in common!"

Lola wondered what else they had in common. And whether it had anything to do with the Otherworld.

Now, Nix and Reiko came to stand at the ice cream counter. Lola squirmed in her polyester uniform. "I wouldn't be doing my job properly if I didn't ask if someone wanted an ice cream cone."

"Nah, leave the ice cream and listen to this," Nix said, her eyes sparkling with the secret she had to tell. "According to Ross, who told Sam, who told Reiko, Ethan is planning on dumping Violet. And he's going to do it in the Maze of Desire." She let out a shivery laugh as though she couldn't decide if she was guilty about how much this delighted her.

"And everybody knows?" Lola's voice rose with surprise.

Nix lifted a bony shoulder. "If we know about it, then it's safe to assume the whole town does. But, I mean, she deserves it, right?"

Walt jogged over to join them, Frisbee in hand, his smile faltering as he processed the information. "Let me guess. Everybody's waiting outside to watch? A public humiliation?"

"We don't know that for sure." Reiko shot a look at Nix as though trying to determine how she would sway on this.

"I know how they work," Walt said, his voice tight with frustration. "They'll be first in line to watch her fall."

Nix flipped her hair back, her tone hardening. "As a matter of fact, I know exactly how that feels. Or have you forgotten like four days ago when Violet set *me* up?"

"I'm not saying that was right," Walt replied, his tone softening. "It's just...two bad things aren't going to make this town any better."

"How sad that the whole town knows about this, and nobody's stepping in to let her know," Lola said. "Doesn't Violet have any friends?"

"Not friends," Walt said, darkness passing over his face. "She has sycophants happy to stab her in the back for a shot at her throne."

An ominous whisper passed by on the breeze, carrying the fading sound of a scream. Lola froze, the air around her thickening. Bright lights flared in her vision, drowning out the summer-blue sky, and the world tilted.

Her legs buckled, and she reached for the wall of the ice cream stand to steady herself. Then everything went black.

She was in the Maze of Desire, the mirrors crowding in, suffocating her. In every reflection, eyes stared back, liquid silver eyes. She spun and came face to face with her reflection—only it wasn't her, but a mask like the ones in the painting she admired, of brightly coloured predators. Then a wash of blood splashed across the mirror.

The screaming came again, a hundred times louder. She squeezed her eyes shut and pressed her hands to her ears, but the noise was inside her head.

"No, no, no." She repeated the word over and over as the vision faded and the ice cream stand came back into focus. She was lying on the ground, her head in Gael's lap. His fingers combed through her hair, gentle and soothing, but his brow was furrowed with worry.

"She's coming to. Did someone call an ambulance?" Gael's voice was tight.

"No," Lola said, struggling to sit up. "No ambulance. What happened?"

"You fainted." Nix was in the back of the shop with them, arms wrapped around her stomach as though she was about to be sick, her lips pressed into a tight line. "Then you had some kind of seizure. Your eyes..."

"They were glowing," Gael said, his voice low and hoarse. "Did anyone else see that?"

Reiko stood to one side of the shack, arms crossed. Her grey eyes were assessing but her skin was ghost pale. "I saw it." Her voice was flat, detached. She clutched something in her hand—an edge of antique bronze caught the light. Lola's mind raced; that was the same device Reiko had been fiddling with before. Who was this girl and why was she here?

Even though her hands trembled with the aftershock of her seizure, Lola wanted to shake the girl to get real answers out of her. As if feeling the pressure of Lola's stare, Reiko twisted away from her, hiding the device. As she did so, the collar of her T-shirt pulled down enough for Lola to get a look at the tattoo at her collarbone. It was like nothing she'd ever seen before, and she tried to imprint to memory.

"You should get looked at, Lola," Walt said, his voice soft but full of concern. "What just happened wasn't normal."

Lola grimaced, trying to pull herself back to the present. Something important had happened. There was something she was supposed to be doing.

"No, it's okay. Or it's not." She tried to stand, but her legs wobbled.

Gael caught her, supporting her against him until she felt solid. "It's not okay?"

"I mean, *I'm* okay. But somebody's in trouble. At the Maze of Desire." She grabbed Gael, fingers digging into his forearms as urgency flooded her. "We have to get there, now. Something horrible is going to happen."

"You mean to Violet?" Gael's voice was tentative.

"I don't know, something bad. And not in a humiliating way. In a bloody way." Lola closed her eyes and tried to tamp down the scream building inside her. Behind her eyes, all she could see were glowing eyes and teeth and splashing blood.

"Lola, are you sure you're okay?" A shadow of doubt flickered in Gael's eyes.

"Yes, we have to get there. Believe me or not, I don't care, but I need to go." She threw ice cream scoops into a bin, closing up the shop as quickly as she could.

Tossing her cap on a shelf, she locked the door behind her, swinging the *Closed* sign around. She was still in her puffy ice cream dress, but there was no time to change.

"Lola." Gael held out his arms, hesitant, as though considering whether he should try to stop her. "If you hit your head..."

"Gael, you know that's not what it is. I don't know how to explain this, and we don't have time. Something is wrong with that maze." Tears built in her eyes as the pressure to act grew.

"We went through it and were fine. We had a good time."

"Did we? Do you remember what happened?" Lola searched his eyes as they clouded over.

"I...think."

She lowered her voice. "Maybe you don't want to believe me, but you've seen enough, haven't you, to know there are things that can't be explained away. After all we've been through, can't you just trust me?"

Gael's eyes cleared, and he gave a decisive nod. "Okay, I'm with you. We'll figure this out. But how do you know?"

"I...saw something. Like a flash. I think it was a warning." Lola tried to make sense of the jumbled images from her vision. She fumbled with the bike lock, her hands shaking so much she missed the numbers the first time. "*Merde.* We need to get there."

"To do what?"

"To stop it, whatever's going to happen."

"Wait." Walt's voice was calm, like a splash of water on her face. "Lola, are you saying you saw something that hasn't happened yet?"

His intense gaze pleaded with her to not mean what he thought she did. She couldn't placate him, though. "I'm saying that I have to get there."

She wrenched her bike onto the Boardwalk, not waiting for the others. The panic drumming against her consciousness told her she didn't have time to stop.

Lola pumped at her pedals, building up a sweat under her silly work outfit. Gael caught up with her within moments. Her heartbeat banged in her ears as she fought the panic that she wouldn't make it in time. Worse still, she didn't know what her deadline was for—or who was going to be hurt.

As she approached the gate, she threw her bike aside and dodged the swollen crowd filing inside. Several people yelled, and one man made a move to grab her, but he ran into Gael, who jerked him aside. A shoving match ensued, and people cheered, but Lola didn't stop.

The Maze of Desire loomed before her, spurring a wave of revulsion she didn't understand.

A group milled around the entrance, a restless sense of dark anticipation crackling in the air. The hyenas. They giggled quietly, nervously, about what was about to happen. Sipping from plastic cups, staring at the curtain as they waited for the show.

Lola grabbed Sam, her nails digging into her skin. "What's going on?" she demanded.

"What the hell?" Sam yanked out of her grasp, then snorted a laugh at Lola's outfit. "Pig girl. Don't you look cute."

Lola stared Sam down until the other girl rolled her eyes, her gossip clearly too good not to share, even with someone like Lola. "Oh my God, Violet went in there to meet Ethan, somehow thinking he has a surprise planned for her. Only the surprise is he's going to dump her."

"Is this fun for you?"

Sam's gaze drifted away, guilt undeniably flashing across her face. "Whatever. It doesn't matter anyways—Ethan never even showed up. I heard he's making out with a tourist at The Gardens. He couldn't even bother to come to her dumping." Sam gave another laugh-snort.

Lola tilted her head at the brassy blonde girl, her lip curling. "Aren't you just the best friend a girl could have."

Sam glared at her resentfully. "Violet deserves to be taken down a peg; she thinks she's so great. Now she can move on with her life and stop obsessing about him. I'm doing her a favour."

"I hope you never do me any favours." Lola's voice dripped acid.

She approached the entrance, heart thudding. The mob behind her shifted and cackled.

"Lola, wait." Gael sprinted up and grabbed her hand. "We'll do this together."

She looked at their linked fingers and hesitated, unsure why this felt like a bad idea. But one look at his face, full of concern and ready to follow her no matter how crazy she was acting, convinced her to pull him inside among the mirrors.

As they entered, a fog lifted from her mind.

She remembered everything that had happened before. It was so clear she couldn't believe she'd forgotten. The scary reflections acting out her desires, the ones she'd never admit to. She'd had no control over herself within this place. Her skin rippled in goose-flesh as her reflection winked at her.

Then the air filled with smoke, heavy with incense, and threatened to bring the fog back.

"This place..." Gael brought his fists up, pushing against his skull. His eyes were wide with horror—and want. His gaze met hers and she was certain he was remembering every desire acted out the last time they were in here.

"It's enchanted. There's deep magic here." Lola was sure of it. When they entered the tent, they entered a different reality—a playground better suited to demons. "It's not safe."

The line of mirrors seemed to stretch on forever, impossibly long for the space it took up. The place was much larger than it appeared from the outside, a labyrinth they could wander for days. She wondered if anyone had ever gotten lost in here, never to find their way out.

A desperate moan echoed from the endless passages, as though from far away, and she suspected yes.

Gael's gaze darted from one mirror to the other. "We should get out while we can. We don't have to do this."

His voice seemed magnified and fractured. Lola wasn't sure if it was him or his reflection that spoke. As if in response, a low sobbing echoed back. Energy crackled around them and the urge to act overwhelmed her.

Lola shook her head. "Listen, I don't understand it, and I have no idea where the vision came from. What I do know is I can't stand back and ignore it."

"Why not?"

"Because, Gael, I've caused so much pain in my life. I can't be responsible for any additional suffering, not if there's something I can do about it."

Gael straightened his shoulders. "I guess we're going to rescue Violet Wynn." He shook his head. "Crazier things have happened."

NINETEEN

Their reflections turned on them, their sneering faces mocking. As if they knew what was coming.

Walt ran into the maze, puffing for air. "Wait for us. Whoa." He stumbled to a halt when he caught sight of his reflection. It stretched out tall until it towered over the real Walt.

"Where are you guys?" Nix and Reiko pushed their way in behind Walt, crashing into him. Lola tried to keep them from entering, but they shoved past her. They stepped into the cloud of smoke and stopped.

Nix gazed at her reflection with wide-eyed wonder, her breath fogging the glass. Reiko, in contrast, had entered the tent cautiously, crouched in a hunter's prowl. When she caught sight of her reflection acting of its own volition, her eyes widened. She whipped out her bizarre device and adjusting the toggles with frantic fingers, muttering to herself. She didn't know what to make of the mirrors, either.

Yet she wasn't surprised that they held magic.

If Lola suspected the new girl was tangled with the Otherworld before, now she had proof.

Lola wanted to warn Nix before her friend fell too deep, but

Nix was transfixed by what she saw in her reflection. She swayed and brought her hand to her face, her grin wide and manic.

"It's magical," she breathed.

"Nix, close your eyes," Lola said sharply, but her friend was beyond hearing.

"All of you, this is a bad place. You need to leave."

"How?" Walt gestured at where the entrance had been. Now, there were only more mirrors.

They were trapped. "*Merde.*"

Lola's reflection approached, a wicked grin of anticipation on her face. Lola flinched away, squeezing her eyes shut until the panic subsided.

"Everyone, close your eyes and hold onto the person next to you," she commanded, grabbing Gael's hand now slippery with sweat. "We'll make our way through together."

The moment she stopped looking at her reflection, the oppressive terror receded until she could pretend they were in an ordinary funhouse. The air remained cloying and heavy, making her head spin. Whispered voices—just on the edge of hearing—echoed around her, pleading, cajoling, demanding attention.

She moved forward blindly, one hand tracing along the mirrored walls. She tugged at Gael, who stumbled after her. With some cursing and shouts, they began to weave through the maze as a human chain.

A familiar whisper slithered into her ear—her own voice.

"What a laugh. You thought you could be normal? You thought you could be one of them? You'll always be a freak."

"Shut. Up." Lola ground the words through clenched teeth and carried on.

"Who are you talking to?" Gael's breath was ragged.

"No one," Lola said, though she wanted to reply, *myself.*

Every few paces, Lola slammed into a mirror, groping for the right way to go. The maze twisted in on itself an impossible number of times.

"This is absurd," Walt muttered.

"It's some kind of enchantment. I don't know how they're doing it or what exactly they are, but the Carnival of Fools is dealing in some very dark magic."

"Maybe the new girl shouldn't have come in with us." Walt's voice was flat.

No, Reiko certainly should not be in there with them, especially since Lola didn't know whether she was a threat to them or not.

Lola banged into another mirror, and a guttural growl rumbled through the glass, deep and dark and right in front of her. Gasping, her eyes flew across all the mirror surfaces, but all she saw was her reflection—

And then she couldn't look away. Gael's reflection came up behind her, his hands sliding around her waist. Although she couldn't feel his hands, a stab of lust passed through her as her reflection arched back against him.

"No," she whispered, putting her hands against the mirror. Her reflection matched her, their hands joined at the palms, and then it began to change.

Her skin withered before her eyes. Flesh drooped, greying, her once-bright eyes clouding over with age. Her scalp shone through wispy tatters of hair. The creature in front of her laughed, a hollow rattle, revealing rotted teeth in a concave mouth.

Gael's reflection transformed too. His skin took on a greenish cast, decaying, one eye melting away.

"This is what you wanted," the corpse wheezed, the echoed whisper wrapping around her.

Lola choked on a sob, wrenching herself away. Her eyes snapped shut.

"You okay?" The deep edge of Gael's voice made her turn back to look at the real him. He was shaking. What had he seen in the mirrors?

Lola risked a look back towards Reiko. The girl studied the

mirrors with wary eyes, then tugged Nix behind her. Without warning, a massive hunting knife materialized in Reiko's hand, serrated and black.

Lola blinked. "What?"

Was it reality or another trick of the mirrors?

Reiko lunged, knife slashing at a mirror. The blade scraped over the glass with a horrific grating screech. The girl shrieked something—guttural, raw—before taking off at a sprint down the corridor.

With Lola's knowledge of languages, she figured Reiko was speaking some Norse tongue, a dialect she didn't fully recognize. It sounded like she'd cried, "Back, demons!"

This brought up a whole encyclopedia of questions Lola had about her.

"Reiko!" Nix tore free from Walt's grip and sprinted after her.

"No, we have to stay together!" Lola lunged to grab her, but Nix was already out of sight, swallowed up in the winding halls of the maze.

"Together, together, together..." the reflections whispered.

A deep growl shook the mirrors, rattling the glass. Lola gasped. "Did you hear that?"

Gael blinked rapidly as he shook his head. His corpse reflection matched his movements.

"I hear crying," Walt said. He frowned and cracked his knuckles, his gaze sharpening as he pressed forward.

A scream ripped through the air, a primal cry of pain and terror.

Then the maze went entirely silent, a suffocating vacuum of sound.

As one, the three of them ran.

Turning a corner, Lola nearly tripped over Violet.

The girl knelt in front of one of the mirrors, sobs shaking her whole body. Her face was swollen and snotty from tears, and she gripped her matted hair as though trying to pull it out.

"No, no, no," she whispered, staring into her reflection. "I'll do better, I promise." She shoved her face into the ground, grinding it into the dirt.

"*Mon Dieu*." Lola rushed to her side, prying her up. "Violet, whatever you're seeing isn't real. It's okay."

Violet's groan came from a place deep inside her chest. "Why can't they see I'd bleed for them if only they'd care?" Lola glanced into the mirror and, for a brief second, could see another Violet holding a knife over a dripping wrist. Lola hauled her away and Violet sobbed, holding hard onto her wrist. "So much blood. I went too deep this time."

"There's no blood, Violet, I promise. You're okay." But Violet's skirt had hiked up and Lola could see real scars tracking up in lines along her thighs.

Lola had discounted Violet as a shallow party girl; she overlooked how much pain she might have in her own life. Bullies often did.

Lola patted her shoulder, unsure what to do. She'd never had a primer in caring. "You don't have to worry. It will be okay."

Violet's eyes flickered open, her gaze drawn back to the mirror. She pulled herself away from Lola and advanced on her own reflection, lip curling. "You're so ugly," she spat, then smashed her face against the mirror.

The surface shattered into a spider web of cracks.

Lola gasped, lunging to stop Violet from hurting herself further, but Walt got there first.

He hauled Violet into his arms, turning her away from the mirror. "Is she okay?" He looked at the girl sobbing in his arms, his eyes wide and frantic.

"She is decidedly not okay," Lola said. "We have to get out of here."

"Violet, talk to me. Tell me you're fine."

Walt's voice seemed to spur something in Violet, and her head jerked up to look at him.

Blood flowed from a cut on her forehead, and her eyes radiated malevolence. "What do you care? I know what you think of me."

With a gentleness Lola hadn't expected, Walt held her against him. "I get it, you know."

"You don't get anything." Violet tried to pull away, tried to hit him.

His muscles flexed as he held her in place, speaking rapidly in her ear. His words were low and intimate but somehow magnified so all could hear. "I know how it is for you because I've been there too. I have a family who doesn't give a shit about me either. I see you, Violet. I know what it's like to be alone in a crowd and I know what it's like when the people who are supposed to be there for you treat you like crap. It can be different."

She let out a shriek of rage and jerked away from him. Her eyes fell on Lola. "Why did you come here?" Her face twisted into a bloody mask, and with fingers clawed, she lunged forward.

Lola reeled back, crashing into Gael. Fighting for balance, they slammed into a mirror.

The panel swung around, sweeping them both into another part of the maze.

Twenty

Lola and Gael fell onto the ground in a long hallway, the hidden door clicking shut behind them. Lola scrambled to her knees, pushing and prodding at the mirror, but it didn't move.

Walt and Violet's voices sounded through the mirror.

"Life is so easy for you," she screeched.

Walt's huff of disbelief whispered around them. "You're self-absorbed enough to think that. You're having trouble seeing past your pretty face. This place must be a dream for you, nothing but your reflection to keep you company."

"You don't know anything."

"I know I wouldn't believe that a set of mirrors would be the thing that brought you down. I thought you were stronger than that."

There was a scuffle, and Lola banged her fist against the mirror. "Walt, Violet! They could hurt each other."

A singsong voice spoke out, high-pitched and eerie—Conri, the artist with the gilded eye.

"What's the point of being human if insanity is the rule?" He broke into laughter that ended on a sob. Nails scraped the other side of the mirror with a shrill shriek, making her shudder as she leapt away from it.

"We have to get out of here!" Gael grabbed her hand, and they ran.

A rush of air brushed her leg; soft, like fur. Nothing was in the corridor. But in the mirror, a flash of black appeared ahead of them.

It paused, an arm's length away, waiting for them. The furry form solidified into a wolf, tongue lolling. It sat within the depths of the mirror.

"What magic is this?" Lola whispered. Her mind grew hazy as the thick, perfumed smoke pumped into the maze, dulling her senses; all she wanted was to forget, let the fog take over.

But a flash of heat at her finger—her silver ring burning against her skin—snapped her back. She stared at the ring, the pain dragging her out of her stupor.

"Follow that," she said, pointing at the reflected wolf.

"Follow what?" Gael stared into the mirror, rubbing his forehead like a deep headache was taking root.

"Gael, trust me. Hold my hand and let me lead you."

He willingly reached for her and Lola pulled him along, following the wolf as it trotted ahead. Having something to concentrate on allowed her to ignore her shifting, mocking reflections.

They reached a dead end, surrounded by mirrors, but only one reflected the wolf. Its silver eyes looked straight at her, a white slash of fur crossed over its left eye.

The wolf nosed against the mirror's edge.

Gael's hand clamped tight around hers. "Lola, what's happening?"

Hesitant, Lola pressed on the side of the mirror, where her reflection overlapped with the wolf's. A hidden mechanism clicked.

With a hydraulic hiss, the mirror swivelled, showing intricate clockwork gears behind it. Lola cringed back, expecting a wolf to leap out at her, but behind the gearwork was another empty hall of mirrors.

"Through here." Gael allowed her to pull him along. The mirror shut with a click behind them, leaving no sign of the machinery.

A howl split the air, and they froze. The sound faded to nothing, the silence ringing in Lola's ears.

"We have to find the others," she said. She was frightened of how far they might sink into this twisted place.

They ran. Rounding a corner, they slammed into solid bodies. Everyone screamed.

"It's just us," Lola gasped, recognizing Nix and Reiko. Dried tears streaked Nix's face.

"This place is a goddamned nightmare." Reiko held her knife in front of her, careful to keep Nix protected behind her.

"We have to find Walt and..." Lola trailed off as she heard bickering.

"And why do you think you know everything—"

"Violet, shut up. I'm trying to find my way out here."

Eyes squeezed shut, Walt came around the corner, dragging Violet by the hand. His other hand slid along the bank of mirrors.

"Don't tell me to shut up! I tell *you* to shut up."

Violet's face was still half-covered in blood, and both were dishevelled. Violet's dress straps were trailing off her shoulders. Walt's lips were red and swollen, a smear of blood across his cheek.

The group gaped.

"Walt," Gael said.

Walt squinted, then opened his eyes. "There you are." A complicated look flitted over his face, guilt and satisfaction in one. "We found each other."

"Or we were herded here," Lola said.

"By what, though?" Reiko's grip tightened on her inexplicable knife, her stance braced for a fight.

The six of them huddled in the hall, shooting nervous looks at the mirrors and each other. Tension fell heavy on them like the weight of ancient spells, and Lola couldn't move, could barely breathe against the pressure.

A scream rang through the silence.

It lingered on and on until it was unbearable to endure, burrowing into their bones.

It ended abruptly on a gurgle.

Like that, the spell was broken.

"I'm out of here," Nix said. She bolted. The rest of them scrambled after her, their reflections chasing them like haunting spectres.

The atmosphere eased, the sickly honeyed fragrance lightening. Ahead, a gap in the tent appeared and blue sky showed tantalizingly behind the flapping curtain.

Too focused on what lay ahead, they didn't see what was underfoot.

Gael, in the lead, tripped, sprawling to the ground.

The rest of the group crashed into him and tumbled in a confusion of limbs and hair. Lola tried to pull herself up, but someone was on top of her. She had fallen on something soft and wet.

Violet's scream punctured the air. A shrill, relentless wail, her voice raw with terror. It was the same scream Lola had heard in her vision.

Her stomach clenched in revulsion at the jarring understanding.

Lola finally saw what she had landed on.

Richie Dawgsby was stretched out on the ground, his gangly limbs askew. His glasses were crooked, his pupils blown wide in endless horror. His mouth twisted in a silent scream.

His throat had been ripped open, leaving a mass of tattered skin and viscera.

His ruined body reflected over and over in the line of mirrors, on into infinity. The smell of blood and something darker filled the air; his belly had been mauled, the blueish tint of what lay inside him visible. His chest was a gruesome cavity where his heart had once been.

Nix was sobbing, Reiko brandished her knife as though she could intimidate mirrors, and Violet wouldn't stop screaming while Walt tried to shush her.

Lola crouched at the side of the body, heaving. Her vision foretold this happening, but she hadn't been able to stop it.

The last time she'd seen Richie was in the library, and he had been scared. What had he known; what had gotten him to this point? His latest story had caught up with him, and he'd been murdered for it.

Gael knelt next to her, holding his hand over his face as though trying not to vomit. "What could have done something like this?"

The first word that came to her mind was *wolves*. She tried to look at the body objectively and swallowed hard.

"It looks like an animal. But any number of demons could be this savage."

"Vampire?" Gael's whisper was only for her. An echo whispered it back and she glared at the hall of mirrors. She was done with this.

"There's too much blood. A vampire would never leave this kind of gore. Besides, the bitemarks don't match." The wound at the throat was a massacre, not made by the precision needle-like fangs of a vampire.

She steadied herself on the ground and her hand brushed something smooth. Hard black leather: Richie's notebook, the one he scribbled in incessantly. She grabbed it and shoved it in her bag.

Gael held his phone up. "No signal. We have to call 911."

"What do we do about him?" Nix asked, her voice breaking.

Her composure crumbling, Lola straightened his glasses with trembling fingers. "Nothing we can do for him now."

The six of them stumbled towards the exit, away from the hellish place.

TWENTY-ONE

"Let me go over this one more time." Greyson stared at his notes and drew out every word, causing Lola to grit her teeth. Sanctimonious jackass: she was beginning to think he was enjoying himself.

After their group had stumbled out of the maze, screaming and covered with blood, it hadn't taken long for the police and paramedics to show up. When Greyson stomped up to the barbaric scene, Lola's heart sank. She shouldn't have expected any less; he was the authority here, and another bloody corpse had been found on his sleepy island.

His glower, directed at her, told Lola everything she needed to know. She was implicated with yet another death, and he was going to hold her responsible.

Even worse, she was the only one who remembered what happened in the maze, not that she'd tell him that. One by one as they emerged from the enchanted tent, her friends had turned to each other in confusion, unsure why they were screaming, why they were covered in blood. The magic of the maze acted so the details of what had happened inside were like a bad dream.

Only this time, Lola remembered everything.

Violet, her head wrapped in gauze, looked like something dragged from a horror film. The hyenas who'd been waiting outside to witness her comeuppance now flocked around her, handmaidens to their queen. Sam and Cassidy were first in line to simper over her, eager to be a part of the unfolding dark drama.

Sam was reapplying makeup to Violet's blood-smeared face, but it was a losing battle. Violet's face was sticky with darkening blood. Sam rubbed a spot too close to her forehead and Violet winced, batting the girl away. She rubbed her arms despite the scorching sun.

Lola couldn't blame her. A deep horror had sunk into her bones as well, and she wondered if she'd ever feel warm again. Her Ice Cream Shoppe uniform was spoiled with blood. The feeling of Richie's body underneath her was vivid; he had still been warm.

Greyson had lost his patience early when speaking to them, his tone sharp as each of them struggled to piece together their fractured memories of the maze. No one could offer anything substantial. Lola could see uneasiness shift over their features as each tried to recall what had happened inside.

Lola watched them all carefully, remembering what it had been like when she'd left the maze the first time. She'd been fleeing in terror, but when she exited the tent, an odd sense of contentment stole over her, like a drug.

The maze was magicked to cause those to forget what happened inside, which was probably for the best. The mirrors showed them things that none of them could process: their deepest emotions laid bare, they were forced to gaze into their dark sides. It would be enough to drive anyone mad.

Lola eyed Violet; her reaction to the mirrors had been more extreme than others. She might be the meanest girl in school, but her demons lay close to the surface. Clearly, all was not right in her world, and despite her ugly behaviour, Lola couldn't help but understand her a bit more. She knew what it was like to be discarded and abused by those in her life.

The blonde girl wouldn't meet anyone's eyes, pushing away her friends with a scowl. She might not remember what she saw, but Lola knew that feeling of dread still clung to her like a shadow.

Reiko, ever the enigma, sat a few feet away from the others, her hands clasped tight in front of her. Her eyes flickered back and forth over the dirt as though trying to read something there, trying to recover her lost memories.

She muttered, again in something that sounded Norse, and again Lola had so many questions.

Reiko was not who she said she was and knew more than she pretended. A bear-like protection of Nix was building inside of Lola. If Reiko was not being upfront about who she was, then was she truly interested in Nix? Because the thought of someone playing with Nix's fragile heart made Lola want to hit something, vampire strength or not.

Nix looked lost, gazing at Reiko. Walt kept his arm around her, rubbing her arms as if trying to keep her warm. Walt's gaze kept flickering to Violet, and Lola's curiosity burned. What had happened between them?

Gael held Lola's hand, but the way their hands came together seemed wrong, like they were putting on a show.

She released him and crossed her arms over her chest as she glared at Greyson. "I don't know why we need to go over this again," she said, digging her nails into her palms to control her temper. *Merde,* she was tired of this all; she wanted nothing more than to go home, but he was making them jump through hoops over and over. "We found a body in the maze. It looked like it was attacked by a wild animal."

She didn't tell him she'd seen a wolf in the mirror. He was the last man on earth she'd try to explain that to. Greyson lived his life in the harsh lines of black-and-white reality, and there was no room for the greyscale of the Otherworld.

The wolf she'd seen in the maze must have mauled Richie, and yet it had seemed helpful, as though it wanted to help them escape. Not at all like a beast that had just ripped a person apart.

Her thoughts chased each other around her mind. Lola rubbed her forehead, feeling the pulse of a headache behind her eyes. *Why did she remember everything now? What had changed?*

And how did her visions play into all of this? Despite becoming human, clearly the Otherworld still held onto her with its clawed fingers. She might no longer be a vampire, but she was something Other, only she didn't know what. Pressure built behind her eyes at the thought; she would always be some kind of freak.

She shivered and tried to pay attention to what Greyson was asking.

"You six went into this maze together."

"We *weren't* together," Violet snapped, her face pinched with pain. Her eyes lingered on Walt; as she caught his gaze, he glanced away, rolling his shoulders.

"Five of us went in together," Walt said, clarifying what had been said three times already. "Violet was already inside. And we got separated."

"Nobody else was in there?" Greyson pressed.

"What about Ethan?" One of the hyenas piped up from the crowd, eager to be part of the spectacle.

"Ethan never showed." Violet stared hard at the ground.

"Then I don't give a shit about Ethan," Greyson continued. "I want to hear about you six and the victim."

"Richie." Lola's voice was a weak rasp. "His name was Richie."

"Did you know him?" Greyson's scowl could have blistered her skin. "Have a personal vendetta against him?"

"No," Lola said, though her stomach felt like an empty hole. Richie had been investigating her. It would look an awful lot like a motive for murder, especially since Greyson clearly believed she was capable of it. She prayed Richie had never reported Gael's assault.

"There was screaming," Reiko said, her face screwed up with the effort of trying to remember.

"It's okay," Nix said, her voice warbling as she tried to reach out for Reiko's hand. The girl gave an infinitesimal shake of the head, and Nix recoiled like a kicked puppy.

Greyson picked on Nix next. "You, redhead, what do you remember?"

Nix's eyes were round and haunted. "That place is effed up. Weird things happen in there." Her voice dropped to a whisper.

"Weird things like brutal murder," Greyson said. He watched them all with narrowed eyes.

"We got lost in the maze, but we eventually found each other," Gael said. "It was creepy in there—we were running to get out and we fell over Richie's body."

Greyson leaned in, eyes sharp. "Creepy how? Can someone provide details?"

All of them stared at him blankly, Lola more than happy to play along. She would almost enjoy Greyson's rage if a man hadn't just died and all her friends were under the effect of a powerful spell.

After a long silence, Greyson let out a low sigh. "Right, so you got spooked by a kids' attraction." Some of the onlookers snickered.

Lola's eyes narrowed. "Have you been in there?"

"Yes, we've searched the entire tent for the attacker. There are some mirrors, which, granted, turn you around. But nothing scary."

The way Greyson's face went fuzzy for a moment, she wondered if that was the truth, or if he also felt the creeping dread that something very wrong had happened inside. "Not that it matters. No one is going in there ever again."

Another officer was unfurling crime scene tape around the tent, wrapping it like a yellow and black present.

Duke Louis sprinted towards the maze. It was surprising he

was only arriving now; surely, he'd been aware of the police and paramedics on the grounds. For once he wasn't wearing his top hat and his long hair was mussed.

Puffing for breath, the ringmaster halted in front of Greyson. His gaze flitted over the crowd; perhaps it was her imagination, but it seemed to linger on Lola an instant too long. She shrank back, instinctively pressing into Gael's side.

"Sheriff," Louis said.

"Sergeant," Greyson corrected, flipping his notebook open again.

"Apologies, Sergeant, of course. I would like to express my horror and utter regret that such a senseless tragedy has taken place under our watch. We had no idea there were dangerous wild animals in the vicinity, or we would have taken more precautions. Something must have slipped in from the forest."

"You think a wild animal slipped into your weird tent in the middle of the day, in the middle of the carnival grounds, without being seen?" Greyson's lip curled as he stared at the man.

"I have no idea how this could have happened," Louis said, his face a blank canvas, devoid of the silvery makeup he usually wore. "Perhaps something decided to nest there overnight, and this gentleman was the unfortunate victim."

He seemed calm, far too calm for the owner of a carnival where a body had been discovered. Lola tilted her head, watching him, and his gaze slipped to hers again. She stiffened. This time, there was no denying it.

"You don't keep dangerous animals on the premises? You don't have some kind of menagerie, do you?"

Louis's smile was sharp, his canines showing. "You can search all the grounds for as long as you like, Sergeant. You'll never find dangerous animals on our premises. We do keep pigs, but they are unconnected to the carnival itself. I have all the requisite paperwork for the livestock; I'd be happy to show you. But from what I heard, it was no pig that did this."

"We'll check it out," Greyson said. "And this carnival is shut down as of this moment."

Louis nodded in oily acquiescence. "Of course. It's the only sane thing to do in the circumstances."

"Hmph." Greyson eyed the carnival owner, then barked at the men milling around the maze. "Wallace! Take Davis and Tartt and move people out of here. I don't want kids to get an eyeful of this."

The officers pushed into the crowds, hustling people towards the exit. One look at the flashing lights and officials guarding the maze with sour looks on their faces, and protests faded away.

Lola stood, stretching out her back, but Greyson spun on her. "We're not done here yet."

"How many more times do you want us to say the same thing?" she asked, her voice rising. "As far as I can tell, this was a dreadful accident with a wild animal. Is there something more to this? We're exhausted and need to get home to get cleaned up." She brushed out her bloodied uniform.

Greyson stared hard and a hint of silver glinted in his eyes. Lola clenched her fists. "Unless we're under arrest?"

He let out a stream of air through his nostrils but finally nodded. "Nobody is under arrest. You can go." He stabbed a finger at them all. "But nobody leaves the island until I've figured out what happened here."

He turned to Louis. "Now show me your permits."

"Of course, this way."

Duke Louis' gaze flicked back to her once more as he turned away. She stood tall and crossed her arms. She wasn't going to be frightened, not by him.

But she wondered what game he was playing here.

Twenty-Two

Garbled voices crackled over radios signalled the paramedics coming out of the maze, maneuvering the gurney through the crime scene tape. Richie's body was draped in a bloodstained white sheet.

While most of the lingering carnival-goers scrambled to leave, a few rubberneckers remained, craning over the EMS teams to catch a glimpse. Some seemed to treat it like another spectacle.

Reiko sucked in a breath. "Right, I'm out of here." She rose and walked off without a backwards glance. Nix blinked hard, eyes focused on the horizon.

Lola fought the instinct to jump up after Reiko and demand to know what she was, what she wanted. She didn't know enough about her, and Lola didn't want to be on the receiving end of that hunting knife.

As the crowd broke up, Violet stalked towards them. "I never want to see any of you ever again." Her teeth were clenched so hard that their outline was nearly visible in her cheeks. Her gaze lingered on Walt, who gave a low, dismissive snort.

"The feeling is mutual, Violet."

Sam's gaze bounced between them, an excited gleam taking light in her eye. "Wait, what happened in there?"

"Nothing," Walt and Violet snapped in unison.

Sam smirked. Her radar for drama had picked up on something between the two of them, and Lola didn't think she was wrong. Not that she'd ever sit down for a gossip with the spiteful girl. Sam had a vicious streak that could rival any of Lola's old crew.

"Freak." Violet stormed away, her sidekicks trailing behind her like shadows.

Gael was watching Walt. "Seriously, man, what did happen in there?"

Walt shook his head. "I...can't remember. I know it wasn't good, but it's like something that happened to someone else. And when I try to think about it, it slips away. All I really remember is finding the body."

"And the screaming," Nix said as though in a reverie. "There was too much screaming for that little space." The rest of them nodded, the weight of it settling over them.

"Duke Louis didn't seem very upset, did he?" Lola's gaze drifted back to the maze. The man hadn't seemed surprised in the least.

"The creepy ringmaster guy?" Gael asked. "About the body in one of his attractions or the fact that his carnival has been shut down?"

"Either one, take your pick. This should be devastating to his business. But instead, he looked...satisfied? As though he knew this would happen."

"Why would anyone want this to happen?" Gael asked.

"Publicity?" Nix suggested, though her usual energy had dulled, her voice flat. "Like, even bad publicity is good publicity?"

"But with the carnival closed, he can't even capitalize from the trolls looking for a thrill. Besides, the one person who would have written about this…" They fell silent as Richie's body was wheeled past them.

The ambulance was getting packed up when a figure emerged from the maze—Otsana. She strolled through the police tape like it was nothing.

Lola sucked in her breath. "I didn't see her go in. She must have been in there the whole time."

"Hey!" One of the officers pointed. "You can't be in there."

Otsana turned, flashing a grin as she slung her guitar over her shoulder and plucked at the strings, staring the officer down. The twang of the chords resonated through the air, picking up volume as the sound travelled. A strange stillness descended on them, captivated by the melody.

A flash of silver lightning arced across the ground, the tendrils reaching out to the authorities in front of Otsana.

The light licked towards them as well, and Lola let out a cry as the light reached their feet.

Everyone but Lola and Otsana froze, trapped in place as though suspended behind glass.

Panicked, Lola shook Gael's shoulder, but he didn't respond. His skin was warm and pliable, but it was as if he was no longer fully present, his eyes glazed.

Otsana prowled towards Lola, her steps slow and predatory.

"Look at this," She purred. "I've found myself a rabbit again. Although you're something more, aren't you, if you're not falling prey to my little melodies." She played another eerie chord, and the crowd of statues quivered, then remained frozen.

Lola's breath caught in her throat. "What did you do to them?" Otsana grinned and continued her approach. Lola stepped back, her voice shaky. "Stop it."

"Or you'll what?" Otsana moved even closer until Lola could smell the rancid blood on her breath. "That's right. You'll do nothing because you are nothing. If you keep your nose where it doesn't belong, you'll end up like your friend Richie. Little

Richie." Her smirk made Lola's skin crawl. "He thought he was so clever spying on me. I let him know just enough to bring him to my lair, and…well, you see what happens to troublemakers."

She tilted her head back, eyes gleaming silver. "But you, I like. So I'll do you this favour. Don't come back, not ever. If I see you here, you'll join Richie. And so will your sweet friends."

She made as if to touch Gael's throat, and Lola jumped between them, heart beating as though it would explode.

"You stay away from them," she hissed.

Otsana stared at Gael for a moment longer and licked her lips. "So tasty." Then she turned to Lola with a wink. "Still here, little rabbit? If I were you, I would *run*." The last word came out as a snarl. Her teeth were pointed and outlined with blood.

"No!" Lola threw her arms out as Otsana strummed a chord.

Her figure warped and stretched like a funhouse reflection. Lola blinked, and the woman was gone, leaving behind only the haunting echo of her music.

Everyone snapped back to life as though nothing had happened.

"We have to get out of here," Lola whispered, her voice tight with fear. Her friends gathered around her, and she tried to corral them away from the maze. "The carnival is dangerous for all of us."

"Lola, you're white as a ghost." Gael took her hand, his warmth a shock against her ice-cold skin.

As she passed through the gate, Lola swore she heard laughter. She glanced back to catch bursts of silver. The grounds were threaded with light, more powerful than before. Emptied of visitors, the carnival pulsed with new, ominous energy.

"Guys, you can't come back here," Lola said. "It's not safe; this place is enchanted, the lead singer is a witch, and I need to figure out why this is happening."

Nix, Walt and Gael all shared a heavy-lidded look; none of them shared Lola's urgency.

"Well, this place is closed," Nix said, her voice dull. "So I guess that's taken care of."

Gael squeezed her hand, trying to hide his worried frown with a smile. "We just need to let the experts handle it."

Lola couldn't help wonder who exactly those experts might be.

TWENTY-THREE

Her headache had morphed into a full-blown migraine by the time Lola stumbled home. All she wanted was to wash off the blood and sleep for a week. Never had the doors to The Pain Perdu seemed so welcoming.

Faye waited for her there, ambushing her at the doors with a tight, unexpected hug. For a moment, Lola drooped in her arms, letting Faye's softness wrap around her. She could almost imagine she was safe here. That the threads of the Otherworld weren't entangling her, pulling her back into the shadows.

But under the scent of freshly brewed coffee in the café was the underlying hum of gossip, faces alive with dark curiosity.

Faye's eyebrows crammed together as she pressed her hand against Lola's forehead. The touch was so motherly, her eyes so tender, Lola had to look away or risk shattering.

"Are you okay?" Faye asked, her voice laced with concern.

Lola nodded. "You've spoken to Greyson." She couldn't keep the edge out of her voice.

Faye didn't answer right away. Instead, she turned and called over her shoulder. "Francine, you've got the front? I'll be back in a minute."

Peeking around Faye, Lola saw the café was jumping, packed full of people. Everyone at the Carnival of Fools must have spilled into Port Despardoux after it shut down, some of them landing here. A sense of shared trauma hung in the air—being a part of the gruesome accident drew them together as they discussed what they knew about the death, their hushed voices laden with speculation.

Lola sighed. Humans could be exhausting. "I'm fine, Faye, I can help too."

"Not looking like that." Faye gestured to her gory outfit. "Just get upstairs." Her voice was tighter than usual.

Once they were in the small apartment that sat over the café, Faye sank into one of the squishy pink chairs in the living room. Only then did Lola realize her shoulders were trembling; how tightly had her friend been holding herself together before?

"Lola, what happened? You found a body? And you're somehow involved with the murder?"

"That's not what happened." Lola clenched her fists at how Greyson had twisted the truth to serve his agenda—getting her away from Faye.

"A young man was killed, Lola."

"The young man was mauled by an animal. And it was horrible to find his body, thanks for asking. But there's no murder."

Although she suspected Richie had, in fact, been murdered, it wasn't in the way the authorities were implying. "What did Greyson say?" Lola asked.

Faye's shoulders sagged, an invisible weight bearing down on her, but she didn't respond.

"Did he warn you about me?" Lola's voice was small. "Do you think I had something to do with this?" Though she'd done little to deserve it, Faye's trust meant everything to her. Sometimes she felt it was her only tie to her humanity.

"Of course I don't think you murdered someone. But I've been worried about you for hours. I got a call that the Ice Cream

Shoppe had closed mid-afternoon, and no word from you. You left in the middle of the shift?"

Lola let out a slow breath. In all the horror, she'd forgotten to let someone know she'd taken off from work. "I'm so sorry about that, Faye. Something came up. I wouldn't have left if it wasn't important."

Like a premonition of death. Which turned out to be accurate.

"Something important. Like going to the carnival with your friends?"

"It wasn't like that. Faye, this was serious."

"Maybe it seemed that way, Lola, but you're going to have to explain it to me because right now I can't see it your way."

"It's not like I left to go to have fun. I thought—" She faltered, unsure how to make sense of the inexplicable feeling that had driven her to the carnival. "I thought somebody was in trouble."

"Like Richie? How could you know he was in trouble?" Faye's tone was skeptical now.

Lola kicked the carpet with her toe. "I just had a bad feeling that something horrible was going to happen." Her voice faded away.

"You had a bad feeling and now somebody is dead." Faye's voice had gone flat.

Lola's chest tightened. "I wasn't involved. I tried to stop it, but...This is coming from Greyson, isn't it?"

Faye's lips pressed together in a tight line. "Greyson's worried about you."

"He's worried about you being around me. He's telling you not to trust me." The words stung even worse because Greyson wasn't wrong. "But I promise you I was trying to help, and I had nothing to do with Richie's death. I'm not a monster."

And maybe if she said it enough times, she'd believe it.

Pressure built behind her eyes, and she pressed her hands over her aching face. Faye jumped to her feet and swept Lola into a hug.

"I don't think you're a monster. I worry about you."

"I don't try to get into trouble; it seems to find me all on its own."

Faye's laugh was caustic. "Believe me, it's a feeling I know far too well."

Lola's heart was in her throat. The worst thing Faye could do would be to ask her to leave. "So where do we stand?"

"Going forward, you need to keep in touch. I gave you that phone for a reason. God, most mums I speak to can't get their kids off their phones, but I want you to actually let me know what's going on."

Lola tried to swallow, but her throat was too tight. Faye had never referred to herself as a mother before. Lola didn't want to move, didn't want to breathe, didn't want to break the spell. She didn't want Faye to take it back.

"I can do that," she whispered.

Faye nodded. "Lola?" She smoothed out the lapel of Lola's stained uniform.

"Yes?" At this moment, Lola would agree to nearly anything.

Faye patted her shoulder. "Give this a soak, see if we can get the blood out. And if you ever run out on your shift again, you're fired."

Lola cringed. "Got it."

"I have to get back to the café. It's like every tourist on the island is there."

As the door shut, Lola swayed on her feet, then followed orders. She showered and put the pink uniform to soak. Baking soda and vinegar to help lift the blood; after decades of bloodshed, she'd learned some tricks of the trade. It was surprising how many stains could be washed clean.

Bracing herself against the door frame, Lola assessed her bedroom with fresh eyes. It was barely the size of a closet found in some of the sweeping mansions and grand apartments she'd resided in over the years. The surfaces were tidy, lifeless. The walls remained painfully bare, as though she had moved in yesterday, not months ago. There were no signs a teenage girl lived here.

She'd seen movies about girls her age, rooms full of colour, posters of places they wanted to visit, pictures of friends making silly faces. Hopes and dreams of the future on display.

Who was she kidding? She wasn't a teenage girl, not really. She had more in common with the monster Greyson sought to expose. It was obvious here, showcased on her colourless walls.

Lola sank into the desk chair. She'd never thought about a future before. When you live forever, there's no point in planning ahead. She'd given so much for this life, but now she didn't know what to do with it.

Because it was too overwhelming to think about all the possibilities that lay ahead of her, Lola instead focused on something more manageable: investigating an Otherworldly murder.

So much was out of her control, but this was something tangible she could do. Not only would it take any blame off her heavily loaded shoulders, but curiosity pricked her, sharp and sweet. With her knowledge of the Otherworld, she might be uniquely suited to solve this mystery.

Otsana had threatened her friends, and now Lola wasn't going to rest until she knew exactly what was going on. And how she could stop it.

A flame of purpose lit inside her.

Rummaging through her bag, she brought out the leather notebook Richie always had on hand and opened it across her empty desk. Anticipation curled inside her.

Richie had been targeted because he got into his story too deeply and discovered too much about the wrong people. He'd finally come face to face with the monsters he'd been searching for his whole life and found they came with teeth.

His handwriting was heavy black scrawl that she would have a nightmare of a time interpreting, but some words and thoughts jumped out at her. *Unnatural objects. Carnal desire. Are we being drugged?*

Interesting. Lola grabbed a pen and a plain spiral notebook and made a note. The air in the maze had been heavy and thick with incense; could they be burning opiates that caused hallucinations? It was possible. The reflections in the mirror were disturbing, and a drug could cause the fogginess and sense of oppressive dread that enveloped the labyrinth.

But Lola was certain dark magic was at play as well, intoxicating the carnival goers. The mass forgetting had to be caused by an enchantment.

Richie seemed to have his own shorthand Lola itched to decode. She translated what she could make out: *Can't correctly remember what happened. How did she appear out of nowhere?*

Lola made a note: *Otsana?* then added *witchcraft?* Otsana was using spells, she'd seen her do it today.

At the bottom of one of the pages Richie had marked in thick ink and circled a phrase several times:

IT HAS HAPPENED BEFORE.

A string of dates followed, and Lola's blood chilled as her pen lingered over them. They went back in time over decades.

TWENTY-FOUR

Lola blinked in the morning sunlight, her eyes heavy after a restless night trying to decipher Richie's notes. Port Despardoux's town square was alive with movement, now that the carnival was shut down. Children ran over the grassy slopes, and people laughed under the shade of the central gazebo. It was an idyllic day, but she sought darker corners than this.

She needed guidance, and the first place that came to mind was the library.

When she first entered the building, she'd thought it bore the same enchantment found in all places of knowledge. But after seeing ghosts playing with the books, she was certain the place was steeped in the Otherworld.

Lola had always felt the most at home in libraries, tracking down treasures and unravelling mysteries one document at a time. She missed that about her life as a vampire.

She slowed as she entered, unsure where to start. What struck her the most about Richie's research were the dates he'd listed, some with a location noted. The internet provided little useful information. One newspaper in Wisconsin referenced a death at a fair the previous year that coincided with one of the dates, but the death was ruled accidental.

She was out of her depth and needed help.

Slowing at the front desk, she tapped the service bell. The chime echoed through the stacks.

A bespectacled head peeked out from the office door. The librarian, the one who'd been sitting with Richie the other day, had a deep frown etched across her face, her eyes swollen and red.

"Can I help you? Our checkout is automated, so you don't need me." Her voice was stuffy as though from crying, but she still managed to look down her nose at Lola.

"You've said that before. I need help with something different."

The librarian sniffed and, after a long pause, reluctantly came out of her office. Even though the space was overheated from the sun, she was swathed in long, grey layers. "Help with what?"

Lola made a face. "I'm looking for events that happened on specific dates, but the internet hasn't been helpful."

As if against her will, the woman crept closer, bringing with her a whiff of elegant French perfume.

Lola pushed her notebook towards her, where she had copied the places and dates; Richie's stolen notebook remained carefully hidden.

"Okay, so you want to look for old newspaper articles that correspond to these dates. That'll be a job, but we have an extensive archive. I'll show you."

As the librarian swept around the desk towards the wooden staircase, several thumps sounded above them. Were more books jumping out of the stacks? The library ghost was restless.

"What's going on with the building?" Lola asked, watching for a reaction.

The girl stiffened. "What? Oh, yes, it's just old. Pipes and stuff." She glared at the stacks as they reached the second floor, as though warning them to behave. "Just ignore it."

"Right." Curiosity about the young woman grew every minute she spent with her, so at home in a haunted library.

As Lola and the librarian passed rows of shelves, streams of light from tall windows picked up motes of dust floating by. In a back room, computers and equipment sat on desks, and rows of labeled drawers hinted at hidden knowledge.

"Here's my database. I've uploaded nearly everything into our digital system." The librarian nodded at a computer. She seemed more at ease in the closed-off space. "What are you looking for?"

"Unusual events." Lola assessed the librarian's reaction.

Her head tilted, seemingly unfazed by the vague request. "Unusual how? Weather phenomena? Disappearances?" Her eyes glinted behind her glasses.

"How about deaths, cross-referenced with carnivals?"

The words had an instant effect. The librarian took a step back, her composure cracking. Her hand flew to her mouth. "Is this about Richie?"

"I'm sorry about what happened. Were the two of you close?" Lola's voice was soft, like she was approaching a frightened kitten.

She didn't need to worry about scaring the librarian off. The girl dabbed at her nose with a tissue, but the look in her eye was steely.

"Not particularly. Richie was a bit odd. He seemed lonely, and I've never been much for socializing, so we had that in common. Sometimes I'd help him with his investigations. But that's about it."

"I think his latest investigation is the one that got him killed."

She slumped. "I warned him about it."

Lola paused. "You warned him about the carnival?"

Another book hit the floor with a decisive thud. The librarian winced and turned to the side. As the light hit her face, it illuminated a delicate, almost ethereal profile; something she seemed to do her best to hide.

"I mean, I told him he should avoid it." She wouldn't meet

Lola's gaze—she was hiding something. "He should have stayed away. He was onto something that scared even him. The last time I saw him; he told me he was being hunted."

"Hunted?"

"That was his word."

Silence stretched between them, but it didn't seem as though the girl would volunteer anything else.

Lola decided to take a different approach. "I'm Lola."

The librarian blinked, lost in her thoughts. "What? Oh, sorry, I'm Marissa."

"Nice to meet you, Marissa." Lola hesitated. Maybe Marissa needed to be shocked into revealing the truth. "Is the library haunted?"

Marissa's eyes widened behind her glasses. "Haunted?"

"By a ghost? Pushing all those books around?"

"That's ridiculous. You sound like Richie." Marissa let out a slightly hysterical laugh.

"You know something about the carnival." Lola spoke carefully as she was on shaky ground. Most people didn't come out and state their connection to the Otherworld. Not if they wanted to survive.

Marissa's posture changed, shoulders scooping in, more guarded. Perhaps she realized she'd said too much. "What of it?"

"I want to help figure out Richie's murder."

"It was an animal attack."

"I think it was more than that," Lola said. "I think he discovered something that got him killed. And I want to know what it was."

"And end up like Richie?" Marissa jumped to her feet and took a step away. "I'm not going to help you get into that kind of trouble too."

"I swear to you I can get into trouble all by myself." Lola's voice was wheedling. She gave Marissa a tiny half-smile. "When has knowledge ever hurt anyone?"

Marissa snorted but held out a reluctant hand for the list of dates. "Basic internet searches aren't turning up anything?" She pulled an elastic from one of her many pockets and swept her hair into a loose bun. "Let's see what we can do. The library computer databases can search through the digitized archives of most major newspapers. For this one"—Marissa pointed at the Wisconsin town and date on the list—"you'll want to look at Milwaukee. We carry that." She tapped away at her computer. "Here we go."

Lola watched her work. What was her story? "You seem young for a librarian."

"Oh, well. My father is the head librarian. He homeschooled me, you know, and I finished high school years ago. I've been taking online university classes, although I haven't quite finished my master's in library science. Come, sit here, I'll show you how to work everything."

Once Lola was well-versed in the system, Marissa stood. "Must get back to the books."

"Books that jump off the shelves?" Lola asked, her curiosity overwhelming.

Marissa pushed her glasses up her nose, peering at Lola as if trying to figure out if she was being mocked. "You shouldn't say things like that." She glanced around as though worried they were being spied on, though nobody else was in the building.

"Why not?"

"I know most people don't believe in that kind of thing—"

"Consider me a believer."

Marissa raised her chin. "Or maybe you're like Richie, messing in things he didn't understand," she said in a furious whisper. "I'll tell you what I told him: there are some things you shouldn't unearth."

With a whisper of her skirts, Marissa left Lola alone in the room with a notebook full of questions—including ones about the haunting librarian.

Lola searched through the archives, trying to find news articles that lined up with the right dates and times.

It was long work, and after hours in the dusty room, Lola was blinking grit out of her eyes. She rubbed her temples, the tiny print giving her a headache. That had never been a concern of hers before becoming human. She wondered if she'd need glasses some-day; the thought irrationally made her smile. Nothing seemed further from vampirism than a pair of glasses perched on the nose.

It wasn't until she noticed how far the sunbeams had drifted in the drowsy library that she realized how long she'd been there; it must be mid-afternoon. She sighed and put in her next search, this time for Kansas City. The date was June 1982, and she went through the fine newsprint, trying not to flip by too quickly. Still, she almost missed it; it took her brain a few seconds to process what she had seen.

The photo was grainy black and white, but Lola recognized the Carnival of Fools; the same arch stretched over the entrance gates, Duke Louis in his top hat at the centre with his arms wide as if to welcome the crowds. Otsana was recognizable next to him, her electric guitar slung over her shoulder. Her hair was teased around her face, but they both sported the same harlequin makeup.

In the crowd behind Louis and Otsana, another face jumped out at Lola. The artist with the gilded eye stared straight at the camera.

"*Non,*" she whispered out loud. They looked exactly the same more than forty years ago.

How could that be? She scanned the article; it was about the body of a middle-aged man found underneath a stage at the carni-val. He had been mauled, just like Richie.

With a surge of excitement, she zoomed in on the photo and printed it.

What were the carnival workers playing at? Dead bodies and immortality went hand in hand, and it usually meant a ritual sacri-fice. The consumption of the heart would seal it.

Otsana's eyes burned from the photo as she smirked, mocking Lola through time.

She must be a powerful witch; she was playing with blood magic and turning back the hands of time.

The door to the back room banged open and Lola jumped, her heart lodged in her throat. Marissa stood there in the door frame, panting, her hair falling out of her bun in frazzled clumps.

"What is going on?" the librarian said through gritted teeth. "The books have never been more active, and it's because of you, I know it! They're desperate to get my attention. Something bad is happening, isn't it?"

Lola folded the printed photo and tucked it into her bag. "What are you talking about?"

Marissa's expression was stony. "You're here looking for death and mayhem, so I'm assuming you know of Duchesne Island's supernatural reputation? There's a convergence of negative energy swirling around the carnival right now."

"How do you know?"

Marissa's eyes glittered behind enormous glasses. "The books."

"I don't understand."

Marissa raised her shoulder. "Believe me, it shook me as well. But at a certain point, you can't ignore something that's staring you in the face. Or that's fallen on your toe. The books speak to me. They open and a passage or word will jump out, like a message."

"Could be coincidence."

Marissa's smile was ancient and sad. "Maybe. But they haven't been wrong yet."

One of them was going to have to say it out loud, and Lola didn't have time to tap dance around the skittish librarian. "Are you a part of the Otherworld?" Lola's voice dropped though no one else was around. She'd been Other for eighty years and now it felt like a dirty secret. Her heart pounded at speaking it out loud.

Marissa shot a look at Lola, cautious as though testing murky water. "What's the Otherworld?"

"You don't know the Otherworld? Marissa, if what you say is true, this is deep magic you have. Does anyone in your family practice witchcraft?"

Marissa's skin paled to frost. "I'm not allowed to talk about it."

"But this kind of power can get out of hand if you don't control it."

Marissa's voice lowered to a furious whisper. "We *don't* talk about it. My mother died when I was young, but my father always said she was killed by something evil. I never knew what he meant by it, only that the occult was a wicked thing I wasn't supposed to know about. But the library is filled with books on it; my father is obsessed. I wonder sometimes whether my mother..." She broke off, breathing hard. "When this started happening to me, this abomination, he took off, saying he needed to track down some resources. He left me here to deal with the book apocalypse that is my life."

"Marissa, if you're developing supernatural powers, it's likely your mother was a witch," Lola said. "Bloodline witches are passed down through the maternal line. But I've never heard of a book witch. How does it work?"

"I don't know how. My father has always been the librarian here, and it's always been the two of us. We live upstairs in the apartment. This is the one place I felt safe, protected, almost as though my mother is watching over me. But these last few months, something changed, and the books started flying off the shelves, sharing secret messages, and I don't know why."

Lola stilled. "Last few months?" An idea itched at the back of her mind. "Would you say this began around the beginning of May?"

Had Lola, diving far past the realm of mortals into the Well of Souls, left a gate open on her way back in, like Otsana insinuated? Were powers found deep beyond the veil crashing through into this world? Dormant magic could have manifested under a barrage of supernatural energy.

"Yes, exactly then. Do you know why?" A hunger burned in Marissa's eyes, a longing to understand. A hushed expectancy hung between them, and Lola reached out with deliberate slowness to take Marissa's hand. It was cold and bony, the skin like parchment.

"It sounds like your father knows more than he's told you. You are a part of what we call the Otherworld, although not many people know about it, and we rarely talk about it because it can be dangerous."

"Oh." Marissa held still. Finally, the ghost of a smile flickered over her lips. "I thought I might be going insane."

"Nope, just a witch living on an intensely magical island. And right now, everyone on the island is in danger."

"What do you mean?"

"There's some kind of spell set over the carnival. It draws people in, making them behave differently. It seems to be gaining power. Wait." Lola's head shot up. "Have you been to the carnival?"

"No." Marissa shoved her glasses up her face. "I don't get out much."

"Interesting. Almost everyone else on the island seems drawn to the place."

A book thumped onto the ground farther out into the stacks, heavy with foreboding. Both Lola and Marissa winced, then tracked down the sound in the stacks, Marissa's heels clacking on the hardwood floors. They found it in the well-stocked occult section.

Marissa picked up the book and opened it with her eyes closed. It fell open to a chapter near the back of the book, and she read it.

"It's about protection spells," she said, looking up at Lola with eyes as round as moons behind her glasses.

Protection spells. Why did that sound familiar?

Her finger grazed over the ring Gael had given her. What had he said about it? That as long as she was in his heart, she would be impervious.

She stared at the lovely silver ring. It had been made by the strange artist, Conri; had it, in fact, been designed with a protection charm within, making her invulnerable to magical enchantment? Like being able to remember what happened in the Maze of Desire.

A wave of affection crashed through her towards Gael. Even when he wasn't with her, he was keeping her safe.

"But what kind of spell do we need protection from?" Lola said out loud.

Marissa blinked, and Lola worried for a moment that she was going to fall apart or deny any of this being true. But the librarian squared her shoulders and gave a firm nod. "Tell me what's going on, exactly."

As Lola described what she'd seen and what she suspected, Marissa scurried around the library gathering books. The rapping of her shoes was punctuated by the thuds of books, and she'd patter over to retrieve each.

"Freud," she said, picking one up. "That's interesting."

A surge of understanding flooded through Lola, and her scattered thoughts reorganized into a pattern.

"It makes sense. It's the *Id*—the pleasure principle. The people at the carnival are acting on their basic instincts. They want what they want when they want it, and they don't care about anything else."

"A spell that causes us to act out our basic desires, looking for immediate gratification." Marissa shivered under her woollen sweater. "So those under the spell have lost the ability to control their impulses? Scary."

"Extremely."

Marissa eyes were intense behind her enormous glasses. "But what are you in all this?"

"Pardon?" Lola took a step back, shying away from what she knew Marissa was asking.

"I'm a witch; you must be something. You know about all this...about the Otherworld."

"Some people do. Like Richie." She wanted to get her off this line of questioning.

Marissa's gaze turned inward. "Richie didn't know, though, not the way you do. He always believed something paranormal was going on around us. He searched out every legend on the island, desperate to prove magic was real. And it got him killed."

Lola snapped her fingers as something clicked. "Killed *inside* the Maze of Desire. I think that's the crux of the spell. There's a magical vortex in there as if reality itself is being warped. The way Richie was murdered..." Lola hesitated, not wanting to get into the gruesome details. "It was a blood sacrifice, a ritual to strengthen the enchantment."

"Good grief," Marissa whispered. She picked at the pages of the book she clutched as though the dry paper could give her some kind of comfort. "This is real, isn't it? A part of me always thought there might be more to the world, but I was never allowed to question it. Holed up in the library, I was kept away from all of this Otherworld."

"It looks like the Otherworld caught up with you."

Lola's phone chirped. She read the incoming message from Gael:

The carnival's reopened. Going there with my fam. Join us? Mum wants to see you.

Lola stared at the message, several thoughts popping into her head at the same time: What the hell is he doing taking his family to the carnival? Why is it even open? as well as: I *bet* his mom wants to see me; that lady doesn't trust me as far as she can throw me.

What was Gael thinking?

"Something's going on," Marissa said. She'd moved to the window, looking down over Main Street. A roar went up from the crowd of tourists and islanders that had been milling around Port Despardoux since the carnival had closed. En masse, people swarmed up the street towards the Granger Farm, mindlessly flocking back to the carnival.

"Carnival's open again," Lola said.

"I can see."

"This is more powerful than before. It's like everybody has been brainwashed. Are you sure you don't feel a pull to run away and join the circus?"

Marissa paused as though considering it. "I don't have any desire to leave this building."

Lola glanced around the arched ceilings and towering stacks of the library, still certain it was imbued with muted enchantment. "I think there might be protective spells placed around the library. You should stay inside until this is over."

Marissa let out a tiny huff of breath. "That won't be a problem. But what are you going to do?"

"I don't know." Lola was already throwing books into her bag. "Stop them? See if you can find the way to break a spell. I'll try to get my friends away from there before anything worse happens."

TWENTY-FIVE

Outside on the streets, Lola had to elbow her way through the throng. What the hell was going on?

Yesterday, Greyson had been determined to get the carnival out of town as quickly as possible, and now the gates were being thrown open in a chaotic free-for-all. Either the authorities had lost control of Duchesne Island, or they were affected by the same madness as everyone else.

Merde, this wasn't good. The entire town had fallen under the carnival's sway. And only Lola knew what had happened. Otsana had warned her against returning.

But her friends were now in the belly of the beast. She needed to get them out of there before something worse happened. Because Lola had no doubt the carnival was ratcheting up to some terrible grand finale, and she didn't think anyone should be around for its climax.

Frantic to get to Gael and his family, she dashed across Main Street, dodging the crowd of carnival zombies. Some people laughed hysterically, some of them shovelled food into their faces, while others were in screaming fights. It was as though everyone on the island had collectively lost their minds.

The gates to the carnival stood wide open; the masses swarmed onto the grounds unimpeded. Lola joined the flow as her fingers flew over her phone:

Where are you?

Gael texted back immediately: *Picnic tables*

It was only then that she registered what that meant—she was going to face Gael's mother. Gael had wanted them to meet again, just as much as Lola wanted to keep on stalling, until potentially they were all adults and no longer lived on the same island.

Anita Smith was a Bolivian archeologist with one foot firmly rooted in the occult. Lola often wondered if her knowledge of the Otherworld had led her to the supernaturally active Duchesne Island, where she had fallen in love with Gael's father and settled down. The Smith family had struggled for years after Gael's father was lost at sea, and then Diego was diagnosed with cancer.

Finally, their luck had turned around with the "discovery" of gold on their land and Diego's miraculous recovery. While Lola had orchestrated most of that, Anita perceived only the dangers that swirled around her.

From their first meeting, Anita had known what Lola was. How she had seen through Lola's human disguise so easily was still a mystery to her. No one had ever been able to sense she was a vampire before.

Anita had warned Lola away from Gael, which, rationally, Lola understood. After all, when they had met, Gael was in the hospital for blood loss after Lola had nearly sucked him dry.

For a mother, some things were simply unforgivable.

Lola stormed past the food stands, panic mounting, scanning desperately for the picnic tables. Finally, she discovered a clearing under some trees near the edge of the grounds.

She assessed the area to see if it was safe, glancing over her shoulder to see if Otsana was stalking up behind her. But there was only Gael, striding over to greet her, silver glinting in his eyes.

"I was wondering if you'd show up."

Lola grabbed his T-shirt. "Gael, you can't be here! Don't you remember what happened, just yesterday?"

His eyes hardened diamond-bright. "Lola, I just want you to spend some time with my family. Is that so drastic? It's a part of being human. If you want to be one of us, you actually have to act like it."

Lola reeled back, stung by his words. "Gael, this isn't like you. I might be new at this, but meeting up with the family and having a picnic where a murder investigation is ongoing doesn't seem particularly wholesome."

"Richie's death was an accident. There's no reason to hold the carnival responsible. Everyone just wants to have a little fun. Why is that so hard for you to see?" He began pacing, agitation vibrating off of him. "Why can't you to see how much I want you to be a part of all this?"

Lola's stomach twisted. If the spell was unearthing Gael's raw instincts, then how much of him was he usually holding back? Beneath his easygoing nature he showed to the world, was he always this intense?

She could use the spell to see what he truly wanted. To understand him.

But it wouldn't be right. Gael was vulnerable in a way Lola wasn't right now. He'd given her the ring that shielded from this magic. Maybe she could share a part of the protection he'd given her.

Gently, she reached out and pressed the ring against his cheek.

His eyes cleared, the silver melting away to golden brown. His smile softened. "Lola, hi. The whole family is over here, waiting for you. Diego can't wait to see you again."

She blinked at his abrupt shift. "Are you okay?"

He shook his head. "I feel a bit dizzy, actually. Maybe we've been in the sun too long. Come over here; we've found some shade."

She stared at him for a beat longer. Gael had no idea what was going on. She needed to get him—and his whole family—away from here before it was too late.

"Yes," she said, gripping his hand, keeping the ring firmly pressed into his palm. "Take me to them."

Anita Smith perched on the edge of a picnic table. She was a tiny woman, but her posture had straightened since Diego was cured, as though the weight of a galaxy had been lifted from her shoulders.

Lola approached carefully and stood in front of Anita. Before she could say anything, something slammed into her, knocking her to the side.

Diego had barrelled into her, wrapping her up in a hug.

"Did you bring me something from the shop?"

Gael had brought his brother a few times to the ice cream stand, and Diego seemed enraptured by the fact that Lola dispensed his favourite food.

He was small for twelve, but it could have been the year of chemotherapy treatments that set him back. Now that he was cured, hopefully he would be back on track. The boy's mysterious recovery from cancer still mystified doctors, and Lola suspected they would be running tests on him for years.

They whispered that he was a miracle boy, but they didn't know how close they were to the truth.

Lola was just delighted she could watch this boy grow into a healthy man.

"Unfortunately, I don't have any ice cream in my back pocket. You'll have to wait for next time I see you at the stand. We just got in this new flavour, Shark's Tooth. Full sugar. I'll save you some."

"Sweet." Diego grinned and bounced away. He, at least, seemed his normal self. Relief warred with urgency. Lola wanted him away from this place as quickly as possible.

Next to Lola, Anita watched Diego gambol like a puppy. Steeling herself, Lola turned to face Gael's mother.

Without warning, Anita reached out with thin fingers and

grasped Lola's wrist, checking for a pulse. Her gaze darted over Lola's face, sharp and searching, as though trying to peel back layers and see straight into her soul.

"How did you do it?" Anita asked, her voice low and hoarse. "I didn't know it was possible."

So much for a normal picnic with the boyfriend's family.

"I don't know if it's been done before," Lola said, trying to keep her tone upbeat. "I guess I'm just a trailblazer."

"Still, there's something…" Anita narrowed her eyes, and Lola's heart flip-flopped. What did she see with her uncanny perception? Did the Otherworld linger on Lola's skin like a tattoo, forever engraved? Did she see something that had to do with her visions?

"There is something going on, Anita," Lola said, hoping she could get through to her, if not to Gael. "This carnival is a part of the Otherworld; we need to leave. It's not safe here."

"No, not safe." Only then did Lola see the sheen behind Anita's dark, solemn eyes: the silver gleam of the spell. "You'll never be safe; you will be the doom of my family."

"*Mamá*, what's going on?" Gael was wide-eyed as his mother's face twisted into a snarl.

"I want this *bruja* out of our lives forever! Before it's too late." Anita swung her hand back to strike her.

Lola caught her wrist. As with Gael before, the silver melted from Anita's eyes when the ring grazed her skin, and the woman collapsed forward as though the strings holding her up had been cut.

"What…what is happening?" Anita's breath hitched.

"*Mamá*, you went to hit Lola." Gael said, stunned.

Anita paled. "I—I would never."

She wouldn't, but she probably had wanted to. A range of emotions flooded her face before Anita was able to school them into blank civility. "I apologize, Lola, I don't know what came over me. Perhaps it was the heat."

"Perhaps it's this place," Lola said. "Since you seem to be clear-headed for the moment, please listen to me. The carnival is enchanted. If you wish to keep your sons safe, take them away from here now. Get back to your cottage and lock the door."

Anita's face set in grim lines. "They're in danger?"

"Yes, and not from me. Gael, can you take your mom and Diego home? Please? It will mean everything to me to keep them safe."

"Lola, what's going on?"

Lola reached up and gave Gael a hug while he was still the Gael she remembered. She let him hold her with his solid strength, his warmth, before whispering in his ear. "Please trust me in this. You have to stay away from the carnival."

"What about you? And Nix—I think I saw her here."

Merde. "I'll find her, but getting your brother to safety is more important than anything."

"Wait for me, then."

"I can't. It might be too late."

"You don't have to do this alone," he said, his voice heating with frustration. "It's not up to you to save everyone."

"If not me, then who, Gael? Don't worry, I'll be safe." She lied as she kissed his cheek and pulled away. Gael didn't understand, not really, how she was uniquely placed to be able to help others. And it wasn't a calling she could just walk away from.

The Otherworld would always be inside of her, and she knew more than anyone how dangerous it could be. It was up to her to keep the people she loved safe.

Twenty-Six

Though Gael seemed torn between wanting to stay with her and safeguarding his family, Lola knew she could count on his devotion to his brother. With a heavy sigh, he went to gather their things. Even as she walked away, she could hear Diego's pleading to stay a little longer, his mother's quiet murmurings.

How long did they have before the spell called to them again? Would they even be safe if they were back in their cottage in the forest, with doors locked tight against enchantment?

Gael seemed so genuinely lost, as though he remembered nothing at all, not even finding Richie's body. Yesterday, they were fleeing through the maze, screaming in terror, and today, he'd brought his family here, as though the very place wasn't saturated in death.

The spell was getting stronger. Lola felt it in her bones. She needed to figure out how to stop it. Or perhaps the better question was, *why*? Was this scheming group of con artists only here to roll the townspeople for their money?

It couldn't be something so mundane. Every fibre of her being screamed that the dark magic here was seeking a larger prize. And all her friends were in the crosshairs.

Her best chance to find Nix lay with the crowd. Everyone was gathering in The Gardens. Tinny organ music was playing over the speakers for the moment; while the sound grated at her nerves, at least The Bayous weren't playing. Every time they played, the spell seemed to grow, and Lola didn't want to be here as things spiralled further out of control.

Her own emotions roiled inside of her, whether or not she was under a spell. Ever since she'd come back as human, she hadn't connected with Gael on the same level as before.

She wished more than anything she could just tell her head and her heart to stop messing around and get in line. But the pull of everything inside of her made that impossible.

Entering The Gardens, she spotted Nix instantly: a copper-headed girl shovelling candy into her mouth with abandon, staring forlornly into the crowd.

Lola approached Nix gently, not wanting any emotional surprises. She still wasn't expecting the tears that welled up in her silver eyes, spilling over her cheeks.

"Nix, what happened?" Lola pulled her into a hug, feeling her bony shoulders shaking under her hands. "Did someone hurt you?"

"No, nothing like that." Nix swiped angrily at her cheeks. "It's so stupid. I can't stop these waterworks…it's like the faucet's broke."

"Nix, you're not plumbing," Lola said, which earned her a watery chuckle.

"I know. It's just stupid." She glanced into the crowd and started crying again.

Lola followed her gaze to see Reiko dancing with a group of teens, laughing, her arms slung around Violet and Sam.

"I see," Lola said, her voice a little quieter. "Nothing stupid about that. Let me try something."

Lola touched Nix's shoulder, pressing her ring against her skin, and watched as the silver gleam receded. "How do you feel now?"

Nix inhaled deeply as though she hadn't been breathing properly for ages. "Whoa, much better. What I felt before, it was… crushing." She turned away from Reiko and the beautiful girls, hunching her shoulders. "Do you ever feel like you're always standing on the outside, looking in?"

Lola smiled softly. She understood. "I'll say this while you're still able to remember, then. I know how you feel. I see you; you are brave and fierce and everything I could have ever asked for in a friend." She pulled away. "I hope that helps put things into perspective."

Nix rubbed her arm meditatively. "How'd you know what to say?"

"Because it was exactly what I needed to hear once."

"It's funny to think of you as needing any kind of love. You were kind of a weird vampire, weren't you?"

"The weirdest." Lola gave a dry smile, her heart aching at the memory. "Now, I don't want you to freak out, but you're under the influence of a spell."

Nix popped a jellybean into her mouth, seemingly untroubled by her warning. "A spell? Huh. Things are always interesting when you're around. What kind of spell?"

"It makes people lose control of their impulses."

Nix nodded. "I can see that. The food stands are like a prison riot. Everybody is super extra, behaving like children." She popped another candy into her mouth.

Her pixie-bright friend was one of the most observant people Lola knew. "That's an interesting way of putting it. I just saw Diego, and he didn't seem affected. Maybe it doesn't work on kids, or kids always behave like that? I think it goes back to Freud's pleasure principle of wanting what you want immediately."

"Yeah, everyone is super extra," Nix repeated as though the

case was closed. "So, you saw Diego? Getting in with the fam, right. How'd it go?" Nix dug a finger into Lola's side.

"Not the best. Anita tried to slap me, and Gael doesn't think I'm trying hard enough to fit in."

"Oh no—trouble in paradise?" Nix prodded, sitting Lola down on a bench and passing her a handful of jellybeans. She tucked her knees up, settling in like they had all the time in the world. "Want to talk about it?"

"About what?" Lola perched next to her as though she could flee. Her heart was pounding like she'd run a marathon, at the thought of what she wanted to confess.

"About how since you've become human, things are different between you guys."

Lola's stomach sank. Nothing got by this girl. "I don't know how to explain it. When I was...how I was before, I wanted Gael. It was so clear in my mind. And not like, as a meal, but there was a connection between us. I'd never experienced anything like that before. But since being...the way I am now—"

"Human," Nix said loudly. Lola swung her head around to make sure they weren't overheard, but no one was paying attention. She glared at Nix, who remained impassive. "Listen, I think it's important that you say it out loud; it's probably something you should talk about more."

Lola contemplated what Nix had said. "Maybe that's a part of it. Gael never wants to talk about it, like I started off brand new when I became human, and everything I was before ceased to exist. But I can't pretend the past decades never happened. I can't forget what I was, and I don't know what it is I've become, because I'm not sure it's entirely human. And I don't know if Gael could deal with that."

Lola's words gushed out like the dam holding it all back had disintegrated. "And I feel like that connection we had is being drowned out by all the other things going on inside of here." She made a circling motion over her whole body. "I'm scared of so many things, and on top of that, I have to think about a future I never imagined for myself. And half of my thoughts are conflicting with the other half. I think I came back wrong."

Nix's smile wasn't as sharp as normal. "Or maybe you came back as a teenage girl and have no experience with hormones. Welcome to reality. Half the time I have no clue what I want but could scream for not having it."

"Yes, exactly!" Lola could have jumped to her feet, happy somebody got it.

Nix made a face. "Lola, I'm sorry to be the one to break it to you, but all of that is normal."

"It's absurd."

"Humanity is absurd." Nix agreed. "But listen, I'm going to lay down some hard truths. Maybe Gael hasn't handled it the best either, but he still feels that connection. Based on everything that's happened between the two of you, he absolutely thinks you're his girlfriend. I mean, everybody does." She shrugged apologetically.

"I want to feel that way," Lola said. "More than anything, I want that connection back, the way it was before. But I don't know if I'm ready for what that means. To be Gael's...person. Because it would be serious, life-changing serious, and I've only just discovered this life of mine. Sometimes I see him looking at me in this way, this urgent way, and I feel like I'm suffocating."

"Not the way you want to feel about the person you're with."

Lola's throat tightened; the tears she wanted to shed were choking her. "I love Gael. I just don't know if I can be the person he wants me to be."

Nix took her hand and squeezed. "Lola, you have the right to figure out your life like everybody else. You're allowed to change your mind."

"You wouldn't hate me for it?"

"You're human now. We change, we evolve, and sometimes things get messy. I wouldn't hate you for following your heart." She paused. "But Gael deserves to know where you're at. None of this wishy-washy I want everything crap, okay? You can't have everything. You need to let him know."

"Right." Lola longed to ask Nix what to do but suspected this was a human thing she'd have to figure out on her own. "*Merde.*"

"I hear ya. Try being gay on top of that." Nix's eyes sparkled sympathetically, and she laughed at her own heartache.

"Do you want to talk about what happened with Reiko?"

She sighed and buried her face in her hands. "Hard to know. I had thought...there might have been a spark. Sometimes I'd catch her watching me, and I'd go all fluttery and just wanted to ask, you know, are you into girls? Or, this girl, in particular. But then the maze happened."

"Have you spoken since then?"

"Not at all; every time I try, she shuts me down. It's like trying to talk to a glacier." Her forehead creased. "I think something dramatic happened in the maze yesterday. But I can't remember what it was."

"We found a body," Lola reminded her.

"Right." Nix still looked hazy and shook her head. "I guess that's a bit of a mood killer."

"Depends on who you hang out with," Lola said with a smile.

Her gaze found Reiko in the crowd. She had been watching both Lola and Nix, but now she turned away. What secrets was she hiding, and what did it have to do with the carnival? Because there was no mistaking she turned up on the island at the same time as the Carnival of Fools.

"You know," Lola said carefully and hoisted Nix onto her feet. She began to lead Nix away from The Gardens, out of the carnival. Nix munched on her candy, complacent for the moment. "It might be for the best. I think there's something off about the new girl."

Nix's eyebrow arched. "That's what I keep on hearing about you."

"*Touché.*" Lola started laughing. "The truth is, you deserve better than both of us."

"Just my luck my life filled up with hot women with issues." Nix sighed and leaned against Lola's shoulder, letting her head fall back as she gazed up into the evening sky. Her eyes seemed to reflect the starlight as silver reflected in them again. "You know, maybe everyone's just acting weird because of the full moon. I've seen it at my mum's shop when I've been working. People always get squirrelly at this time of the month."

"What did you say?" Lola gazed upwards with dawning horror towards the pale disc rising in the deepening sky. "Is the full moon tonight?"

"Um, I think it's tomorrow. But it's close enough for the lunatic inside of us to come out; I swear it's true."

Dots connected inside Lola's head and the mystery of the Carnival of Fools began to unravel. The full moon, the wolf, the mangled body.

Things were far more dangerous than she'd imagined.

Anxiety quickened inside of her; Nix had to get home, but Lola had to stay at the carnival. There was someone she needed to speak to. "Nix, you have to get out of here."

"No! Let's stay and have fun."

Lola pressed her ring against Nix's cheek, watching the swirling silver in her eyes fade again. "You weren't having any fun at all here. And it's you who has to get home. Please, get into your house with your family, and stay there. Promise me, Nix."

Eyes huge, Nix shoved more candy into her mouth and nodded. "Okay, you're the magic boss. I'll do what you say. But Lola?" Her eyes narrowed. "When it comes to Gael? And I say this with love. But figure your shit out...fast. He doesn't deserve to be played by you."

TWENTY-SEVEN

Lola waited until Nix was on her way down the road before she spun back towards the carnival. Nix had given her an idea—one that filled in the gaps as to what was going on at the carnival. But now, she needed answers from the source.

She needed to find Chann, the pickpocket who definitely knew more than he'd been willing to share. She had to figure out where all this magic was heading.

She weaved through the throng of boisterous people, her heart racing as she approached the strongman game, the first place she'd seen him. Somebody grabbed her as she passed, and she wrenched out of their grasp, a sob building at the back of her throat. The chaos of the crowd made her feel vulnerable, like at any moment they would turn on her and tear her apart.

The squeal of an electric guitar blared through the speakers, and Lola cursed. The Bayous were gearing up for another set.

As the music kicked in, an insistent beat that pulsed with her own heart, a sinking feeling in her gut told her the night was about to get wild.

A large group of older men gathered around the strongman game; they had the look of tourists. They struggled with the hammer, never getting it above 2. One man turned puce red and smashed the hammer into the ground again and again as he screamed incoherently.

The carnival worker's painted face was impassive as he called, "Next."

"Step aside, folks." Chann shoved the men aside, swaggering up to the game. "Thank you, princess." He plucked the hammer out of the raging man's hands, who seemed too dumbfounded to react.

Lola held her breath. Chann was playing a dangerous game, with the group of men jostling and seething behind him. Pushing up his sleeves to reveal defined muscles, he hefted the hammer. With a powerful swing, he brought it down with a deafening clang. The slider shot to the top and the whistle blasted.

"What do I win?" Chann flashed a cocky grin to the worker, who jerked his head at the man behind him.

"A trip to the morgue!" the man screamed and jumped on Chann's back, a knife clenched in his palm.

Lola froze, her breath caught in her throat, unable to warn him in time.

But Chann was quick—he dodged at the last minute, and his attacker slammed into one of his companions. Immediately, they turned on each other, snarling like dogs as they fought.

Chann surveyed the fight with detached interest before casually relieving a few of the men of their wallets.

Lola sidled up beside him. "Is that seriously your only move?"

Chann's eyes widened when he took her in. "Lola, you shouldn't be here." He stopped to peer into her face. "Wait, what's wrong with you?"

"What do you mean? Ouch!" She yelped as she was jostled from behind by one of the fighters.

Chann shoved the man back and bared his teeth. A deep growl emanated from his throat, vibrating in the air between them.

The man glanced between Chann and Lola before evidently

deciding they weren't worth his time and disappearing into the melee.

"Come on. This night is getting crazy."

Chann wrapped an arm around Lola's shoulders, guiding her away from the crowd of yelling people. With him at her side, nobody dared approach them. He led her to an empty stand near the edge of the grounds. Here, in the quiet, they could speak without shouting.

Chann released her and stared, a puzzled frown pulling at the scar over his eyebrow. "How do you feel?"

"How do I *feel*? Confused by what's going on. Maybe a little nervous of the crowd."

Although if she were being honest, she felt safer with him than she'd felt in days, like he was the calm centre of the storm swirling around them.

"Huh. But, how do you feel about *me*, specifically?" His voice was too casual, too curious.

"You? How am I supposed to feel?" She took in his smirk. "Mainly irritated at the moment."

His grin widened. "Not overwhelmed by the urge to ravish me, then?"

His cockiness surprised a laugh out of her. "You're cute, Chann, but you're not *that* cute."

He grabbed her hand, turning it to reveal the ring Gael had given her. "Ah, I see. You're into guys who bring you trinkets. I could bring you trinkets, you know." He pressed her hand to his lips with exaggerated flair.

Lola blushed and tugged her hand away. "I'm all good."

Chann narrowed his eyes. "That was my best effort, and nothing."

"To be honest, Chann, you didn't put a lot of effort into it."

He laughed, scratching the back of his neck. "Guess I'm rusty. Normally, I don't have to try very hard."

"What are you talking about?"

"At this time of the lunar cycle, with Otsana playing..." He leaned closer, voice lowering. "Most women are ready to go at it on the pavement with me."

Lola's lip curled. "You think highly of yourself."

"No, I mean..." Chann pushed his hair out of his face and stared at her, fascinated. "I don't mean figuratively. It always happens. I know how people react. I literally have to fight them off."

"A side effect of putting a spell on all of them." Lola raised an eyebrow at him.

Chann didn't deny it. "Yeah, the carnival's got a way of stirring up...animalistic urges. But you're different."

"Maybe I don't desire you."

He tilted his head, and his eyes flashed silver. "I know you do, Lola."

The way his gaze slid over her made Lola shift, uncomfortable. When she was a vampire, she could sense arousal in others. If she was right, Chann likely could as well, and she flushed at the thought.

She crossed her arms as though that could provide a barrier between them. "And you always fight them off? Surely sometimes it's easier to give in?"

"I would never. I never have."

"So, what, you're a *werewolf* with a heart of gold?"

She held her breath. Calling him out was risky. Antagonizing a werewolf the night before the full moon was reckless at best.

He stilled as she spoke the word. "How did you know?"

"I guessed. It's clear the carnival is deeply connected to the Otherworld. Add in the wolf I saw in the maze and it's pretty obvious. I should have picked up on it earlier, but you hide your true self well, don't you? I bet all those dates Richie found line up with the full moon."

He let out a snort, shaking his head. "Damn, I shouldn't be surprised you'd figure it out. To answer your question, I'm hardly a saint but I would never take advantage of a person who's under the influence of magic."

His eyes flickered between night black to silver, and Lola wondered how she'd ever believed he was human. "Well aren't you a hero," she said, half mocking.

"But you, you're different. You're immune from the spell. What you're feeling right now is real." His mouth lifted in a half-smile, and he took a step towards her. With the enchanted music pressing in on her, licking over her skin, Lola held her breath, wondering what she was going to do; would she give in to what she wanted?

She thumbed the ring on her finger as she pulled back. "Not immune. Protected by the heart of another."

His voice was low and teasing. "Doesn't mean you're not feeling what you're feeling. That means I have a shot."

She needed to get them back on track. "What does the spell do? What's all this for?"

Chann's smile disappeared, his face going stony. "I don't want to talk about that. You don't have to worry about it as long as you keep that ring on. It'll protect you."

"Protect me from what?"

He shook his head. "Listen, you shouldn't be here. You already know too much, and you're attracting attention. That makes you a target."

"A target?"

Chann glanced over his shoulder and his voice dropped low. "I told you that he likes to collect people. People who are special."

"He? You mean Louis?" Chann didn't answer, his jaw clenching. "You were collected," she guessed.

"Yes." In that syllable were lifetimes of bitterness.

Lola shoved the printout of the carnival picture from the 1980s into his chest. "How far back does it go back? Because it looks like nobody's aged for decades, and I've never heard of werewolves being immortal."

Chann's head jerked and he snatched the printout from her hands. "How did you get this? Lola, if they know you know…" His voice trailed off, dread creeping into his tone.

"Know what? I still don't understand what the spell is. Does it have something to do with the maze?"

Chann grabbed her roughly, pressing her back against the fence. She struggled against him, but he was unmovable as granite.

"Lola." His voice was a low growl. His eyes glimmered with Otherworldly light. "Stay out of the maze. You have no idea what danger you're in. You and your friends already got lucky once, but there won't be a second time. I can't help you again. They'll kill me for it."

She glanced at the scar slashed across his eyebrow. "You were the wolf in the mirrors, weren't you? But how did you change? It wasn't the full moon."

"The mirrors reflect my true spirit, the wolf inside." He loosened his grip on her. "Humans normally can't remember what happens inside the maze; there's too much chaos magic to hold. It would turn you insane." He stepped forward, his growl deep and threatening. "So, what are you?"

Lola forced herself not to cringe back from his accusations. Wouldn't she like to know the answer to that question. "I'm human."

He stared at her for a long time, then smirked. "Is that what you tell yourself? You're as Other as me. It's all over you; I can sense it."

"Not anymore."

His eyes sharpened. "That's not possible. There is no going back." Sadness flickered over his face. She understood, having once been trapped by the endless cycle of her immortal life.

"I was human first. So were you."

"That was a long time ago." His eyes pinned her in place. "You couldn't have been a werewolf; you don't have the energy for it. There's a coldness that lingers." He pressed his face close to her neck and breathed in, pulling back with a snarl. "Vampire."

"Not anymore," she repeated. It seemed desperately important that she convince him. She brought a hand to his face, cupping his cheek. "See? I'm alive."

He grabbed her wrist and sniffed. "Alive, yes; you're mortal. But you're smoking something if you think you're human. Your aura is fragmented. You have one foot in one world, one foot in the Other."

She swallowed hard, allowing Chann to reel her towards him. The unnatural heat emanating from him was a balm against her coldness, her confusion. He knew she wasn't human, that she had come back as something Other, and it didn't horrify him.

As she tilted her face up to his, a smile lit his eyes, and his gaze lingered over her mouth. "Have you ever considered hot over cold?" His lips were close now, so close she could lean in and press hers against his. A ripple of desire passed through her that had nothing to do with spells or magic.

"Sounds dangerous." Lola could bridge the gap between them, and a part of her longed to do so. She stood still as a statue, unsure which path to take.

His eyes gleamed. "You have no idea."

Then he was pulling away, holding her at arm's length. "Listen to me. Otsana suspects something is different about you and everything she knows, Louis knows. That means he has an eye on you. You have to stay away from the carnival tomorrow."

"Will you all turn into werewolves? And attack everyone at the carnival?" She shook her head; that didn't make sense. "You couldn't possibly get away with a massacre every month, not for decades. What do you do under the light of the full moon?"

Chann let a growl slip out. "Dammit, Lola, just promise me you won't be here tomorrow. Even I won't be safe to be around."

She grabbed his arm before he could leave. "Please, how do I stop it?"

His silver eyes were full of regret. "There's no stopping it."

"But I have friends. They could get hurt."

He snorted. "Do you think they care about you the way you care about them? Would they risk their life for you?"

Lola twisted the ring on her finger. "Of course." She raised her chin, daring him to tell her differently.

His eyes shimmered, and his look became one of pity. "Maybe you should check out The Gardens before you leave. Because they're all there."

She didn't try to stop him this time. From one second to another, Chann had melted into the crowd. She took a deep breath, then pushed her way towards The Gardens. In the distance, she heard the squeal of an electric guitar, and a sense of foreboding settled over her.

Twenty-Eight

The carnival grounds grew more perilous with every hour that passed, the hidden chaos rising to the surface. It took Lola longer than it should have to shove her way to The Gardens. She ducked and weaved like a prizefighter, narrowly avoiding the brawls breaking out. A part of her was desperate to flee, to hole up somewhere safe.

But she couldn't be a rabbit—not when her friends were in danger.

The Gardens were packed shoulder to shoulder, the crowd pressed together so tightly it was impossible to move freely. The stage erupted in a flood of light against the night sky, searing her vision.

Otsana stood at centre stage in a patterned corset and black leather pants, her harlequin makeup smudged across her face like war paint. Long bangs fell into her eyes, but the silver gleam beneath her heavy eyelids was unmistakable. With her smile stretched wide, she reminded Lola of people caught up in the ecstasy of drugs, like she was floating high above them.

The crowd moved as one, bodies pulsing to the relentless rhythm of the music. A single organism possessed by the sound, no longer individual souls but a part of something all consuming. The music connected them, taking over their bodies and minds.

Lola used to love festivals. The chaos, the recklessness. The way people left themselves unguarded, excellent places to find easy victims. She'd done terrible things in places like this, in plain sight.

The Carnival of Fools seemed like all those past festivals combined.

Wild fear pulsed through her, but she forced herself to carry on into the heart of the madness. All these emotions, these wants, cascading under the surface, the veneer of civility people normally wore brittle and thin. A crowd without control was the most dangerous place to be.

Then she saw him.

Gael.

Her stomach dropped. What was he doing here? He was supposed to be taking his family back home and keeping himself safe.

Instead, he was dancing, head thrown back in careless laughter. His arm was slung around Cassidy's shoulders as he laughed at something Ethan said.

Lola's vision tunneled as Cassidy's hand traced up Gael's arm. The girl's eyes gleamed, hungry. Grabbing his shirt front, she yanked him towards her, wrapping her arms around his neck and kissing him full on the mouth.

Gael's eyes flew open in surprise. Then, he tossed his drink aside and encircled Cassidy's waist, lifting her so he could deepen their kiss.

Lola froze, her entire body locking up. She couldn't find any breath to protest.

Ethan spotted her first; a cruel smile played over his face. He nudged Gael to get his attention, but it had no effect. Laughing openly, Ethan had to pry Gael off Cassidy to point in Lola's direction.

Rooted to the spot, Lola was unable to get past the splintering pain in her chest. She hadn't been certain what her future with Gael would look like. But she hadn't expected this.

As Gael spotted her, he had the gall to smile. His entire face lit up, warm and bright, as if he had no idea he'd just crushed her.

Cassidy clung to him, reluctant to let go, and he had to scrape her off, tossing her into the group of the others who encircled them. All of them laughing, their giggles too high, too sharp; hyenas scenting blood.

"Lola," Gael said, striding towards her.

Too late, she tried to dash away, but he caught up to her, his hand at her wrist.

She tried to jerk away from him, but he didn't let go. His expression clouded with confusion. "What's wrong?"

"What's wrong?" Lola's throat was so tight she could barely get the words out. "You and Cassidy. That's all wrong." Her insides were coming undone.

"Cassidy?"

"My replacement?" Her voice cracked, brittle as ice. "Funny. I hadn't realized we were seeing other people."

"Wait—you want to break up?" His brow folded, confused and hurt.

"Don't you? You were just making out with someone else."

His lips parted, as if he were about to argue, then he hesitated. His smile was sheepish. "She's not you, Lola."

"You had your tongue shoved down her throat. Like, less than a minute ago."

"Oh." He blinked as if trying to process that. "That must have been an accident."

Her hurt turned to rage, hot as pit fire. "You *accidentally* placed your tongue in her mouth?"

His eyes were solid silver, and tendrils of fear wove through her, pooling in her belly. This wasn't his fault, not really; he was too far under the carnival spell to reason with.

But still—some part of him wanted it, wanted a normal life.

And he hadn't stopped himself. Her heart felt like it had been sandblasted.

She swallowed hard. Focus. This wasn't about her. "Gael, you have to leave. Where's your family? Do you have any idea what's going on?"

Gael paused, and when he laughed, it was mean and low. "You always want me to get away from you. I'm not stupid, you know. You liked me better when you only wanted my blood."

Gael's comments hit far too close to home, punching the air from her lungs. "I'm here because something weird is going on, and I'm trying to figure out what it is."

"Then talk to me," he snapped. "Tell me what's going on."

"You're as caught up in the spell as everyone else. You wouldn't listen!"

Gael snorted. "I always listen to you."

Her fury was crackling now, sparking behind her eyes, and it had nothing to do with the spell. All her confusion swirling around Gael and the idea of them together seemed to crystallize into that moment. "Liar. You don't want to hear anything about it." She spun away before her tears overflowed.

He grabbed her and pulled her back. "Yes, I do."

"No, you don't. You want to hide the past away like it doesn't touch us. You want me to be a normal girl, but there's nothing normal about me. You could never understand."

His expression faltered, something breaking behind his silver-washed gaze. Before he could speak, Ethan slung his arm around Gael's shoulders, smirking. "I told you this bitch is crazy. One of the workers is handing out pills, if you think that might work on her."

Lola choked in fury. "They're drugging people, now? Can't you see what they're doing? You're all sheep, lined up for their consumption." She batted Gael's cup onto the ground. His drink flew out and splashed over the crowd. People jumped back with cries of disgust.

"What a psycho," someone shouted.

Gael sneered like he'd never seen her before. "I thought you'd be better at this."

She stumbled back as though he'd physically struck her, and he stalked away.

"Lola, there you are!" Nix was pushing through the crowd, tugging Walt behind her. Though her face was stained with tear tracks, her eyes sparkled in silver mania. When she went to hug Lola, she forgot to let go of Walt and the three of them ended up in a tangle of arms and legs.

"Nix, why are you here? You were going to go home, remember?"

"Was I?" A moment of uncertainty swirled through her eyes. Her mouth was stained blue from the candy she was devouring. "I heard something...the music. It makes me feel good, like *me*, you know?"

"Why is everyone acting like this?" Walt asked. His eyes were huge and silver, staring at the crowd around him. "Everyone is irrational." His face had an open quality like that of a child trying to puzzle out the world.

Lola grabbed him and Nix. "Listen to me. It's not safe here. Please, get away from the carnival. I'll explain it all, but not here."

"I..." Nix was also staring into the crowd; her gaze caught up on two girls coming towards them. Sam was leaning heavily on Reiko's arm, but when she caught sight of Lola and Nix, she stumbled forward.

"Well if it isn't Hix," Sam said, slurring through her smeared pink lipstick. "You know what I'll always think about whenever I see you? Pig shit."

She started oinking. Others joined in, forming a circle around Nix, getting tighter and tighter.

Nix, stricken, stared at Reiko, her eyes filling with tears. Reiko stood outside the surrounding circle, observing. She held the device again, glancing at it occasionally. Her grey eyes were cold, impassive, and didn't shine with enchanted light.

"That is enough," Lola muttered. "Walt, listen to me." She snapped her fingers under his nose, getting his attention. He came to with a start. "You have to get Nix out of here."

"What are you?" he asked, fascinated by Lola's face. Lola reached out and caught his wrist, pressing her ring against his skin. The effects of the protection spell didn't seem to transfer for long, and she suspected even less while The Bayous were playing, but it was a relief to see his eyes clear for a moment.

"Walt, do you understand me?"

He looked around, spooked, as though he didn't know where he was. "Lola, what's going on?"

"Help me get Nix out of here." Lola forced her way through the crowd mobbing them.

Lola and Walt hustled their friend away, though she resisted, frozen in shame. Finally, they broke out of the group of bullies, who started dancing again as the music picked up.

The effect of The Bayous' melody washed over the group again. Gael came up behind Lola, wrapping his arms around her. "You're not leaving already, are you?"

Lola shoved him off, releasing Walt and Nix in the process. "What are you doing? You were just making out with Cassidy. I don't want to see you right now."

"Cassidy? She's nothing. You, you're everything."

Cassidy stood to one side of them, tears streaming down her face.

The swirling chaos seemed overwhelming, and Lola pressed her hands to her ears. "Stop it!"

The music stopped suddenly. The dancing crowd jolted forward as though they had been held up by sound alone and now slumped.

Lola turned to the stage. Otsana was at the edge, grinning at her. The stars and moon painted on her guitar flashed silver.

Otsana started playing a new song then, one that was loud and wild. The music crashed over the carnival and people screamed and jumped to the beat.

Otsana tilted her head behind her. Lola followed her look to see Gael pull Cassidy against him again, their bodies moving in perfect sync, lost to the rhythm.

The lead singer, the witch, laughed in triumph as she cast her spell, her silver eyes locking onto Lola's. She knew she had won.

TWENTY-NINE

Furious tears blurred Lola's vision as she shoved through the crowd. The music pounded, bodies pressed together, lost to the thrall of the beat. Nix and Walt had vanished, swallowed by the shifting mass of dancers. Lola threw her hands up, ready to scream. Herding those two was like wrangling ghosts —impossible.

Most of the people were pushing forward, desperate to be closer to the stage. The song built to a fever pitch, a crashing wave of sound slamming into Lola as she fought through the press of bodies. She craned her neck, searching for familiar faces. Nothing. Just a frenzied, spellbound crowd.

Only one other person wasn't dancing.

Reiko.

She moved with purpose, shouldering people aside, her delicate features hardened with focus. Gone was the wide-eyed, too-sweet girl playing innocent; she'd dropped the act. No one else was paying attention to her. Her eyes flicked over everything, taking in the carnival like a predator surveying its territory.

Reiko cut through the crowd like a blade. Lola fell back, struggling against the crush. By the time she broke free, Reiko had already reached the carousel. The organ grinder music twisted around the pulse of The Bayou's song, the two melodies clashing in a way that put Lola's nerves on high alert. Children shrieked, and she cast a glance around to see whether they were laughing or fleeing in terror.

Reiko slouched against the frame of an unused game stand, her face bathed in flickering red light. She toyed with her device. Lola approached until she could get a good look at the thing—the face was crowded with too many dials and arrows spinning in different directions.

"What's it do?" Lola asked, startling her.

Reiko snapped to attention, her clear grey eyes two arctic moons. Shockingly fast, she dropped into a crouch, her hand darting to the small of her back as though seeking a weapon.

Lola took a careful step back, palms up. "I just want to talk. Honestly, for once."

Reiko's eyes hardened as she straightened, and her voice was cold and indifferent. "What are you?"

"I could ask you the same thing." The words snapped out with a bite.

Reiko studied her as she counted out facts on her fingers. "You resist the spells here, and you know about magic. Also, visions. So, what is it? Psychic? A hedge witch?"

Lola crossed her arms over her chest. "Would that worry you? Maybe I'm about to hex you."

Reiko snorted, unimpressed, and returned her attention to her device. Her bracelets clinked as she adjusted her grip—wooden beads, etched with runes. Protective charms, likely the reason Reiko wasn't drawn into The Bayous song the way the others were.

It was rare to find humans who knew of the Otherworld; rarer still that they sought the forces out, rather than run the other way.

"Well, what about you, then?" Lola mused, circling Reiko, who turned so her back was never to her. "You know about the Otherworld and seem to assume you're safe here at the carnival; you're not, by the way, but you're deluded enough to think you are, so you must have some power. Based on what I saw in the maze, you know how to fight."

Reiko stilled. "You remember the maze?"

"I do. I guess your protective spells don't go far enough. Do you have any idea what's going on here?"

Reiko had taken a fighter's stance against Lola, subtly shifting on her feet for better balance.

"Oh, I'm not going to fight you," Lola said, shaking her head. "I want to know whether you're here to hurt my friends. More than you have already." Cold fury burned through Lola, and she clenched her fists.

Something flickered in Reiko's expression. "It wasn't my intention to hurt Nix. She was...easy to be with. With time she would have been willing to share secrets. It was impossible not to—"

"I already suspected you were some kind of monster, but now I know."

Reiko's jaw tightened. "I have orders. Study the massive uptick of energy on Duchesne Island and report back on the cause. You were my first person of interest—of course I was going to figure out a way to get close to you."

"By using my best friend?" Lola sneered, though not too long ago, she used similar techniques herself.

She had been right. Nix deserved far better than both of them. She needed to get back to the point at hand, though. "What energy on Duchesne?"

"Don't you know? A few months ago, there was the equivalent of a sonic boom of energy, the epicentre right here on the island, which up until now had barely been on the radar. Like a dormant volcano suddenly erupting. Since then, the island has been putting out essentially a beacon to the Otherworld. Of course we were going to come study it. Something crawled out of its hole and needs to be stuffed back in." She tilted her head, flashing the device at Lola. "Your energy is chaotic, and that's saying something in this place. So I'm wondering if the thing that crawled out is you." She took a step forward, the threat evident in every line on her body.

Lola's pulse skipped. "Who is *we*?" Best to keep the scary girl talking rather than fighting because Lola wouldn't come out on top in hand-to-hand. "Does it have to do with your tattoo?"

Reiko froze. "What tattoo?"

"That tattoo." Lola pointed to it, the upper half visible over the collar of her shirt. Although up close, she could see it wasn't ink; the skin was puckered around the mark. She squinted. "Or is that a brand?"

Reiko recoiled from her. "How can you see it?" she hissed.

Before Lola could answer, a voice rang out: "I said stop it!"

The panicked words were screamed behind her. She glanced over her shoulder to see Violet half-jogging down the path, Ethan in pursuit.

When she whipped her head back, Reiko was gone, leaving behind all the unanswered questions Lola had just unearthed.

"What the hell was that?" Lola asked out loud. She searched the crowd for the girl hunter, but she was gone. Cursing, she turned to Violet.

"You don't get to walk away from me." Ethan grabbed Violet's wrist and pulled her back to him, sticking a finger in her face.

"You don't want me." Violet's voice cracked. Her forehead was wrapped in a dirty bandage. "You made sure everybody knows it. So don't you dare come at me telling me I can't walk away from you. Go find one of your groupies."

"Violet, stop being stupid. I was just having a little fun; everyone else seems to be able to do that but you."

"A little fun." Her voice dripped with derision, even as it

shook. Her beautiful face was crumpled from crying. "You left me alone in that awful place. You did that on purpose!"

"You can't even take a joke anymore."

"I found a dead body, Ethan! It wasn't funny."

He sneered. "You're so boring nowadays. You're not even taking care of yourself. No wonder I've been looking elsewhere."

Violet shivered as though something inside of her was shrivelling. "Then go find those girls and leave me alone." This part of the carnival was quiet enough that Lola could hear her whisper, full of fear and loneliness and defiance. "I am through with you."

Violet wrenched out of his grip and stormed down the path.

Murder in his eyes, Ethan went after her.

Lola dashed onto the path, running into Ethan and knocking him off track. "Oops," she said with a girlish laugh. "I just keep doing that, don't I?"

He tried to sidestep. She shifted, keeping herself in his way. His gaze fixed on Violet's retreating figure, his eyes silver orbs.

After a moment, when it was clear Violet had gotten away, Lola dodged away from him. "We have to stop running into each other like this."

His silver eyes flicked to Lola, glowing with the strength of the spell. It was warping him, stripping away everything that held him back from his baser instincts. She must have been unhinged to get involved.

They stared at each other for one breathless minute, then she spun and fled.

She hated herself for doing it. Old Lola would never flee, but she was far too weak now. Ethan could slap her down in a second.

The worst part of it was that she would never be strong again, and the thought flooded her with despair. She knew too much about the dangers that lurked in the shadows to ever go easy again; she'd always be watching over her shoulder and running away.

Footfalls behind her told her Ethan had taken up the chase. Lola's head whipped from one side to the other, looking for an escape. Leaving the grounds wasn't a good idea; there was nobody out there, no lights, no one to find her if anything happened. The people around her couldn't protect her—they were all too far gone in the spell—so she plunged deeper into the carnival, rounding the carousel of swirling predators.

Ethan laughed, then, and it chilled her to her marrow. This was his basest desire—the joy of the chase. She'd laughed that way once too. But would he know when to stop? Everything she knew of him spelled casual disregard for others; how far into the spell did he have to be before murder was a real possibility?

Maybe she deserved it. This was how she was meant to end her brittle human life, hunted the same way she chased down so many.

But she couldn't let it end here; there was too much to do. The spell was leading to something major tomorrow night, and she still wasn't sure what was going to happen, let alone how to stop it.

Her friends were in danger, and she would be damned if she would let anyone hurt them.

She weighed her options, then changed course and ran full tilt into the cordoned-off area where the workers stayed. It was a risk. A crowd of werewolves the night before the full moon shouldn't be trusted.

And yet her instincts told her she was safer here than anywhere else. For this night at least, the werewolves still had control over themselves. All bets would be off tomorrow.

She dodged behind a tent, then around back, weaving between them until she finally took a chance and dove inside one. She didn't know where she was; she hoped Ethan didn't either. His breathing was heavy on the other side of the canvas as he stopped, panting.

After being surrounded by deafening music for so long, the silence rang in her ears. She could hear the banging of her heart; surely Ethan would hear it too. Holding her breath, she bit back a whimper.

He moved away, stalking along the line of tents. She hesitated at the entrance of her shelter, wondering if she could make a break for it back to the carnival grounds. As she tensed, ready to flee, a large, dark figure bolted towards her and grabbed her, slapping a hand over her mouth to keep her from screaming as she was hauled back into the tent.

THIRTY

Lola thrashed against her attacker, but his iron grip held her tight.

"It's okay, Lola. You're safe." The voice rumbled in the chest she was pressed against, and she stilled, her heart still ready to explode.

She let out a shaky breath as Chann turned her to face him.

"Chann, thank goodness." Her knees trembled like leaves caught on the wind, and only his arms kept her upright.

He studied her, a bemused smile playing on his lips as though half torn between amusement and confusion. "What are you doing? I told you to stay away from the carnival, not lurk around the camp. Do you have any idea how dangerous this is?"

"I wasn't lurking," Lola hissed, her voice shaky. "I was hiding. How did you know I was here?"

"I smelled your fear," he said, his voice matter-of-fact. "You left a trail a mile wide leading here, and I won't be the only one to notice."

Her gaze darted to the flap of the tent, and she peeked outside. "Fine, I'll go then." She didn't want to leave—not with Ethan out there. At least here she knew that if it came to it, Chann could protect her. She'd back the werewolf in a fight with the bully any day.

But would she need protection against Chann? She eyed him warily.

As though he could sense her thoughts, he backed away a step. "What's wrong?"

"Everything," she said. Her mind was spinning with all she was trying to take in. "Someone was following me."

"And you decided werewolves were safer?"

She sniffed, trying to hold back the fear threatening to overwhelm her. "Honestly? Given everything going on right now, it seemed like the best option. People out there have lost their minds."

His gaze turned serious. "It's only going to get worse," he said. "That's why I told you to leave. You don't understand the trouble that will find you if you stay." He paused, then raised his scarred eyebrow. "Unless...that's what you're looking for?"

Something dark edged his tone, but it didn't scare her. Instead, she wanted to step into it. She lifted her chin, meeting his gaze. "What do you mean?"

Chann's voice lowered to nearly a growl. "Humans are weak. Vulnerable. You're not quite human, but you are weak. I could make you strong again." His eyes flared silver, but his tone was shy. "You could join me. You wouldn't have to be a victim anymore."

To become a werewolf.

The longing that surged through her was a surprise. But to hunt again, to know that she was going to win, she missed that. She missed the power that came from being Other.

Still, it wasn't what she wanted.

"I worked too hard to become human, Chann. I can't throw it away now, not because things got difficult."

His expression softened, eyes wistful. "I've never known anyone who was able to do it, to find a way to walk away from it.

Most people only want more power. They never stop to consider the downside. Look at Conri."

"The painter?" she asked, frowning.

Chann nodded. "He used to be a famous artist. When he learned about the Otherworld, he was determined to join it, to go deeper into the darkness. He thought it would improve his work, taking him to new levels of talent and fame."

"How'd that turn out for him?" Lola asked, her voice quiet

"Have you met him?" Chann's voice was laced with pity. "He gouged out his own eye in a fit of madness. He sleeps in the maze, you know. He designed it many years ago. He was an inventor as well, and he discovered a way to magically amplify Otherworld power."

"He sleeps in there?" What would dreams be like inside that space, already warped by magic?

"He thinks of it like his baby—or his prison, depending on the day." Chann shrugged. "Life with the carnival is hard, but it's better than what it could be if we didn't have Louis and Otsana holding us together with magic. At least we don't lose ourselves entirely when we change like most werewolves. We don't massacre people. That's how we stay under the radar."

Lola drew in closer to his warmth, wanting him to spill all his secrets. "How does it work?" she whispered.

His breath hitched as she moved towards him. "We travel to a different town every month, cast a spell on the townspeople and increase our power through ritual sacrifice. It allows us to remain young for another month. I told you that Louis collects people—interesting, powerful people." Chann's voice dropped low. "Otsana was a witch when she was human; she's ten times stronger now. Conri was a world-famous designer-inventor when he was human. Even Anton, our sausage maker, was the best of the best. Louis had to have him.

"Once he finds someone who he thinks will improve the carnival, he stalks them, then bites them when he's transformed. Once bitten, you're changed forever. Louis is the alpha, and our obedience is absolute. Nobody can stand up to him. We're all stuck here, playing out this same cycle month after month."

"Young and powerful forever," Lola said quietly. "Not everyone would say no to that."

"Interested?" Chann's voice held an edge of teasing.

Lola let out a scoffing breath. "Been there, done that."

His smile faded. "What about you? Did you seek out that power, Lola?"

Lola gave in to the impulse to touch him. She trailed her fingers over his cheekbone, brushing his hair aside as her voice softened. "Did you?"

"No, I never wanted any of this." He sat on the army cot, pulling her down next to him. "Some people might seek it out, but I didn't choose this life." Sorrow pulled at his features.

"Why were you collected?" Lola asked.

Chann laughed bitterly, looking up towards the ceiling of the tent as though he could find answers there. "It was 1968, in Belfast. I was working the carnival, seeing if I couldn't pick up some cash for my family. But I picked the wrong pocket."

"Louis?"

Chann nodded. "He caught me red-handed. His fury was unreal. I didn't know where my family was; everyone was behaving so wild. Louis knocked me out, and I woke up surrounded by mirrors."

"The Maze of Desire."

"Yeah," Chann said, his voice grim. "It was...terrifying. The things I saw there. When the full moon was at its highest point, I heard screaming outside. I tried to escape, but I couldn't find my way out of the mirrors. I heard him coming before I saw him, and I could smell the blood on his breath. Then, he bit me." He pulled back the collar of his T-shirt, showing a jagged scar across his shoulder. "When I came to, it was with this wound. And a special surprise the next full moon. I've been a part of the freakshow ever since."

"A punishment for stealing from him," Lola said.

"He doesn't mind if I steal from his customers, but nobody steals from Louis."

Lola tried to puzzle it out. "So that's what happens tomorrow? Someone becomes a werewolf?"

Chann shook his head. "He rarely looks to recruit. Every month he gets Otsana to perform this ritual. A few people in the crowd are compelled into the maze, and the spell consumes them. The sacrifice gives us power, and we have enough to feed for the month, so we don't go crazy when we wolf out again."

"How can you go from town to town every month, eating people and not get caught?"

His face darkened. "Because she only brings those people that nobody would miss anyways."

Lola stayed silent, her mind spinning. She understood that far too well—how to feed without leaving a trace. How to pick off the lost souls, the ones no one would care about.

"And so, you go on like this forever."

He looked away. "Almost forever. We do age, but slowly. I was twelve when I was bitten."

Lola's heart ached for him. "I'm so sorry, Chann. You were just a kid."

His hand brushed hers, his gaze soft. "It's been a long time since I was that kid."

A howl of laughter echoed somewhere beyond the tent, and he jumped up. "Listen, it isn't safe for you here, not this close to the full moon. The spell Otsana casts can keep us under control so we don't massacre the crowds, but that doesn't mean we're not getting more and more animalistic as each hour goes by. You shouldn't be near me. And you can't come back. You've drawn Louis' attention, and not in a good way. Otsana may have convinced him to collect you." He let out a long sigh. "And Lola, under the full moon, I can't go against the alpha. I won't be able to help you. If you don't want to become a werewolf, don't be here."

She went cold at the thought. "But I can't sit by and let people be hurt tomorrow."

"Honestly, why not?" His voice was rough. "It's not like anyone would do anything to help you. You're different, and they know it. You were chased here by someone who wanted to hurt you, right? Why do you think you were targeted? If there's anything I've learned about humanity, it's that nobody is going to step in to help the outsider. You and me, Lola, we look in from the outside. There's nothing you can do to change it."

Not even become human, apparently. She had done so much to be a part of it all, only to end up on the outside once again.

"I can take you as far as the gates," Chann said, looking outside the tent. "Nobody will hurt you if you're with me."

She remembered the fury in Ethan's gaze and shivered. "How can you be sure?"

"Because I'll kill them if they try." His voice was a low growl. This close to the full moon, his predatory nature was unveiling itself.

"You've killed before." It wasn't a question; she was certain of the answer.

She knew she should leave. She shouldn't be here at all. And yet she lingered, speaking one murderer to another.

His eyes darkened. "Listen, you have to understand."

"That's just it." Her emotions were tumbling around inside of her like an out-of-control pinball machine, but one thing she could focus on was that Chann *did* understand. He wouldn't judge her for her past. "I have killed more people than anyone in my life could possibly understand. None of them will ever be able to accept all of me."

He watched her with guarded eyes, taking in her every movement like a hunter about to pounce.

The pull towards his heat was irresistible. "I'm pretending to be a person I'm not. But when I'm here with you, I don't feel bad about who I am."

She didn't mean to do it until it was done. Whether it was to say thank you or to feel better after watching Gael kiss someone else or any number of messed up reasons, she leaned in and grazed her mouth across his.

Chann's lips were soft and warm, and she pressed harder, wanting to feel his heat against her.

He made a sound low in his throat and grabbed her by the shoulders, pushing her to arm's length.

"Is this actually what you want?"

"I have no clue what I want." She wanted him; she wanted answers. She wanted to be normal, but that seemed out of her reach forever.

The tornado of emotions seemed to be swirling at an all-time high inside of her, seeking an outlet, and she reached for him.

He yanked her towards him, pressing her body against his as he took her mouth. The swirl of lust consumed her as her eyes closed, her fingers tangled in his thick black hair. On a curse, he pressed her back against the cot, taking their kiss even deeper.

"God, you're so lovely." Chann trailed his mouth down her throat, making her shiver. "Everything about you is lit up; you shine in the crowd."

She gasped as his tongue reached the juncture between her neck and shoulder, and she shuddered against him. Her hands travelled along the solid planes of his back.

She pulled away, keeping a teasing distance between them. "Tell me about the ritual, Chann. What do you do to them?"

"I can't tell you that." He went to kiss her again, but she hovered a breath away.

"How do I stop it?" She nipped at his lip.

"I told you, once Otsana starts, there's no stopping her."

"So, I have to stop her before she starts."

He growled in frustration. "Are you only using me for information?"

"Among other things." Lola gave a fleeting smile. "I thought you knew what you were getting into." She dodged him, biting her lip as he cursed and grabbed her.

Pinning her down, he kissed her deeply. Lola let him plunder her mouth, the sensation lighting her up from the inside. She felt as drugged as the rest of the crowd

He dragged himself away and let out a bitter laugh. "I don't know why you care. These people don't care about you. My family was starving before I became a monster, and do you think anybody ever tried to help us? Certainly not the good, righteous people who like to tell people like me what to do. We were trash to them, and they treated us like it. But now, nobody can hurt me."

Lola fluttered a kiss over his eyelid. "Not everyone wants to hurt you."

"The humans do. They would in a heartbeat. Have you seen them out there?"

"You're drugging them, bewitching them. You can't hold them responsible for their actions."

"Can't I? You know why people can't stay away from the Carnival of Fools? Because deep down, every human wishes to give in to the animal inside. They beg for it, and we give them what they want." His lip curled and he pulled away from her. "You're still on their side, aren't you?"

"I don't want anyone to be hurt. Can you say the same for Otsana? Or Louis?"

At the reminder of Louis, Chann's expression darkened. "Don't be here tomorrow night. If you do, consider yourself a target. I won't be able to do anything to stop it." He nuzzled her neck, his teeth grazing the sensitive skin there and sending tingles that shuddered through her body. "I'm not even going to pretend I wouldn't want to be the one to bite you. I could show you so many things."

Flashes of her old life burst into her memory. To be the hunter rather than the hunted. Lola's desire rippled over her again, responding to more than the lust in his eyes.

It took supernatural effort to push away from him while her entire body cried out to stay within the circle of his arms.

She dragged in a gasping breath. "I have to go." If she didn't get away from him now, she didn't know what would happen. But she did know she wasn't in the right state of mind and would probably regret it.

He reached for her, but she darted away, out of the tent, towards the carnival grounds. The crowd had swelled further, as though the entire population of the island was squeezed onto the small piece of farmland.

She ran into a figure and stumbled back. Had Ethan been waiting for her the whole time? She drew in a breath to scream.

"Lola, are you okay?" She recognized Gael, the steady warmth of him, his spicy scent hidden under the alcohol wafting off him.

"Gael, why are you here?" Her voice broke.

"I came to find you. I don't know what's going on, but I wanted to make sure…"

His voice faded away as Chann swaggered out from the shadows of the tents. "Don't worry, she's been well taken care of."

Gael looked to Chann, then to Lola, his face hardening. "So, it's like that?"

"Gael, let me explain."

"I think it's pretty clear, actually." Fury played over Gael's face, and Lola tensed, moving between the two. If Gael went after Chann, he would lose, and badly.

Then Gael's anger spent itself. He stepped away from her, arms up in defeat. "You know what? I'm done."

He turned his back on her, returning to the madness of The Gardens. Probably back to Cassidy.

She let him go, her heart breaking as he disappeared into the crowd.

She knew he was kissing other people, too, but this was differ-ent. She wasn't bewitched, just confused.

She spun on Chann, tears in her eyes. "You did that on purpose!"

He snorted. "You did that all on your own." Leaning in close, his breath seared her skin. "You ever want to use me again? I'm more than happy to oblige."

She fell back a step, then turned and ran away from the carnival as though she could outrun the storm brewing inside of her.

THIRTY-ONE

The Pain Perdu was shut, the closed sign tilted as though someone had left in a hurry. Every light in the apartment above was burning.

"Hello?" Lola called as she reached the top of the stairs.

A muffled shriek pierced the silence. Fear jolted through her, and in an instant, she was upstairs, shoving open the door to the apartment she shared with Faye.

Inside was chaos. Faye was screaming at Greyson, who was in Lola's room, tearing through her belongings. Sobbing, Faye clutched at his sleeve, trying to pull him away.

"What the hell is going on?" Lola squeezed past them, heart hammering. Her normally pristine room had been ransacked. Drawers lay overturned, books had been pulled apart and her mattress had been thrown aside. The last remnants of her carefully constructed life lay in shambles.

"Care to explain this?" Greyson's eyes glowed with the eerie silver sheen of the spell. Lola's heart stuttered. The spell wasn't limited to the carnival grounds—the entire island could be affected.

And Greyson, heavily spelled, had one singular desire: to get rid of Lola.

He pointed at the desk. Several passports were fanned out beside a roll of cash in different currencies—the last of Lola's emergency funds. "I don't know what you're involved in, gangs or smuggling or worse. At this point, I don't care. I want you off this island tonight." His thick finger jabbed inches from her face.

Lola's hand flew to her throat, fury and shame battling inside her. Her past lay exposed like evidence of a crime. "You had *no* right."

"On this island, I have every right," he snarled. "As far as you're concerned, I'm your judge, jury and executioner. What I say goes."

Lola sidestepped him and grasped Faye's trembling shoulders. Tears streamed down the baker's face, her eyes glinting the same unnatural silver. Lola pressed her ring against Faye's skin, lending her protection from the charm.

It had an immediate effect. The tension drained from Faye's frame like air from a punctured balloon. Her eyes cleared, blinking in confusion.

"Lola?"

Relief washed over Lola. "Hi."

Faye took in a shuddering breath, the weight of what happened sinking in. "Greyson, you can't be here."

Still wild with the effects of the spell, he whirled on her. "You are not spending another night with this criminal under your roof."

She held up a placating hand. "You had no right to go through her things. Breaking into our home like this is beyond unacceptable."

His triumphant smile twisted into an ugly sneer. "Can't you see? She's not who she says she is. She's playing you, Faye, and it won't be long before she takes you for everything you have. Or worse. Who's to say she's not responsible for the murders a few months ago?"

"Greyson." Faye's voice was steel. "You are way out of line. You need to go. Now." She gave the front door a meaningful look.

"There is no way I'll allow her to stay here."

A long, simmering pause hung between them. Faye straightened to her full height, smudged makeup and swollen eyes doing nothing to diminish her authority. "I'm sorry, did you tell me what to do in my own home?"

His bravado wavered. "No, Faye, you're getting this all wrong." Greyson's voice cracked with desperation. "She's manipulating you! You can't see it, but she's dangerous."

His hand grazed his belt, reaching for his gun.

Faye screamed.

Lola acted on instinct. She lunged, grabbing Greyson's wrist and letting her ring sear against his skin. She just needed to break through the spell enough to get him out of there.

His eyes cleared—then widened in horror as he looked down to see his hand wrapped around his gun. "I...don't know what happened."

Faye shoved him back towards the front door.

"I think you've had enough to drink and it's time to sleep it off," she said, speaking through her teeth.

Greyson hesitated, his breath strangled, gaze swinging between the two women trying to fight him off. He raised his hands, unarmed now, and a thin sheen of sweat broke out along his forehead. "I'll go, I'm sorry..." His voice was unsteady as he stumbled out the door.

Faye slammed the door behind him, locking it with a loud click. She rested her forehead against the wood, eyes closed.

Lola trembled. The protection charm would be short-lived on Greyson. Would he remember what he'd found out about her? How long would it take before he came back and did what he felt was necessary to protect Faye?

Lola had made an outright enemy of Greyson; that much was clear. And he knew some of her secrets or guessed at them, at least.

"Faye..." she said, unsure what to say.

Faye lifted her hands to her temples, eyes squeezed shut as though she wasn't ready to deal with anything. "Just sit."

Lola perched on the sofa, clutching a cushion against her stomach. Faye disappeared into her room, then returned with the passports and money, laying them on the coffee table. She sank into the chair opposite Lola, her eyes shiny with unspent tears.

"We need to be honest with each other."

"I know," Lola said, but it was a lie. Honesty was impossible.

"When I was a kid, I spent a long time living on the streets or passing from the sofa of one so-called friend to another." Faye let out a shaky breath. "I didn't respect the law, and I sure as hell didn't respect myself. I was forced to make choices I never want you to make."

Lola's heart shattered at what Faye must have endured in the past. And yet she had survived.

"I know the world can be cruel," Faye continued. "And I know that you've seen some of that throughout your life. More than I realized. I'm assuming you've been involved in criminal activity."

Lola closed her eyes. "Faye, I would never hurt you. Greyson is trying to turn you against me. He's paranoid."

"That's not paranoia!" Faye stabbed her finger at the table, to the proof of Lola's damning past. "Five passports, Lola. Five! What are you running from?"

"I can't tell you," Lola said. She stared at her fingers. There was no way to make Faye understand what she was or where she had come from.

Faye's jaw tightened. "Then I can't keep you safe. If you can't trust me, then this isn't going to work."

Lola's stomach clenched. Faye was right, of course. Still, she blinked back tears. "I understand."

Faye sighed, a sound as heavy as the whole earth. "Listen, I'm exhausted. We'll talk about this in the morning." She stood as though lifting an enormous weight and trudged towards her own bedroom, her footsteps dragging.

Lola's throat closed. She shouldn't stay here; she'd known it for a long time. But she had been so tired from her transformation, so vulnerable, she'd allowed the kind woman to take her in, to care for her. Greyson was right; she *had* been using Faye, manipulating her to think they were the same.

But who was she kidding? Lola would never be like Faye. No matter what the baker thought, there was darkness in Lola they didn't share, and she didn't want to taint the first person to have ever cared for her. She was stronger now; she should leave.

She gathered up her passports, flipping through them without real interest. She had the contents memorized: British, Canadian, Russian, American, French. Everything she had needed to pass through this world when she had belonged to another.

Here, on Duchesne Island, Lola had thought she'd found herself. She'd dug into the womb of the earth to find her soul.

Yet now she was on her own again, without friends or family. She'd given up all her power and gained weakness and confusion instead.

She settled her bed back into place, tidying the sheets. Then she methodically went through the rest of the room, putting everything away. It didn't take long. A few used books and some clothes someone else had purchased for her. Everything could easily fit into the backpack she'd brought to the island.

Maybe she should take Chann up on his offer and run away with the enchanted circus. She wasn't very good at being human.

She would be one more disappearance that followed the Carnival of Fools. One more teenage runaway with no hope, no prospects.

Lying on her mattress, staring at the dark ceiling, she contemplated her options. None of them were good.

She must have dozed eventually because when she woke, the sun was rising, and the apartment was empty. Downstairs, the café was still shut, something that had never happened before. The cursed carnival had called Faye, along with everyone else in town, judging by the abandoned sidewalks.

Outside, the air was already warm and heavy with humidity. It smelled of briny ocean, and a part of her longed to head to the shoreline to hop on the next boat off the island. To feel the salty air whip her skin again as she sailed away, disappearing into the big wide world. That's what she would have done as a vampire.

But the thought brought her no real joy.

She had far too much to do, and people who were counting on her, whether they knew it or not. She turned in the opposite direction.

The streets were devoid of people, tourists or otherwise. Was everyone sleeping off their hangover, or were they still caught up in the party?

A chill crept up her spine despite the heat as she figured that's exactly what happened. The spell was getting stronger. Nobody could leave the carnival—they were still dancing, still mindlessly giving in to pleasure, no matter how destructive.

All of it was building to a climax under the light of the full moon. She needed to figure out what was going to happen for the grand finale.

Thirty-Two

The Port Despardoux library was as quiet as the rest of the town. Had the librarian finally given in to the spell beckoning everyone to the carnival?

But as Lola entered the main level, three books tumbled from a shelf, landing with a soft thud on the floor. Lola smiled. "Marissa?"

The librarian dashed into the room, her clothes unchanged from the day before, deep shadows pooling under her eyes. She was pale and her movements jittery, as if from the weight of a sleepless night. "I should've known it was you. The books act up like crazy when you're around."

A book banged onto the ground next to them, making them both jump. A cloud of dust puffed up from the floor.

Marissa glared at Lola as though she'd done it on purpose.

"You haven't left?" Lola asked.

The librarian blinked, owlish, her voice weary. "I thought it safer to stay put with everything you told me."

"Well, we might be the only two people on the island not under the spell right now." Marissa's skin had the same greyish tone of old oatmeal. "Have you slept at all?"

"Sleep?" Marissa's laugh was dry. "Not possible when the books are talking to me like this." She rubbed her temples, her eyes squeezed shut as though the morning light hurt her.

Lola frowned. "What did you find?"

Marissa grabbed a book and opened it at random, placing her finger on the page without looking. Then she read it and sighed. "This, every time. Lycanthropy."

Lola relaxed, nodding. "Yeah, I figured it was werewolves last night. I haven't checked yet, but I'm guessing the dates I gave you line up with the full moons."

Marissa looked as though she wanted to throw the book at Lola. "And you didn't think to let me know?"

Lola winced. "Sorry, that was an oversight. I had a lot going on at the carnival." She paused. "This pack is unusual, both in its size and its sophistication. Werewolves usually stick to quiet forested places and live alone until they die. Rogue wolves that get too close to a human population are tracked and killed within months because they always leave a bloody mess behind. They're too chaotic to be organized enough to do something like this. Being bitten by a werewolf is a horrendous curse and leads to nothing but a bad ending." Lola tapped a finger against her lips. "But this carnival, it's slick, and they're using magic."

Marissa thrust a printout of a photograph. "I would say so. I found this last night; it corresponds with the earliest date you gave me."

The picture was even grainier than the one from the '80s, and Lola had to squint to resolve the black-and-white image. At the centre of the Carnival of Fools' arch was Louis. The women in the crowd behind him wore dresses, their hair curled and elaborately swept back. The men wore suits, most of them sporting boater hats.

"This was taken in Paris." Marissa's voice was barely more than a breath. "Summer of 1936."

Lola recoiled from the photo. She would have been ten—and

human—living in Paris. Did she go to carnivals? Had she been there that day? She looked away so she didn't desperately search for the face of a familiar dark-haired girl in the crowd.

Instead, she scanned the article. It referred to Louis as Monsieur Garoux. *Loup Garou.* Cheeky.

"I don't know how they do it," Marissa said. "I haven't found any documents in my research to support that werewolves don't age. Some immortal beings remain forever the same, but werewolves used to be human and still exist on the mortal coil."

Lola only half-listened as she read the article. Three young people were reported missing after the carnival left Paris. "Vampires were human once, and they don't age."

"Yes, but that is specific to the process of vampirism." Marissa shot her a look, then hurried over to a stack of leather-bound books at the back. She seemed relieved to have someone to discuss it with. "I've been reading about this stuff for years, wondering what I was going to do with all this bizarre information. A vampire is a human corpse."

"*Mon Dieu.*" Lola shuddered. She had never thought of herself as a corpse before. "Like some kind of zombie?"

"Not a zombie. Zombies are mindless. Demonic energy allows the vampire to be animated with brain function. They rely on a steady intake of blood to stave off decomposition. As long as they have blood, they don't age because they're not alive. But they are trapped between life and death." Then Marissa turned on her, her gaze sharpening. "Or at least most of them are."

An uneasy feeling settled in Lola's chest. "What do you mean?"

Marissa's shoes rapped slowly on the wood as she came around the front desk, picking up a book as she did so. "The books have been screaming at me. About you." She held out the book to Lola.

With trembling hands, Lola accepted it like an offering. When she looked at the cover, she nearly dropped it.

Stephenie Meyer's *Twilight.*

Lola groaned. "Are you kidding me?"

"Sorry." For the first time, Marissa's eyes filled with mirth. "I don't choose the books. They choose me."

"At least you could have found some Anne Rice," Lola called out to the library at large.

Marissa grinned. It was a bit hollow, but it was the first time Lola had seen her show something other than stress. Even Lola managed a chuckle, though she wavered as she set the book down. "So, you know my secret."

"It's a powerful one. Vampire?"

Lola nodded. "Once upon a time. Not anymore. Are you terrified?"

Marissa hesitated, then shook her head. "You don't scare me; you intrigue me. You see, the books have more to say about you."

She went to the counter to a massive, leather-bound tome. She didn't take her eyes off Lola as she opened it, pointing at a word. Lola gave her a wary look, then finally approached to peek at the word.

"Changeling." Her head shot up. "What does that mean?"

"Changelings were commonly thought to be human-like creatures, put in the place of a stolen baby." Marissa sniffed. "Changelings were generally in the realm of faeries."

"I'm not a faerie."

"Most of those stories were nonsense, of course," Marissa said agreeably, flipping through the pages. "It was usually colicky babies driving their parents insane that instigated the legend."

"But if I'm not a faerie, then why are the books telling me I am?"

"Not a faerie, a *changeling*. You have undergone a transformation, a powerful act. It often creates its own magic. You were one thing; now you are another. Vampire; not vampire."

"But not a normal human?"

Marissa snorted. "Even if such a thing existed, you would be far from it. You can't pass through worlds untouched. I believe what the books are trying to say is that you are something else. Not human, not Other, but somewhere in between."

"And covered in magical residue. That's how I feel sometimes."

"How did you do it?"

Marissa's gaze felt pointed as a dagger, and Lola grimaced. Some knowledge was unsafe, no matter whose hands it found itself in. "It's a long story. And it's not something that can be repeated."

Marissa finally nodded. "Do you have any side effects? Lingering cravings for blood?"

Lola shook her head, disgusted at the thought. "Nothing like that. But I've had visions, powerful ones that knock me off my feet. I knew something was going to happen at the maze, before Richie...but I didn't get there in time." Her voice trailed off.

"A seer, perhaps; your psyche is still connected to the Other-world though you're human. Darker elements cling to you, despite your humanity."

"Darker elements?"

"Your soul may be intact, but not untouched from your un-life before this."

Lola's breath hitched. "Like the monster is still inside of me?"

"Or the memory of what you've done while a monster. I wonder if a price must still be paid?"

The thought was like plunging into a dark well of water. "I've done so many horrifying things, Marissa. How could I possibly atone for them?"

"Atonement derives from intention. Your desire to make up for past wrongs goes a long way. But you must pay attention when your Otherworldly powers are trying to tell you something." A book crashed to the floor, and she rolled her eyes. "A burden we share."

Marissa swept around to pick up the fallen book, perusing it with a frown. The old book was open to a page with hand-painted phases of the moon. "Back to the task at hand," she said.

"Whatever is going to happen, it's going to happen tonight with the full moon," Lola said. "The werewolves will shift."

"Good grief, in the middle of the crowded carnival?" Marissa froze. "It will be a massacre. Somebody would have stopped them by now."

"No..." Lola tried to work it out. "The spell keeps things in control, apparently. Only a few people are affected."

"Affected how? Eaten by werewolves?"

"I'm not exactly sure. Only the worst of us, my source told me."

"Oh. Well, isn't that a good thing?" Marissa shrugged at the look Lola shot her. "What? On a scale of the entire island massacred versus a few of the worst of us, one looks better than the other."

"I don't want anyone on this island to be harmed. It's not up to us to decide who lives and who dies." It was her role to stop whatever was happening. She felt it in her bones. "They killed Richie, and he wasn't bad. He was just poking his nose in something far too dangerous."

Marissa's face paled. "Of course, I don't want anyone else to be hurt."

"The spell acts on our primal desires. Everyone is behaving like toddlers, going for what they want in that moment without any reflection on consequences. Nobody's paying attention to what's going on."

"Is that why they do it, so everyone is easier to control? They eat a few people, then it's over?"

Lola chewed her lip. "The spell is more than that. It has to do with how they barely age."

"To counteract the process of aging is considered dark magic, going against the principles of mortality. Life forces must be sacrificed."

"Yes, I think that's what they're doing," Lola said. "Under the full moon, they perform a ritual, and it allows them to slow their aging. But if it's not eating people, then what do they do?"

Another book thudded to the ground from inside Marissa's office. "That's the rare collection," she said with a frown and returned quickly with an ancient book. "This is unusual," she said, reading the front. "*The Odyssey.*"

"*The Odyssey?*" Lola's brow furrowed. "There was magic and monsters in Odysseus's journey." She took the book from Marissa. "Ooh, is this the original Greek?"

"You read Greek?" Marissa asked.

"Among other things." Lola skimmed the page the book had opened to, the thrill of discovery shuddering through her bones. "Of course. Circe."

"The witch? She turned Odysseus's men into..."

"Pigs." Lola closed the book with a snap. "*Merde*, Chann even told me as much. He said that people were swine, and the worst of us would be chosen. I didn't realize he meant it literally, but some people are turned into pigs. You said it yourself; a transformation can create magic." She gasped at the thought. "They keep a pen of pigs and make sausages out of them. That's what they eat."

Marissa pressed her hand to her mouth, nostrils flaring. "Every month on the full moon, they turn people into pigs, then proceed to make sausages out of them?"

"So there aren't any deaths, not at the carnival site. The disappearances that surround the carnival are people who are turned into pigs and taken away as livestock. No one would be looking for that." She glanced up to stare at Marissa. "How do we stop it?"

Marissa shook her head as though to rid herself of the visual she was caught up in and refocused on the books. "A spell of that magnitude would need a catalyst. An object to direct energy and amplify magic. It would probably be in a location of sympathetic power."

"The Maze of Desire! There is no doubt it's magical; it's a place out of time and space. It's filled with mirrors that act out our desires."

"That must be it. Mirrors amplify spells. And if the catalyst is placed within this magical vector, the energies could be magnified to something enormous."

"So I need to find this catalyst and destroy it before moonrise tonight to break the spell?"

Marissa stared at her books. "I think that would do it. The catalyst is a vessel for the power. If it is broken or even altered too much, the power can't be contained and will defuse."

Lola stood. "Well, I better get my sledgehammer, then."

"Lola, wait." Marissa grabbed her arm before she got to the door. "Why you? You're just a girl."

"Not just a girl," Lola said. "We've already determined that. And somebody has to stop it. Maybe somebody with a lot of supernatural baggage." She gave Marissa a little smile. "Thanks for the help."

"Take this at least." Marissa handed her a thin volume with a gilded wolf's face on the cover. "It spells out how to kill a werewolf."

Lola took the book. "*Coles Notes*?"

Marissa grimaced. "Got any silver bullets?"

"You know, I used up my last one the other day. I'll have to figure something else out."

"I also read that a wolf can be killed by another werewolf."

"Right. I'll just convince one of the wolves to attack and kill their pack leader, who has total control over them. No big deal."

Marissa's laugh was weak. "Right. No big deal."

"Listen, there's another thing I need to look up, and maybe you would have more luck with it. I don't know how it's connected to all this. Have you ever seen a symbol like this before?" Lola found a loose piece of paper and scribbled a sketch of the brand on Reiko's skin, the one she wasn't supposed to be able to see.

"This? I don't think so. Although it somehow looks familiar..." Marissa trailed off as she wandered towards the stacks.

"Okay, thanks for looking into that for me," Lola called. "I'll just be off to face mortal danger."

Marissa came back to herself and turned, her lips pressed tight. "It hasn't been terrible meeting you, Lola. Don't get yourself killed."

Lola smiled at that heartwarming speech. "It's been okay meeting you, too, Marissa. Maybe stay inside the library until the sun comes up tomorrow. I'm not sure what's going to happen tonight."

The reflection caught Marissa's glasses, so they were two white discs. "I don't have to be a witch to tell you there will be wolves."

THIRTY-THREE

People were bottlenecked at the entrance to the carnival; the entire island funnelled to the small space. Families dragged their sleepy kids towards the grounds. A couple, locked in a messy makeout session, stumbled into Lola as they pushed forward. She elbowed them aside and shoved through the crowd.

As she struggled to get in, she sent a text to her friends. She assumed they were at the carnival; everyone was.

Stay away from the Maze of Desire

Lola forced her way to the front, ignoring the outraged cries behind her. The security guards in their harlequin makeup grinned and ushered her through. Their teeth were long and curved, as though the wolf inside was already creeping to the surface.

An elderly woman barged past Lola. No one was willing to miss today's events, though none of them knew what surprises lay in store.

The air was thick with the smell of old fried foods, laced with something rancid. Lola peeked behind a food stall, recoiling at the sight of burgers that had clearly been left to sit out for days. She gagged, but a man came up behind her, tossing money on the counter for one.

"You don't want that," Lola said, but the man ignored her. His eyes were silver and blank.

She skirted The Gardens, where most of the people had gathered, sticking to the less populated areas. The games section was nearly deserted now. The hammer from the strongman game lay abandoned in the dry grass. Lola picked it up.

As she passed Conri's booth—abandoned by both carnival-goers and workers—she hesitated. Where was the crazed artist? Preparing for the night's festivities?

She stopped abruptly, swerving towards his display despite the urgency that pounded in her veins. His ring protected her from enchantment—could his other pieces be imbued with helpful charms?

Every piece of jewelry shimmered the same colour: silver. Lola picked up a pendant, holding it up to the light. She'd categorized enough treasure to know it was sterling.

Interesting choice. The one metal that could hurt werewolves. A self-destructive joke? There were no silver bullets to be seen, but her fingers hung over an elaborate hairpin, its length wickedly sharp. She plucked it from the display and secured it into her hair.

A familiar figure stood motionless in the middle of the path, staring at the candy apple in her hand. Violet's eyes were half-closed, and she swayed as though dead on her feet. She wore the same outfit from the day before, now stained and wrinkled.

Lola placed a hand on her shoulder, her ring brushing over her skin. "Violet? Are you okay?"

Violet jerked at her voice as though coming out of a trance. "What?" Her cracked lips curled into a scowl. "What's it to you?"

"You seem a little out of it. Maybe you should get some water."

"I'm fine." She glanced at the candy apple. "I kinda feel weird, though. Like I've lost something that I had."

"What, like a conscience?"

Lola's biting remark seemed to snap Violet back to herself. Her gaze sharpened. "God, you're so high and mighty." Her voice was pure poison.

"Sorry I asked." Lola held her hands up in surrender. "Have you seen Gael?"

"Worried he's with Cassidy?"

Lola was more worried that he was going to be turned into a pig or mauled by a werewolf, but the image of Gael and Cassidy wrapped around each other made her stomach curdle. "I wanted to make sure he was okay. Bad things are going to happen. If there's any way you can, you should leave."

"Taking care of everyone, aren't you?" Violet rolled her eyes. "If you must know, I managed to shake off Cassidy about two minutes ago. She was crying over how Gael ditched her in The Gardens. Don't get the appeal, honestly. I know he got all tall and rich, like, overnight, but seriously, what's the deal? What makes him so special?" Her head tilted as though truly curious.

"Gael is kind and thoughtful, and when you speak, he listens and—oh, never mind." Violet's eyes had glazed over. "Where did he go?"

Violet shrugged. "I saw him go off with Nix...and Walt." She stumbled over his name and that lost look came back to her. "They were going to the maze."

"What? No!" Lola spun and dashed to the centre of the fairgrounds, leaving Violet swaying behind her.

Though the Maze of Desire was still technically closed, the crime scene tape had been pulled away.

Gael stood at the entrance, arms crossed. Whenever someone approached, he shook his head. Nix and Walt flanked him, redirected people elsewhere.

Lola stormed towards her friends, the hammer resting heavily on her shoulder. "What are you doing here?"

"Lola." Gael's face lit up, his eyes glowing silver. He moved forward to embrace her, but she stiff-armed him.

"Gael, no. We need to figure things out when you're not under a spell."

"Spell?" His voice was fuzzy with confusion. She sighed and placed her hand on his cheek, allowing the metal ring to graze his skin. A spark of recognition flooded over his face, and he frowned. "Oh."

"Exactly," she said with a dry tone. She did the same with Nix and Walt. They both came back to themselves, blinking heavily.

"I don't know how long that will help, so let's do this quickly. I told you to stay away; why would you come here?"

Nix crossed her arms. "Lola, do you *ever* check your texts?"

"No, I..." She fumbled to take out her phone. In reality, she wasn't well-versed in technology. Her creator Jacquotte predated the telegraph and bore an inherent suspicion of human devices, something she passed on to her creations.

Lola quickly scrolled through the string of responses to her first one that warned them away.

What's going on Lola?
People are heading into the maze. We should stop them
Meet you there

Lola put her phone aside, sighing. Their first impulse was to head towards danger. Her friends, these amazing people, were driven by a desire to help others—to help her. She glanced away, overcome, fighting between her swell of affection and exasperation.

"No, *you* need to stay away from here. Just being nearby could be dangerous. A spell's been cast over the carnival, and the magic is amplified here."

"This is where Richie was murdered," Walt said, looking into the mirrored halls. "Bad things happen here, right? I remember... parts of it." He ran his hand over his face and looked appalled.

"More bad things are going to happen here tonight. Terrible things. All the more reason to stay away. Listen, you need to remember this. The carnival workers are werewolves. And tonight's the full moon. The spell attracts people and makes them behave animalistically, focusing on their most base desires."

"That's ridiculous," Nix scoffed, then got distracted by a carnival worker walking by with a tray of snacks, being mobbed by people shouting for more. "Anyone want candy?" she murmured.

Lola grabbed her arm again. "Focus."

Nix turned back to her, her eyes clearing. "I'm sorry, did you say *werewolves*?" Her eyebrows arched.

"Is it so difficult to believe? There are vampires; there are werewolves. And this pack has set up a ritual tonight."

"You were going to go in there on your own? Alone?" Gael's frustration boiled over. "With a *hammer*?"

"I'm the only one here not enchanted. You guys have to get away from here. This is the catalyst for the ritual. The people most affected by the animalistic spell will be called here and turned into pigs."

"Holy shit, people are going to turn into pigs?" Nix said.

"What's a catalyst?" Walt asked.

"Lola, when are you going to stop acting like you have superpowers?" Gael's eyes were dark with worry.

"I might not be a vampire but there are some things that I can do," Lola said. "I'm still connected to the Otherworld. I can sense paranormal things, and the spell doesn't affect me the way it does others."

She didn't tell him it was because of a protection spell he unwittingly gave her. They were too caught up in their emotions right now; she would figure out what it meant later. "I can at least remember what happens in the maze."

"What do you mean?" Nix asked.

"What do you see when you look in the mirrors?"

"Myself, obviously." Nix scowled, then her face changed to the same lost look Violet had. "But something funny, too, right? Why can't I remember?"

"You see things that you want, way down at the bottom of

your soul. The whole place is spelled to have us act on our deepest desires, and the mirrors amplify it. While you guys are thinking clearly, you can leave the carnival. Get as far away from it as possible, potentially out to sea. I'll find the catalyst and destroy it."

"That doesn't make any sense." Gael grabbed her arm roughly. Desperation lined his face. "Leaving you doesn't make sense."

"Please, Gael, I want you to be safe."

"What about you? You're not going in there alone."

"Listen, it has to be me. Alone. I can't have you guys hurt in there."

Nix shook her head. "Try and stop us. We'll follow you anyways."

"Worked last time," Walt said.

Lola let out a frustrated laugh. "Fine, follow me in, but for the record, this is a terrible idea. Like last time. And Gael?" He looked at her hopefully, and her insides squirmed with guilt. "Stay away from me while we're in there, okay? Nix and Walt should stay between us."

His face fell and Lola felt like a monster again.

"Why do you have to...oh, it's a desire thing." Nix's finger flicked back and forth between them. "You act on your wants? Like you guys—" She frowned as she thought it through. "That's super messed up."

Gael's jaw was clenched, but he nodded. "If that's what you want."

"It is." Lola turned to the maze. "We need to find our way to the centre."

One by one, they slipped in, Lola leading the way.

THIRTY-FOUR

Everywhere she looked, a string of Lolas stretched out to eternity. One of her reflections grinned too widely, and she felt a shot of horror at the wrongness of it.

Behind her, Nix sucked in her breath. "I remember. Oh God..."

Walt covered his mouth, eyes flicking between mirrors as though searching for something—or someone. Lola wondered what happened between him and Violet that caused that look on his face.

Beyond her own reflection, she caught a glimpse of Gael's. His gaze burned into hers, filled with longing and despair in equal measure. For a moment, she wanted nothing more than to go to him, to wrap herself around him and forget all the chaos.

Her reflection did just that, stepping into his arms. But the real Lola turned away.

"We have to stay on task. Don't look at the mirrors. They show things that aren't real."

"Aren't they?" Walt's tone was quiet, almost reverent. "A maze designed to reflect our deepest desires. In a way, it's more honest than we are."

"Don't get all philosophical on me," Nix said.

"It doesn't show truth; it feeds on our basest wants. Strip a person of their inhibitions and sense of self, and they become a dangerous animal."

A harrowed look crossed Gael's face, and his eyes snapped shut.

Lola's reflection winked at her, and she scowled before moving on towards the centre, where they'd find the crux of the spell. But she had no real way to chart their path. Every turn brought them deeper into the maze but showed her only more distorted reflections.

She slapped the surface of one in frustration and turned quickly again—

And froze.

Duke Louis glowering at her from one of the mirrors, his eyes painted black. A mad grin spread across his face.

Her scream echoed across the mirrors.

"What is it?" Nix rushed to her side.

But the only thing to be seen was their reflections, smirking at them.

"I thought I saw—" Her voice was a raw whisper. Lola shot a nervous glance over her shoulder.

From the depths of the maze, a low growl rumbled.

The sound curled through the air, thick with menace. It rose into a snarl, vibrating across the mirrors.

"Run!" Gael shouted and grabbed Lola's arm, spurring them deeper into the maze.

In blind panic, they sprinted forward, banging into mirrors as they went. All the while, the growls chased them, multiplying, surrounding them. Every crossroads forced a desperate choice, the snarls and vicious barking funneling them in a single direction.

They were being herded.

Something latched onto Lola's ankle. She screamed as she crashed to the ground. Her hammer skittered from her grip. Frantic, she clawed for it, fingers closing around the handle just as Gael scooped her up into his arms.

"You know, you might have been right," he panted. "This was a bad idea."

The growling stopped suddenly.

Gael slowed, easing her back to the ground. They had lost the others. The mirrors around them reflected only the two of them, wrapped around each other.

Gael stared at her, exhilaration lighting his face, his eyes wild. "But don't you think—"

The mirror behind him swung around, sweeping him up and bearing him away behind it. She heard his strangled curse, quickly cut off as the mirror slammed shut.

"Gael!" Lola lunged, but he was gone. She ran her hands over it, trying to find a release mechanism, but she couldn't even find a seam or hinge.

Her sobbing breath was the only thing she could hear. She stared into her reflection. It wasn't doing anything magical. It only stared back at her. Alone. Afraid.

Laughter echoed, high-pitched and mocking.

White-hot fury ignited inside her. "I don't like being played with," she snarled.

The laughter continued.

She hoisted the strongman hammer, weighing it in her palms. Then, with a primal roar, she swung it into the glass.

The mirror exploded into shards.

Somewhere deep in the maze, a howl ripped through the air.

"Didn't think you'd like that much." She went to the next mirror. Her reflection stared at her, hate shining deep within glowing eyes. Lola blew her a kiss— then shattered her doppelgänger.

She stormed forward, swinging her weapon from one side to the other, delighting in the splintering of glass that followed her. A trail of shards on the ground crunched under her feet. The destruction felt so good; satisfaction rose inside of her, and the carnage made her feel alive.

She hoisted the hammer to swing again, but somebody grabbed her from behind.

She gasped, her gaze meeting Chann's in the mirror. His grip was unyielding, his eyes glimmering with Otherworldly light.

In the mirror, his face shifted into something inhuman, stuck halfway in his transformation. His breath came out in ragged pants.

She turned in his arms to face him, pressing her ring against his cheek.

It worked; for a moment, the tension eased in his shoulders, and his eyes darkened to black.

He spoke rapidly as though trying to get all the words out in one breath. "It's different this time," he whispered. "I only found out now. Otsana's going to turn *everyone*. The whole island. She's mad with the magic she found here, and Louis is happy to go along with it."

"Everyone?" Lola stumbled back, releasing her hold on Chann. Immediately his eyes morphed to glowing silver. "How is that possible?"

"It's never been done before. But the power on this island—it's unfathomable. She said we could capitalize, being the first to tap into it." His look darted one way then the other, a wild animal trapped in a cage. "She wants to make us immortal. She promised we'd never have to scrape for a meal again."

He growled, the sound tearing the air between them. "I told you not to come back. You could have had a chance. I can't help you now."

He grabbed her wrist with an iron-like grip and slowly twisted her hand until she dropped the hammer with a cry.

She struggled, pounding at his chest, an ungiving wall of muscle. "No! You can't let this happen!"

"I'm sorry, Lola." His voice was almost gentle. "I'll make it as easy as I can."

A cloth pressed over her mouth

She gasped. The scent hit her—a cloying, herbal sweetness.

Then darkness swallowed her whole.

THIRTY-FIVE

Lola's eyelids felt sticky, unwilling to lift, and for long moments, her sight was a foggy blur. It took a few blinks before she realized she'd been dumped face-first into the dirt, the earth digging into her cheek. Her arms were bound behind her back, twisted at an angle that made her muscles scream.

She forced herself to move, struggling to shake off the lingering lethargy from the drug. Her throat was dry, a ragged cough wracking her chest as she tried to roll over. A groan slipped from her lips as agonizing pain shot down her arms.

Above her, light filtered through a glass skylight. The sky had deepened to indigo—the evening was near. How long had she been unconscious?

Her mouth went dry as paper as she realized where she was— bound at the heart of the maze.

She was surrounded by five mirrored walls: a pentagon, a magically powerful shape. In the centre, a towering altar of mirrors caught the last of the light. The catalyst, the object giving the spell its unnatural power, must be somewhere inside. But what was it?

"Lola, Lola."

The voice cut through her haze, and Lola managed to roll herself up onto her knees. She shook her head, trying to clear her vision, and caught sight of Nix on the other side of the room, her voice low and insistent.

"Oh, thank God. You were out forever. I thought you were dead." Tear tracks smudged Nix's face.

Lola's throat ached as she croaked. "How long?"

"For hours! They kept coming to check on you. I would pretend to be passed out each time."

Gael and Walt were also bound, their faces puffy and eyes red as though they'd only just woken up as well. They struggled against their restraints, but neither had made much progress.

Lola glanced at her circle of friends, her heart sinking. "Was everyone drugged?"

Gael nodded, his mouth pulled into a thin line. "All I remember is the mirror moved. Then I saw Louis."

"For me, it was Conri." Walt's voice was hoarse. "I saw the gold of his eyepiece."

"Drugged and tied up at the centre point of the spell." Lola glanced uneasily at the darkening sky above them. "They've singled us out. We know too much."

Nix's gaze darted to the mirrors, her voice trembling. "What did you say about being turned into pigs?"

Lola swallowed. "Everyone on the island. It's going to change us all to pigs. A massive spell. I've never heard of anything so ambitious."

Nix struggled harder against her bonds. "And after we're all pigs...?"

"You're a pig and you're surrounded by werewolves. There really isn't a bright side here."

Gael's eyes narrowed. "How do you know all this?"

"Because I've spent the last few days doing nothing but trying to figure this out." The words came out sharper than she intended, a jagged edge of frustration cutting through.

"Why didn't you tell any of us?" His voice was thick with accusation.

"I tried," Lola snapped. "But you were all enchanted by the spell. Too busy with...other people, and you didn't want to hear about it."

She hadn't realized how much anger had been building inside her until she saw her reflection in the mirror, twisted with ugly fury. She flinched away from it.

Gael's look was equally enraged. "All on your own? I'm surprised you had time to get anything done in between sneaking off with that werewolf. That's what he is, right? You and your monsters"

"Not really the issue right now," Walt said.

Nix turned to Lola, eyes wide. "You've been sneaking around with a werewolf?"

"No, I...he helped me. Before he tied me up. It's complicated. Can we sort this out later? Right now, we have to get out of here."

A bright flash of light blinded her, and the room suddenly filled with smoke.

As they all choked, cringing away from the stinging vapour, a flurry of movement surrounded them. By the time Lola blinked away her tears, Duke Louis stood in front of them, his arms up as though he had performed a miraculous feat.

"Apologies for the theatrics." His voice boomed through the maze. "You've proven to be our most curious spectators in a long time."

Walt laughed, the sound rough and strangled by the smoke. Louis's arms dropped, eyebrows raised, clearly thrown by the unexpected laughter.

"What?"

"You actually use smoke and mirrors," Walt managed to wheeze, a hint of a grin breaking through.

"Anything to keep them looking in the wrong direction," Lola said, her eyes streaming from the smoke bomb as she worked frantically at the rope binding her. "All the way back to 1936, isn't that right? I know about the carnival in Paris."

Louis's smile was not kind. "1936. Now that was a time to be alive. The chaos, the violence of Europe, the way people looked the other way, certain that if they didn't acknowledge it, the evil creeping over the land wouldn't get them." He paced the room, his eyes growing misty as if recalling an old memory. "But it always does." He lunged as if to grab Nix. She shrieked and jerked away.

"The true show came later, though, when the streets ran with blood. We didn't even need to hide. Nobody cared. Life was cheap back then, and we were there to cash in."

Lola's heart beat faster at his words, and a wave of nausea gripped her. She remembered—she had been there. Her first memory as a vampire was still crystal clear, on the streets of Paris.

The streetlights were bright on her eyes, and noises, smells, rushed at her in a flurry of sensation. Surrounding her were bodies. The cobblestones drenched in blood. She too had been there when life was cheap; she had reaped the rewards of the monsters during that time.

The world blackened and she squeezed her eyes shut, willing the memory to go away. But it was engraved in her mind.

A body pressed against her, warm and grounding. Gael. He'd shifted over next to her and said her name in a whisper. When she looked at him, he held her gaze, anger forgotten. "You're okay. Stay with us."

She let out a shaky breath until her ribs trembled. Colour returned to the world.

Louis continued, oblivious to Lola's crisis. "As much fun as that was, we go much farther back. I started my travelling show more than a hundred and fifty years ago, and we're still going strong. One of the longest-running attractions in the world, not that anyone remembers us after we leave. But they'll always keep on coming because we give them what they want."

He stared at his reflection. In the mirror, a wolf stared back, hackles raised. "I created the Carnival of Fools when I was a young pup in the Old World, but there's something about the Americas that has pulled me in for decades. The gluttony, the greed; you don't even try to hide it. It's intoxicating."

"There is so much passion here, so much energy, and we use it all." In a swoop, he was crouched by Lola's side. "But you seem hell-bent on ruining the show. Otsana tells me you're different, worthy of my collection. I'm sure I could find a way to work with your talents. So, little troublemaker? Care to join us?"

Louis reached out and tilted her chin back, exposing her neck. He eyed her with a calculating gleam.

Lola tried to jerk out of his grip, but his long nails dug in deep. "What makes you think I'd want to join you?"

His smile grew. "It wasn't really a choice."

"Get away from her." Gael struggled to rise, but Louis slapped him aside with a single swipe.

Lola screamed as Gael's body crumpled to the floor with a sickening thud.

Her thoughts raced, desperation flooding her. She had to act fast.

"Let them go," she said to Louis. "They have nothing to do with this. I'll do whatever you want if they're safe."

She had fought so hard for her humanity. Messy as it was, it was hers alone.

But she would give it up if it would help them.

Louis' lips curled into a twisted smile. "Brave words, but you're in no position to negotiate." He stepped back, eyes gleaming with cruel amusement. "They know too much; we'll feast on them and leave nothing but their bones. Now tell me, what are you? Your energy is fractured." He waved his hand around her. "I can't make sense of it."

"I don't know what you're talking about." She spoke through gritted teeth.

"Oh yes, you do. You are *something* and I'll find out soon

enough. It only takes one bite." His smile soured and he yanked her up to whisper in her ear. He smelled gamey, like a wet dog. "I like my special people, my little freaks with all their powers. I keep them with me forever."

Lola flinched away. "But don't you hate us too, people with power?" she said, hissing around the pain as he twisted her arms backwards. "Because you don't have any?"

He dropped her with a mirthless laugh and his mouth twisted. "I have all the power. All of you freaks obey me and only me. I'll keep you obedient; you'll see for yourself." His eyes glowed silver. "Conri!" he shouted.

A sudden howl pierced the air, shaking the room. The artist was at his side in an instant. One second, he wasn't there; the next, he was—silent, swift, like a shadow.

Louis himself jumped, as surprised as the rest of them.

"You called, Mr. Garoux?" Conri's voice held a mocking lilt.

"Saints, Conri, stop lurking in the shadows and watch these troublemakers. Soon, they'll have front-row seats to the best show in town." He winked at Lola, which made her shudder. "Be back soon."

He threw his hands in the air, releasing another explosion of smoke.

Conri waved it away, his face wrinkled with distaste. "Ridiculous spectacle," he said under his breath.

Walt watched him closely. "How did you do it?"

Conri stared at the skylight, not appearing to hear. When he glanced down at his one-eyed reflection, he flinched and seemed to come back to himself. "Do what?"

"How did you get in here?" Walt asked. "I'm positive you weren't here before. Nothing opened; you just appeared." His eyes were bright.

"You weren't looking in the right place, were you?" Conri said. He shook his head this way and that as if to clear his ears. "Mr.

Garoux is anything but stealthy. He's all flash and shimmer. Unbearably loud. He treats magic like it's a show, makes it impossible to look away from him." His single eye glowed silver. "Don't look too long in his eyes, child. You might get lost in them."

"Is that what happened to you?" Lola asked.

"I got lost, yes, in the promises. Everlasting glory, he said. Nothing could bring me down until I found myself in the dirt." His fingers traced over the gilt eyepiece.

"So you use your boss, a thundering showman, as your distraction," Walt said. "Nobody's looking anywhere else, so you can appear or disappear at will."

Conri grunted.

"Could you teach me?" Walt squirmed against his ties.

Conri cocked his head, and an amused smile flickered over his lips. "You're going to be ripped apart by wolves, boy, and that is what you care about?" He lowered himself until he was face to face with him. "Oh yes, you would be adept. I can always tell. I wish I'd met you in another time. But this is no place for wishes. Soon the moon will be overhead, and you'll have disappeared inside my belly."

Walt cringed away as Conri let out a little howl, barely more than a whimper. Conri's hands shook as he stared at them.

"It's agonizing, you know. Nothing quite like being turned inside out. All the flesh and blood and gore. And then everything that makes me a man." He held up his gnarled hands for inspection, then tapped his temple. "These thoughts, they change as well. I am nothing but a vessel for the deeper urges. It's a swirl of colour, of smell, of violence and instinct."

"Your paintings," Lola said. "It's how you perceive your time as a wolf."

Conri sneered. "My paintings used to be celebrated at the Louvre. My inventions were displayed at the Crystal Palace, unparalleled for their combination of art and science." He held up his hands, lost in memory. "Now, I am nothing more than a beast, scrabbling in the garbage for meat scraps, eating the worst that humanity has to offer."

"You designed this maze, didn't you?" Lola said. "No beast could do this. It's masterful."

"I have no sway over this; chaos magic holds court here."

"You mean Otsana's desire spell?"

"Desire *is* chaos. There is no order or reason to want. It infuses the mirrors with its own designs, and I have no more control. My beautiful work turned against me."

His reflection moved of its own accord. A wide, wicked grin stretched out towards his ears, then kept on stretching until his face split in two. A grinning wolf's head emerged.

Lola's skin prickled at the grotesque show. Nix turned her face away, eyes squeezed shut.

Conri shouted a laugh, whirling around in circles. The prisoners pulled themselves up against the mirrors to avoid his dancing, stomping feet.

"He's insane." Gael watched him with wide eyes.

"He's a genius," Walt said. "But it broke him."

"It's this place that broke him." Lola wasn't even sure the madman could hear her or understand. "He sleeps in here. Imagine what that would do to you? Imagine dreaming in here." She flicked a nervous look at her reflection.

"It is you who broke it. Crash, crash, crash. My beautiful work smashed to pieces." He halted in front of Lola, panting.

She shrank away from his gaze. Dark fur crept up his neck to cover his face and his nose lengthened, his fingers sharpening into claws.

He held the claw up to Lola's face and she went completely still.

"I'm sorry," she whispered.

"I should kill you." His voice was a snarl ripped deep from his throat. "I should thank you. In your destruction is freedom."

He stared at his wolf-man reflection, leaning against the glass, breathing heavily. Then, so quickly she couldn't follow it, he slashed towards her, knocking her down to the ground. Gael screamed from the other side of the room.

THIRTY-SIX

Lola slowly sat up and brought her hands to her face. Conri had severed the ties at her wrists. A thin stream of blood trickled from where his claws had sliced the skin sent a shudder through her.

His head jerked to the side, his glowing eye riveted to the ruby gleam at her wrist.

"Such pretty blood inside of you. Must let it all out." In a wild, whirling dervish, Conri danced around the room, claws flashing like knives in a storm. In a moment, all of them were freed.

"Soon, soon. Blood will run. Can't be late," he sang, spinning once more before vanishing with a suddenness that make Lola's head ache.

Gael ripped off the last of his bindings and rushed to Lola's side. He pulled her into an embrace.

"Are you okay?" he asked, his voice tight. "You seemed to get lost somewhere inside of you."

She leaned into him, pressing her face into his chest. "For a minute, I felt trapped in my past," she whispered. "I have some dark places inside of me. Thanks for bringing me back."

"Always." His voice was rough with emotion.

"So we're untied," Nix said, dusting herself off as she stood. She limped around the room, shaking out her legs. "That's great. What do we do now?" She went rigid, and Lola turned to see what had startled her.

Their doppelgängers were circling them within the mirrors, staring with manic eyes, lips twisted in snarls.

Nix backed away from her furious reflection. "You don't think they can...come out, do you?" Her redheaded reflection took a swipe at her, fingers curved into claws.

"Impossible." Walt stared at the reflections as Nix and Gael shared an alarmed look.

Gael pounded on the circle of mirrors surrounding them. His reflection's eyes darkened, taking on a murderous glint as he slammed against the inside of the glass as though trying to break free.

Lola's mind raced. "We need to find the catalyst."

"The thing that will turn us into pigs?" Nix shuddered. "Right. How the hell do we do that?"

Lola approached the central altar, her eyes focused on the intricately arranged mirrors. "The catalyst to the spell is inside here, I'm sure of it. It soaks up the energy of the moonlight coming through the skylight, and the mirrors are spelled to amplify its power. Tonight, with the full moon, its power will be at its apex." She swallowed. "And then..."

"Pigs," Nix finished.

"But if we destroy it, the spell will lose its power."

Walt crossed his arms. "What exactly is the catalyst?"

"I don't know. It could be anything, but I believe Otsana has it on her when she casts her spells."

"Something she wears?" Nix asked, raising an eyebrow.

"Maybe." Lola ran her hands over the cold surface of the mirrors, probing the edges, the corners.

Gael was doing the same. "This is impossible; everything fits together perfectly."

"If it was designed by Conri, there would be a release some-where," Walt said. "He would have made sure it was unseen, tucked away where no one would notice."

"Dammit, we don't have time to play escape room." Nix stomped her foot on the ground. "I just want to get out of here."

Her words triggered a thought in Lola. "Of course. That's what we want, more than anything right now."

She faced her glowering reflection. "These mirrors reflect our desires. If what we desire is how to find the catalyst…"

She stepped up to the mirrored altar and her reflection shifted, meeting her eyes with unsettling intimacy. Lola reached out and brushed her fingertip against the mirror. Now that she was paying attention, her reflection preened under her gaze.

Gael came up behind Lola to watch, and Lola's reflection cuddled up with his. With a grin, she slipped a hand under his shirt. Lola could feel Gael stiffen behind her.

"Enough of that." The real Lola held up a stern finger. "What I want is to find the catalyst. Can you show me where it is?"

Reflection Lola released Gael and pouted. Real Lola leaned forward, giving her a flirty smile. "Please? I really, really, *really* want it."

Reflection Lola perked up. She walked to the side of her mirror, then passed seamlessly over the edge to the adjacent mirror. Lola's stomach did a flip at the unnaturalness, but followed along the perimeter of the altar, keeping pace with her reflection as it continued its eerie journey.

On the other side, her reflection stopped and crossed her arms. Gael's reflection followed her closely, and Lola could see the same tension on his face.

"What's wrong? What's she doing?" Nix asked.

"I think she's showing us something." Reflection Lola was pointing to the top corner of the mirror.

Lola frowned. "What do I need to do?" Her reflected self

placed her hands on her hips and shook her head, then curled a finger towards someone.

A shadow shifted and Walt's reflection stepped forward.

His reflection seemed older—more hardened—than the real Walt, whose eyes were nearly popping out of his head as he watched.

"Walt!" Lola turned to him. "Do you understand?"

The real Walt hesitated, then glanced at his mirrored self, who had rolled up his sleeves and seemed to fiddle with the corner of the altar.

Realization dawned on Walt's face. "The lock is hidden there." He stepped forward, patting his pocket. "Let me see what I can do."

He slipped out a small lockpick set.

"I can't believe you can do that." Nix came up behind him, watching in admiration as he began to work on a tiny hole in the altar—exactly where his reflection had indicated.

"Ha," he said with grim triumph, as a soft, metallic click resonated.

The mirrors shuddered.

Gears whined in protest, grinding against each other. Whirring and clicking, they shifted on an elaborate clockwork structure, reforming to fit together like puzzle pieces. The mirrors moved with eerie precision, transforming into a raised stage.

Sitting at the centre was Otsana's midnight blue electric guitar, hand-painted with silver moons and stars.

"Is this it?" Nix's fingers brushed over the strings. She yanked her hand back, shaking it hard. "Ouch, this thing is charged."

Lola stepped onto the stage and braced herself, picking the guitar up from its stand. A flood of energy surged through her, and she let out a choking gasp. Her muscles stiffened as the raw power shot through her like lightning.

Gael made as if to grab her, but Lola shook her head.

"Let me do this. I think I can get a handle on it."

She closed her eyes and breathed slowly, rhythmically, until she could bear the current of magic coursing through her. "*Merde*, it's potent," she said through gritted teeth. "But we need to find a way to destroy it."

"Shame to ruin it," Gael said, his fingers nearly brushing the paintwork on the surface. "It's a beauty."

"Pigs, Gael." Nix reminded him.

"Right." He straightened. "Smash it to bits."

"I guess I'll do it the old-fashioned way." With one last glance at the gleaming instrument, Lola swung it over her head and brought it down with all her strength. The impact sent a shock that jangled up her arms with an amplified screech.

The guitar remained intact.

"I guess I didn't give it enough." Lola was panting from the buzz of the energy through her. She drew in a deep breath and tried again. This time, a thin stream of smoke came up from the body, but it didn't even crack.

The air began to hum, and the stage glowed as silvery light flooded the maze.

As one, they gazed up, transfixed, as the full moon came into view from the skylight.

THIRTY-SEVEN

Outside, a howl rose in the sky, then another and another, then a dozen more, the call of something primal and ancient. Laughter, wild and unhinged, joined the chilling symphony.

"Time's up."

The silky voice curled around them. A mirror wall swung open, revealing Otsana. Her sharp teeth curled over her lips, grey fur spreading up her face and over her arms.

She moved before Lola could react. One clawed hand seized the guitar, the other wrapped around Lola's throat, lifting her as easily as a doll.

Dangling in the air, Lola's feet kicked wildly, her fingers tearing at Otsana's grip, but the woman was unyielding.

Gael lunged forward, only to be yanked back by a carnival worker as they flooded the room. Nix shrieked as a hulking figure lifted her from the ground, his face distorting, mouth elongating. The air thickened with the scent of fur and musk.

Otsana's eyes glimmered and she gave Lola a sharp-toothed grin. "And so, little rabbit." Her voice lowered to a growl, and she shook her shaggy head. "You want to play with the wolves?"

Lola's nails dug into Otsana's wrist, her vision flickering with bright bursts as claws punctured her throat.

"Don't kill her." The command cut through the chaos.

Chann stepped up to Otsana, his dark eyes burning. "You know Louis has plans for her. Nobody's to hurt her." His voice resonated through the crowd, and the workers grumbled.

"But the others are fair game," one of them snarled. Hands clenched; grips tightened. Tears streamed down Nix's face as she sobbed.

"I wasn't going to hurt her." Otsana purred, shaking Lola as she choked. "We were just playing." With a curled lip, she flung Lola aside. Chann caught her effortlessly, his arms gentle but unyielding as she gasped in breath after breath. Her hands came away bloody from her throat.

"Chann, let me go," she croaked, struggling feebly, but he was infinitely stronger than her.

His eyes were downturned, showing unbearable sadness. "I can't. The closer we get to the change, the less control I have over myself. I have to obey." He rested his forehead against hers for a moment. "I'm sorry."

His breath shuddered, and then his body. He turned his head away as his jaw lengthened, bones shifting beneath his skin. Otsana watched in triumph.

"Otsana, stop this." Lola's voice cracked with desperation. "You can't just turn people into pigs."

Otsana looked thoroughly amused. "Of course I can," she said. "I learned how a long time ago. A man tried to rape me once, in Russia. So I turned him into a pig." She tilted her head, eyes glinting, and let out a bark of laughter. "It was fun. You should try it sometime."

"Can you change them back?"

"Nyet, little one. I call on the heart to show their true nature. After that, it is finished. No more man, just pig. There is power in that. Now, I must play while I still can." She strummed the strings with her warped fingers.

The sound, amplified magically, slithered out into the carnival night.

Wild whoops of laughter sounded from outside the maze.

"You stopped one man from hurting you once," Lola shouted, trying to distract Otsana. "But you're still in the power of another, aren't you? How does it feel that Louis has complete control over you? You don't have any real power at all."

Otsana's eyes glittered with hate, her face darkening. "I will live forever, feasting on mankind. I am powerful."

"But you don't get to decide anything. You don't even have control over your body. Did you know what would happen when Louis bit you? Did he even offer you the choice?"

Her smile dropped. "What do you know of it?"

"Everything," Lola said through her teeth. She struggled against Chann's grip, but it was like fighting a marble statue. "But you do have a choice now. You don't have to do this."

"What if I like it?" Otsana's face twisted, her transformation accelerating. "What if this is all I've ever wanted?"

"You'll still belong to Louis."

Otsana snarled. "Perhaps you'll be my gift to him."

"I'll enjoy that," Louis's voice rasped through the air like a razor over rocks.

Lola stilled in fright like the rabbit Otsana accused her of being.

He stood at the entrance to the maze, eyes glowing and a mad smile stretched across his face.

"Now, play."

Louis's command rang out in the air, and the pack howled. Otsana played in earnest, the music warping the air. The workers convulsed, bodies contorting. The music was electrifying—a part of Lola wanted to move to the beat, to thrash wildly and without control until she lost herself in it entirely.

A flash of silver light exploded from the guitar like a sonic boom.

Chann's grip on her slipped. His hands were changing, and as the muscles flexed and moved under the skin, she ripped herself out of his hold. He made a swipe at her but fell heavily to the ground, clumsy in his transformation. Lola dodged.

"Now!" she screamed at her friends. "They're vulnerable right now."

She drove her foot into the knee of the brute holding Nix. His leg was grotesquely bending the wrong way, and he dropped her with a grunt. Nix pulled away as Gael and Walt fought their way free.

Lola vaulted onto the stage, seizing the guitar out of Otsana's clawed hands. The werewolf was too surprised to stop Lola, and the catalyst came into her hands easily. The guitar blasted energy into her palms. Though her skin felt as though it was blistering off, Lola held on.

Otsana reeled back, howling. "Stop her." Her words were garbled as her jaw snapped.

"Run," Lola said, and the group of them plunged out of the room, dodging the reaching hands of the werewolves as the change took them.

Lola kept expecting her reflection to lunge at her. But it seemed her reflection was finally in agreement with her; the desire to survive surpassed everything. They showed her the way out, as dozens of Lolas sprinted to save their lives.

At the exit they found themselves in the middle of pandemonium. People convulsed, bodies contorting, shrieks twisting into something high-pitched and unnatural. The first sacrifices.

Ethan stood in the crowd, his hateful silver eyes intent on her.

Several werewolves stumbled out of the maze, deformed monsters halfway through their change, led by Louis. He found Lola in the crowd.

"Kill them!" he commanded.

Lola's friends scattered in all directions as the crowd rushed them. Every face was twisted with emotion: fury, anger, hatred marring them all. Their hands curled in on themselves and their shrieks took on a squealing edge, but still, they came after her.

Lola sprinted with all the strength she could find in her human legs, her muscles burning from the effort. The crowd would rip her apart with their bare hands if they got her.

But her desire to live spurred her on.

The Ferris wheel loomed in front of her. No riders were left, called to the maze and the pull of the spell, but the ride continued to wheel around its endless loop, and Lola got an idea.

She timed it, then dove between the spinning seats, making it to the central shaft. Above her, where the massive wheel turned around the axle and the grinding gears churned, was a space large enough to swallow a guitar whole.

Lola slung the guitar over her shoulder, burning her skin, and climbed the ladder-like frame. The crowd still followed. It reminded her of the time she needed to climb out of the treasure pit as it flooded, Gael over her back. Then she had been a vampire, recently fed on fresh blood.

This time she was only human, hurt and tired at that. How could she possibly make it?

The mob was beneath her, brushing at her heels, their faces caught up in vicious sneers. At the front of the pack was Ethan, eyes lit with joy and rage in the chaos.

She scrambled up the ladder, fueled by fear. She would make it because there was no other choice. The grinding of the wheel sounded right above her.

She missed the next rung and fell, clinging to the bar with one hand. Ethan lunged to grab her.

Lola drove her foot into his face, grinding her heel for good measure as he yelled and fell down a rung, delaying the climbers behind him. She launched herself upwards, making it to the centre.

Bracing herself on the ladder with her legs, she jammed the guitar deep into the gears.

It was yanked out of her hands.

Time stood still as the guitar got stuck. With a high-pitched whine, the wheel of chairs shuddered and ground to a halt.

An overwhelming rattle shook the entire frame of the structure, but still the guitar wouldn't break.

Merde, the spell was too powerful for even this.

But the pressure grew.

Then—a shrieking metallic rip.

With a bang and a flash of silver light, the guitar shattered, splintering into a thousand pieces.

The explosion knocked Lola off her perch, and she plunged from the frame.

Thirty-Eight

As Lola plummeted through the air, someone grabbed her, swinging her back onto the frame. Her breath came in ragged gasps as she clutched at her rescuer, her heart hammering against her ribs.

"Gael, what are you doing here?" she choked out, pressing against him despite the crush of panicked teenagers around them.

"I was always right behind you." He met her gaze steadily, his small, relieved smile sending warmth curling through her.

Screams of fear cut through the air, the crowd of people now terrified to find themselves on the Ferris wheel high above the fairground. Below, the ride ground to a halt, its mechanical whine fading into eerie silence. People scrambled down the ladder, desperate to escape.

Lola waited until the ladder had cleared entirely, making her way down on shaky legs. She didn't want to let Gael go, unwilling to lose contact with him.

When they reached solid ground, Lola flung her arms around him, inhaling his familiar scent, anchoring herself. Here he was, protecting her to the end. Despite everything between them—all the mistakes, the betrayals, the unspoken words—he would always be there for her.

The longing she felt for him had nothing to do with magic. It had always been real. But too much stood between them now, so many questions and other people and mistakes that maybe couldn't be overcome. She didn't know how to bridge the gap between them.

Gael's eyes showed the same flicker of uncertainty. His fingers brushed her cheek, tilting her head to inspect her neck. "You're hurt."

"I'll survive. Thanks to you."

Around them, the chaos spell had broken and the people who had been writhing on the ground stood. With relief, Lola didn't notice any pigs squealing in the mob. She had made it in time.

People who had been dancing and drinking for hours, some of them for days straight, stared at their phones in disbelief. She heard frantic children and teenagers calling out for their parents, searching for comfort in the crowd.

A guttural snarl sliced through the night sky, freezing the breath in her lungs.

The crowd's panic swelled into sheer hysteria as shadows moved at the edges of the fairground. Then the screams came.

Wolves emerged from the darkness, their glowing eyes reflecting the silver moonlight. They spread in a semi-circle, hemming the terrified humans in like prey.

And at their centre stood Louis.

He had yet to fully shift, his misshapen body caught between man and beast. His barrel chest heaved, his unnatural eyes gleaming with savage glee. To his right, a sleek grey wolf's intelligent gaze locked onto Lola. Otsana. To his left stood a massive black wolf, a tuft of white fur over one of his eyes. Chann.

The pack bristled, hackles raised, their saliva-drenched maws twitching with hunger. They were poised to strike.

"You thought you could stop me?" Louis's voice rumbled with

an Otherworldly growl, his lips peeling as his mouth broke open, and his voice garbled as he transformed. "You've only changed the game. Watch your friends die."

The moon shone bright silver over the scene as Louis unleashed a howl of pain and ecstasy, his body cracking and breaking as it reshaped itself. On an explosion of blood and fur, he dropped to four legs. He was dark grey and enormous, his powerful shoulders tensed as though ready to pounce.

Lola turned to Gael, grabbed his face and kissed him hard. "Get them out of here."

"Lola—"

"Now! Take them to the exit; go calmly, don't run. I'll take the wolves." She pulled away, her heart cracking as she whispered. "I love you, Gael." Then she turned and ran towards the wolves.

Louis' gaze snapped to her, and the pack tensed, their primal instincts sharpening.

The mass of people began to move, obeying Gael's urgent commands. The wolves hesitated, whimpering as they followed the fleeing people with their gaze.

Lola waved her arms, drawing their focus. "It's me you want, isn't it?"

She faced the pack of hungry wolves as Louis's predator gaze sharpened on her.

Out of the corner of her eye, Lola spotted a nearby building. The wolves were hungry; she could feed them.

"Can't catch me," she said, turning her back on them and taking off like a rabbit.

Louis plunged after her, and the pack leapt into action behind him, the chase irresistible.

She sprinted for the old Granger barn, her lungs burning. Their teeth snapped at her heels. Lola was fast, but not as fast as a werewolf on the full moon, and she had only seconds before being overrun. Rancid breath heated the back of her neck as she ducked and veered, dodging snapping jaws and hurling herself over the pigpen fence.

The stench of pig offal and raw animal fear hit her like a fist. The werewolves followed her, clearing the barrier with ease and finding themselves surrounded by tender flesh.

It was too much for them to resist. The shrieks of pigs were maddening as the wolves lost themselves in a feeding frenzy.

Lola kept on running through the slaughter, dodging the blood and chaos to make it to the loft. If she could get up there, the wolves wouldn't be able to climb after her, and she could wait out this terrible night.

Her fingers grasped the wooden ladder when a wolf barrelled into her at full speed. She flew back, slamming into the ground on her side with her breath knocked out of her. Rolling, she tumbled towards the dark back corner of the barn. She was trapped.

Louis slinked forward; his lips curled in a lethal snarl, mad fury in his eyes.

He was going to rip her apart. Or worse, bite her, and next month, Lola would be working the carnival, dining on people turned to pork sausage.

Either way, her human life was over. It had been short and confusing, but she didn't regret it.

She brought her hands to her hair, releasing the sharp silver pin. It glinted in the dim light, trembling in her hand. At least she wouldn't go down without a fight.

Louis snarled and pounced. In the instant before his jaws closed, Lola dropped to the ground, and he leapt right over her. She scrambled to her feet as he slid in loose hay, his powerful limbs scrabbling as he fought to get his footing underneath him.

Going against every instinct to flee, Lola leapt onto the werewolf's back. She grabbed Louis around his thick neck as he tried to shake her off and jammed the silver pin deep into one of his eye sockets.

His shrieking howl rivalled the screeches of the pigs as they were ripped apart. Lola was thrown against the wall of the barn with a crack, and she wasn't sure if the sound was the wood or her ribs. She crashed to the ground, white-hot pain lancing through her side.

Louis pawed at his face frantically, but the pin was buried deep and without fingers, he couldn't remove it.

He turned to her with an agonized snarl. It hadn't been enough. Injured but not mortally, Louis's one good eye promised endless pain as he approached her. Lola whimpered, frozen in fear. She had no other play.

Another wolf broke away from the bloody feast. The massive black wolf snarled, leaping between Lola and Louis as if to defend his master. Blood dripped from his jowls, and his eyes glazed over with the indulgence of flesh.

"Chann," she whispered, taking in the slash of white over his eyebrow. He growled, so deep in his throat it was vibration rather than sound. He was bound to obey his homicidal master.

Lola had nothing left; she couldn't fight anymore. She raised herself to her knees, anyway, wanting to face the end.

Chann tilted his head then, his eyes sparkling with intelligence. Perhaps there was a flash of recognition somewhere deep inside.

"He's right there," she said, her voice little more than a rasp. "He's injured, and he's yours."

Chann whimpered, then shook like a dog. Panting, he turned to his alpha, blinded on one side.

And the boy who'd been punished for decades for stealing from the wrong man realized his master was weak.

The pack followed strength. And Louis' reign was ending.

Louis pounced on Lola, and she shrieked, bringing her hands up to protect her face. Louis's hot breath seared her cheek as his teeth missed skin by a thread. Then Chann crashed into him, and Louis was whipped to the side by the younger, stronger wolf.

The two predators circled and snapped until finally Chann drove into Louis, teeth flashing.

Strong jaws grasped Louis's throat. The alpha let out a throaty howl and slammed Chann into the side of the barn wall. Blood sprayed across the wooden beams, the brutal clash shaking the foundation of the barn.

Groaning with pain, Lola dragged herself farther from where the furred bodies grappled with each other. From her vantage point, all she could see was carnage. Pigs were being slaughtered, the smell of warm blood thick in the air.

Louis dodged an attack by Chann and came back at him, snapping. He grabbed the younger wolf by the throat and brought him down. Chann whimpered. Now that he had challenged his alpha, he was fighting for his life, and if he lost, Lola was as good as dead too.

A rusted pitchfork lay next to her, hidden under the hay. Every muscle in her body fought against her, but Lola crept forward, pulling the fork towards her.

"You overrated asshole," she screamed, hoisting the weapon. "Come and get me!"

With a savage snarl, Louis lunged for her. As he pounced, she drove the pitchfork up with every ounce of her strength.

The tines punctured his throat, his massive body jerking. It wasn't silver, but it was enough to stop him in his tracks. Chann was on him in a second, ripping at his throat.

Blood gushed and with a final, gurgling snarl, Louis's body went limp.

Lola let out a shuddering breath as Chann turned to her. He approached, fangs dripping with blood, she backed away on hands and knees. There was no escaping. If he wished to bite her or to kill her, he could.

She closed her eyes as she felt his nose, surprisingly cold, nudge her cheek. She looked up to meet his eyes, and he let out a huff of breath. He rested his muzzle on her shoulder for a moment.

Then he turned away, bounding into the middle of the pack as they fed. He let out a long howl that echoed all the way to the moon.

The other wolves stopped to circle him, joining in his ancient song. They rubbed against him, bowing their heads, as Chann took his place at their centre.

Under their chorus, Lola found her legs again. Stifling her sobs, she scrabbled along the back side of the barn. The wood was rotted, and it didn't take long for her to wiggle one of the planks loose, giving her an opening wide enough for her to squeeze through the splintered wood. She pushed through, ending up at the edge of the woods.

The relief she felt at her sudden freedom quickly faded as the dread of being pursued coursed through her. She ran, though her breath was squeezed out of her lungs with every step.

She didn't dare look back, for fear the werewolves were behind her. But no one came, and she left them to their feasting.

THIRTY-NINE

With nothing chasing her, the adrenaline that had pushed Lola forward suddenly ebbed, leaving a hollow emptiness in its wake.

She circled back to the carnival grounds, praying the werewolves would remain preoccupied gorging on pork.

The carnival grounds had been destroyed. Tents torn apart, rides empty and vandalized, carts creaking as they swung in the wind, all the music silenced. Food littered the ground, dropped when people had come back to themselves. Under the heavy odour of grease, it smelled like a slaughterhouse. Lola didn't think she'd ever eat fried food again.

A few straggling carnival-goers wandered the littered paths, crying or staring with blank eyes. "What happened?" A girl her age grabbed her arm, her eyes hollowed with fear. "Where are my friends?"

Lola took her arm, guiding her down the path as quickly as she could stumble. "You have to get out of here; you're in danger here." She rounded up the dazed people, directing them to the front entrance. Lola didn't know how long the werewolves would be distracted by the pigs. "Get somewhere safe. Lock your doors."

People responded to her urgency, perhaps happy to have someone giving them direction. Lola could only imagine what it would be like to wake up, disoriented, unable to remember how they'd ended up here, unsure of what had happened to them. They needed to find shelter. Fast.

"Lola!"

She stopped, her heart leaping into her throat, and turned to find Gael running towards her, his face a mixture of relief and raw panic. She threw herself at him and he caught her, spinning her into his arms and tucking her head against his shoulder.

"Is everyone okay?" Her voice was hoarse from screaming. Gael set her on the ground and ran a thumb over her cheek, trailing the tears that still flowed.

"Because of you, everybody made it out. You led the werewolves away from the crowd and saved them all. God, Lola, what were you thinking? You could have been torn apart." His hands shook slightly as he cupped her shoulders, desperate fear laid bare in his expression.

She would never let him know how close she had come to dying. "I needed to protect them."

His smile was exasperated, but his words were soft, incredulous. "And who made you the guardian of the island?"

"I have to make up for everything I've done, Gael. All that death and destruction. I've been given a second chance at life. But I can't pretend I wasn't a monster before. I need to make amends."

"By risking your life?" Gael brushed her hair away from her face. Though he tried to smile, his eyes betrayed him "You're not Otherworldly anymore."

His words tore at her heart. He couldn't understand, not really. She swallowed hard and looked away. They stood in front of the Maze of Desire, deflated and magicless. Nothing but ripped canvas and broken glass glittering in the moonlight. It mirrored how Lola felt on the inside.

A howl split the air, dragging her back into the moment.

She brushed her tears away. "We can't stay here; it's not safe." She was speaking too fast, the emotions bubbling up inside of her too fast, too much to deal with.

Clinging to each other like shell-shattered refugees, they stumbled through the ruined fairgrounds.

"Lola? Gael?" Nix and Walt called out for them at the front arch as though reluctant to step over the threshold back into the hellish carnival. They looked exhausted, propping each other up. But when they spotted Lola and Gael, relief washed over them.

"Thank God," Nix said, glowering at them as they reached the exit. "What the hell took you so long?"

"Werewolf stuff," Lola said. "Is everyone out?"

"I think so. Everyone but you." Nix frowned at her. "I thought you were dead when the pack went after you like that." She pulled Lola in for a hug, bone-crushingly strong for such a small girl. Lola clung to her, resting her cheek on her hair, happy they'd all made it out alive.

"We did it," she said, giving one last look at the sign for the Carnival of Fools, which tilted drunkenly to the side.

They trudged down the midnight-black path towards Gael's cottage on the outskirts of town. Lola's heart beat harder with each step. She needed to talk to Gael—about everything.

"Nix, Walt," she began, her voice tight. "Can you give us a minute?"

"Why?" Walt asked.

Nix elbowed him, a shrewd look on her face as she took in Lola and Gael. "I'll tell you later," she muttered, tugging him away by the arm.

Once they were alone, Gael put a hand on Lola's cheek. She went fuzzy at his gentle touch.

"Listen, Lola, I know a lot of weird stuff has happened over the past few days. I don't remember it all, and I don't understand it. But we were under some kind of spell, right? Making us do things we wouldn't have normally done." He grimaced. "I remember kissing Cassidy, and it kills me. I never thought I'd betray you like that. You're everything to me and I don't want to lose you. I get you kissed that...wolf too. We were all messed up."

He was offering her an out. They could pretend nothing had ever happened, that it was all a crazy spell, and now that the effects had worn off, they could go back to the way things were.

She pulled out of his arms and took his hands in hers.

"Gael, we need to talk."

He eyed her warily. "And no good conversation has ever started that way."

She tried to smile, but her lips twisted as she forced the words out. "Ever since I've become human, my life has been turned upside down. Everything is confusing; everything I thought I wanted maybe wasn't what I wanted. I've been dealing with emotions that I haven't felt in nearly a hundred years, and it's still a tangled mess."

"I know," he whispered.

She shook her head, feeling helpless. "I don't think you can. You don't know who I was before I came to Duchesne. I was a monster, Gael, worse than the werewolves."

"Not worse than Louis."

"I mean, okay, he was a real piece of work. But so was I. I murdered without a second thought. I have taken so many lives, and I have been drowning in guilt because of it. I'm struggling to deal with it all, being a human with a conscience and a bloody past."

"I still love you despite all of that."

A smile broke through her tears. She believed him, but would he have loved her if they hadn't been to hell and back together? If Lola had never shown up on Duchesne Island, where would Gael be now? Would he be happier?

If what he really wanted, deep down, was to be a normal boy with a normal girlfriend, she would only get in the way. He had the right to try, without her Otherworldly interference.

"You have always had my back, without question," she said, her voice raw. "I trust you entirely with this life of mine. But that doesn't mean we should be together."

"I don't care what you were, what you did. I only want you."

"The thing is, Gael, I don't know what *I* want."

A long, stuttering silence stretched out between them as he held up a hand, as though to stop whatever she was going to say.

She swallowed hard and cleared her throat. "I don't know who I am. I don't know who I was before I became a monster. All I know is that I have to figure that out—alone."

"Let me be the one to help you through this." His voice was a whispered rasp. "I'll wait for you."

"But it might take a lot of time. And I can't promise you I'm ever going to figure things out." Her voice cracked. "I can't promise you *anything*. I wasn't under the spell when I kissed Chann."

He staggered back as though she'd struck him. "But..."

"He understands, Gael, what it is to be a monster. He lives his life in darkness and magic. You want me to be this normal person. And I'll never be that girl." Her hands tightened on his arms, then released him.

Her heart shattered as she saw the hurt in his eyes. He blinked rapidly. "You'll need others in your life, Lola. Nobody can survive all by themselves."

"I know. I have my friends, and I hope that you'll be one."

Gael's forehead wrinkled and he blinked quickly. "But Lola, there's something between us. We're *connected*. You can't tell me what happened in the Well of Souls was nothing."

"Never. What I feel for you is more than I've ever felt before. Gael, you're in my heart, imprinted on my soul. But right now, I need to explore the world on my own, without expectations. I need to be able to mess up, to figure out what's right for me. I can't be what you want me to be right now, and it kills me." She took in a shuddery breath. "But you should have the life that you want. There are other girls…"

"Lola, no." He let out a long breath. "None of them are you."

"I'm sorry." Lola dissolved into sobs, and Gael wrapped his arms around her. She clung to him. She wanted to comfort him, even as she ripped both their hearts out.

They stood there for a timeless moment, unwilling to let each other go because it would mean it was over.

Finally, he pulled out of her arms. The loss of his warmth was like losing a part of her soul again. He gave her one last wild look, then turned away quickly as though he couldn't bear to look at her anymore. He strode down the dark, shambling path towards his cottage until he was lost from view in the darkness.

FORTY

"They found two bodies?"

Faye's voice was low as she navigated the wreckage of what had been the Carnival of Fools. The sun had only just risen and shone with golden light on the broken rides. An early morning mist hung over the ruins, the whole thing like a painting of a dystopian landscape.

They picked their way over smashed food stands destroyed during the worst of the full moon riots. It was the second morning since the madness, and people were starting to put themselves together again after the events of the carnival.

With no reports of wolf sightings or ritual murder, Lola wanted to see what was going on at the Granger Farm. To see if the werewolves had moved on.

To distract her from that thought, Lola opened the *Duchesne Daily* that had appeared on the front stoop that morning, still warm from the press. She scanned it before responding to Faye's question. "Two deaths, that's what this article says."

"But who wrote the paper?" Faye asked. "Richie died, and the rest of the town has been under the influence of whatever the carnival was giving out."

That was the theory put out by the article: hallucinogenic drugs had been given en masse to the islanders and caused memory loss.

Lola flipped to the front of the article. "Written by Matt Vernon. I guess he took over from Richie."

Faye sucked in her breath as she read over Lola's shoulder. "Both deaths were carnival workers. One of the bodies had a six-inch pin embedded in his eye. And the other death appears to be from self-inflicted wounds. He also had an eye missing but wore a golden eye plate...what the hell were they getting up to at this carnival?"

Faye's face got that hazy look as though she were trying to remember what happened, her mind puzzling over pieces she couldn't quite fit together. Lola wasn't sure if she should fill in her blanks.

She also didn't want to bring up the fact that Faye had said she wanted her out of her apartment, but it was a discussion they needed to have.

Slowly, Lola folded the paper and shuffled along the path littered with garbage. "Listen, Faye, there are some things we need to talk about."

The shine in Faye's eyes told her she remembered at least some of what happened. "Like cash and passports kind of things?"

Lola nodded. "You asked me to leave if I couldn't be honest with you."

"Lola, it was said in the heat of the moment." Faye's face crinkled and she reached out as though to stop Lola from speaking.

"But you weren't wrong." Lola stopped and faced her. "How can we share each other's space without trust? You want to know about my past, but the truth is, there are a lot of things I can't tell you. And I don't know if I'll ever be able to. Whether you believe me or not, it's safer if you don't know."

Faye's face softened, her tears quick to rise. "After everything

I've been through, I end up acting like every adult in my life who refused to listen to *me* when I was in trouble."

"No, it's not like that." Lola wrapped an arm around Faye.

"I didn't handle it well," Faye whispered. "I know you have a past, and it scares me. I thought I could offer you something I didn't have when I was your age, but I messed it all up."

"You have every right to question me. But you also have to accept that we must keep some secrets from each other." Lola gently eased back, and Faye mopped her face with her sleeve. "I'm not the same person I was, in part because of you." Faye's face crumpled at her words, and Lola squeezed her hand. "You saw me and gave me a safe place to land. I'll never forget that."

"I would do it again in a heartbeat. I don't want you to feel that you have to leave."

Lola nodded. "I'd be happy to stay, Faye. But we need to come to a different understanding. Having me as your ward will not always be easy, but I need my freedom. I'm not a normal teenage girl, and it won't work if we try to pretend that I am."

"I get it, Lola. I was trying to keep you safe."

"I'm trying to keep you safe as well. And you need to trust me enough to let me do my own thing. One thing we need to discuss is that I'm actually pretty wealthy. I'm only going to stay here if I pay you rent and contribute to the household."

"But I thought you were..."

Lola could only imagine what she was thinking. Homeless? Orphaned? Poor?

"But," Lola continued, "to access my wealth, I'm going to have to take a trip."

"And your wealth comes from where exactly?"

Lola held her gaze for a long time. "I could tell you it's the inheritance from a wealthy relative."

Faye looked away. "Right. This probably has to do with all your passports."

"Are you going to be okay with this?"

Faye raised her chin. "I don't care how you made your money. I've done what I've had to do in the past, and I won't respect you any less, no matter what you've done."

In those words, Faye undid a knot that had been sitting inside Lola's heart. Love and support that bore no strings, that had no conditions. This was her true, deepest desire.

She turned back to the ruined carnival, unable to face the woman who was filling her with such light. "I didn't realize how much I needed to hear that."

"Can I come with you? Wherever you're going? I could get the others to cover the café for a few days."

Lola shuddered at the thought of Faye getting involved with her contacts in the Otherworld. "I don't know how long I'll be gone. It's something I have to do on my own. But I promise I'll come back."

Faye sighed. She still feared Lola would skip town and never return. "I'll take you at your word, then. Are you planning on being here in the fall? Because I just put in the paperwork for you to start at the high school. That was presumptuous of me, but there was a deadline, and I didn't know how to ask. You don't have to go if you don't want to."

Lola let out a breath. Of course, she would be expected to go to school. It wasn't necessary. Lola's knowledge and resources were more than enough to get by in the world. But it would be something her friends would be doing. She could join them and have the typical teenage experience. Even the awkwardness of having to sit in class next to her ex-boyfriend.

"I'd like that," she said, realizing how true it was.

Faye hesitated, then looked up at her. "I am sorry I've handled things badly. I'm protective of you, Lola. I want you to be safe above all."

"The world isn't a safe place, though. We have to take the risks to get to the joy. That's the only way to have the full human experience."

As they passed through some abandoned stands, a splash of colour caught Lola's eye. Under the folds of a fallen pennant, she spotted the corner of one of Conri's paintings, the one that reminded her of the thrill of the hunt.

She teased the artwork out from under the wreckage and angled it for Faye to examine.

"What do you think?"

Faye stood back and inspected it as though she were in an art gallery, studying it from all angles. "It's interesting," she said finally.

"There are some similar pieces at the National Gallery I remember seeing when I was in Europe."

Lola grinned; little did Faye know that they could very well have been by the same artist.

"I like it." Lola gave a firm nod and rolled the painting up and brought it with her. It would be the first thing she'd decorate her room with—a reminder of the part of her she couldn't forget and a memory of a man who had struggled with his monster as she did.

Figures emerged from behind the carousel, hazy in the morning mist.

Lola froze, instinctively stepping in front of Faye. Would they have to make a run for it, or was it only other townspeople, drawn by the wreckage?

Then one of the figures approached, his strides long and confident, and she recognized Chann's broad shoulders. Despite the horrors she'd endured the past few days, a smile tugged at her lips.

"Faye, there's someone I need to talk to. Alone."

"Are you sure?" Faye gave the carnival workers a dubious look. But there was no need for a fight today.

"Don't worry, they're...friends." Lola wasn't sure if a group of werewolves who tried to rip her apart could be considered friends but had no idea how best to describe them.

Faye's eyes were shaded with worry, but she nodded. "This is probably one of those times where I just have to trust you, isn't it?"

"It is. I'll see you back at the café?"

"The pain au chocolat will be waiting for you."

The very idea sounded delicious; Lola didn't plan on lingering here.

She stepped forward to meet Chann, her arms wrapped around herself. Seeing him in the stark daylight, after what they had done in the dark hours, made her feel raw, exposed.

Chann seemed different—he radiated a new, powerful energy.

If she had doubted whether he'd become the alpha of the wolf pack, she didn't anymore. His movement was deliberate, his steps purposeful with a quiet power. The air shimmered silver around him as though he warped the space he moved through with magic.

"How's my favourite former vampire?" he said. His voice was rich with his Irish brogue, but she sensed the softness of apologies behind it.

She let out a little laugh. "Still alive, which is more than I thought I'd be a few nights ago. How's my favourite alpha werewolf?"

His silver-tinged gaze held steady as he bowed his head in front of her. "Extremely sorry for everything you were put through." His voice dropped lower. "Lola, what happened the other night...what could have happened—it makes me sick to think of the part I played in it."

Lola held up her hand to stop him. "Chann, I understand. It wasn't you."

"What you did was incredible, though. I'm free, thanks to you."

A growling snort came behind him.

Otsana stalked forward as though to attack Lola. Chann lifted one of his hands calmly, and she stopped short, a few paces from Lola.

"Not all of us are free, though." Otsana bared her teeth, still somehow too large for her mouth.

"I guess not," Lola said. "But doesn't it matter who you're bound to? I mean, Louis is gone. That must count for something."

Otsana tilted her head, her silver eyes glittering under her heavy lashes, and finally she shrugged. "I will not miss him."

"And no more turning people into pigs?"

"We'll see about that." With a furious glare at Chann, Otsana stalked away.

"So now things can change." Lola raised an eyebrow at Chann. "They are going to change, aren't they?"

He nodded slowly, deliberately. "I intend to do things differently. I've had a long time to think about it."

"So you won't be killing people anymore?"

His gaze sharpened, silver knives, and Lola forced herself not to flinch. "We're still monsters, Lola, and we were made to hunt. My first responsibility is to the pack, to ensure they're taken care of."

Apprehension bubbled inside of her as the full effect of Chann's power crashed over her. He was promising that werewolves would behave on their instincts, but would that mean hunting down humans? Would Chann become more of a monster than Louis?

But then he smiled, and a flash of the Belfast pickpocket he'd once been broke through his serious demeanour. "Don't worry, Lola." He winked. "I'll make sure nobody's enchanted by the carnival ever again."

"No more desire spells?"

Even as she said it, a twinge of longing for him rose inside her, and she forced it down. The werewolves were leaving, and Chann along with them.

His smile was knowing. "No more desire spells. I'm sticking with the real thing from now on."

His gaze lingered, appreciative, frank enough to cause Lola's cheeks to flame with heat, and he chuckled, dimples forming. His charm was even more potent with his newfound power, and Chann needed to get off the island before she lost all her self-control.

She squared her shoulders. "Right, but you plan to continue the carnival?"

Chann shrugged, surveying what was left of the midway. "Why not? We'll have some work to do to get things into shape again, but it's what we know. It makes us money and keeps us moving. A werewolf life is nomadic; it works for us." His eyes were silver discs like the moon, and in his words, she could almost hear the lonely howling of a wolf pack. "Besides, I think I'd make an excellent master of ceremonies." He lifted his hand to his forehead and bowed with a flourish as though he had already stepped into Louis's top hat.

"As long as you're not luring people in to eat them, I think it could work."

He let out a bark of laughter. "I'll work on that."

His humour faded quickly. "In all seriousness, though, I'm not the only one dealing with changes. The power on the island is only growing, and it's attracting the Otherworld. I'm worried about what other creatures are going to be drawn to Duchesne Island." His gaze settled on her. "You seem to be at the heart of everything, too, and I don't want you to get hurt."

"I'll be fine," she said, though his concern was justified. She'd like to be fine, but Lola had no idea *why* this power was overflowing, let alone how she could stop it. How could she protect everyone if she was the reason they were in danger?

Chann's look was rife with skepticism. "Sure you will. But if things get out of control, or if you need help, you can always reach out. You've earned my loyalty, Lola; in giving me this power, I owe you a great debt."

She smiled at the thought. "Should I just send a text to the Carnival of Fools?"

He grinned and reached under the collar of his shirt. He pulled out a long chain with a dog tag at the end of it and lifted it over his head, handing it to her. The metal was still warm from his skin.

"Silver," she said turning it over. "Conri's work?"

Chann nodded. "An interesting spell is attached to that one. If you wear it, I'll get the message that you want me." His gaze was penetrating and his cheeks flushed. "I mean, if you need my help, I'll come."

Lola slowly let the chain pool in her palm, staring at it so she didn't have to meet his eyes. "Thank you, Chann. This is a great gift, although I hope I don't ever have to use it."

His smirk returned, lazy and devastating. "Well, if you're ever interested in someone warm-blooded, you can use it too. I'll be by your side in a flash."

"Chann..." He was going to make her say it. "I'm taking some time on my own right now. Figure out the whole human thing without men or monsters to distract me."

"Well, you can't blame me for trying." He flashed her a silver wink and turned back towards his pack. "Be seeing you around, Lola."

FORTY-ONE

Lola still held the dog tag in her hand when she strolled down Main Street, the early morning light casting long shadows across the pavement. She wasn't looking for anyone in her life right now, but Chann had a way of making her moony.

She was nearly at the café, picking up the smell of fresh coffee and chocolate, when an out-of-place figure jolted her back to reality. She tucked the dog tag into her pocket and veered towards the library.

Marissa stood at the top of the stairs, squinting in the sunshine like she hadn't seen it in years

Lola smirked. "Nice to get confirmation you're not a vampire."

Marissa didn't respond. Her skin was blanched as white as parchment, her breath coming out in short, rapid bursts.

Lola's amusement faded. "What is it? What happened?"

Marissa shoved a paper at Lola, the one where she'd scribbled the symbol she'd seen burned into Reiko's skin. "Are you sure this is what you saw? Branded into someone's flesh?"

Slowly, Lola took the paper out of Marissa's hand. It had been softened, nearly shredded by worried fingers. "Yes, this is the symbol. Did you find something?"

"The books turned up nothing."

Lola frowned. "So...we're at a dead end?"

Marissa shook her head. "No, you don't understand, Lola. The books *never* tell me nothing. They've never been so silent; to be honest, it's the first real peace I've gotten since they started acting up months ago." She swallowed hard. "For them to have nothing to say, it must mean that information regarding this symbol is . protected."

"Protected how? By who?" Lola let out a sigh of frustration. "I guess that means we're nowhere."

"I didn't say that." From out of her skirt pocket, Marissa pulled a small leather tome and handed it to Lola with trembling hands.

The mark was seared into the cover.

Lola sucked in a breath. "Where did you find it?"

"My father's personal effects. This is his journal.

Lola's fingers traced the burned symbol. "And this? The mark?"

"It's the Order of the Hanta Cythraul."

"Hanta Cythraul." Lola sounded out the foreign name. "Never heard of them."

"From what I've learned from the journal, they're a secret society of demon hunters." Marissa's voice dropped to a whisper. "And I think my father is one of them."

Acknowledgments

Writing may seem like an individual sport, but the process of getting a book created and ready for consumption is decidedly a team effort. Even when you're "doing it alone" you need to have a whole team backing you up, and I'm lucky to have an amazing team on my side.

Thank you to Marilyn Boake for her insight and eye for detail. Your support of this series has been monumental and I couldn't ask for a better editor.

Thank you to Steph Whitaker, who is such a talented writer, who critiqued the manuscript (and called me out when I tried to be lazy!). I really appreciate your author's intuition.

Thank you to Nika Teran for your continued support and insight into this series. And thank you to the Brown Cat Press team for the enthusiastic encouragement as I continue my journey as an author.

As always, thank you to my family. To Marilyn Smith for being my number one fan, always, and for always being there for me. For Zach Magnan, without your support and encouragement I would have never made it this far. And to Alexandre and Élodie, because everything I do, I do for you.

ABOUT THE AUTHOR

Cordelia Kelly is the author of the YA paranormal series *The Port of Lost Souls* and the standalone fantasy novel *The Sibyl and the Thief*, which earned the *BookLife Editor's Pick* designation. Her short fiction has been featured in numerous horror anthologies, including "Herbalista" in *Prairie Witch* and "Dare to Survive" in *Dark & Stormy*. She also released a chilling collection of horror shorts, *Then She Said Hush*, featuring her award-winning post-apocalyptic tale "Unfreeze."

When she's not crafting spine-tingling stories, Cordelia designs francophone greeting cards, creates intricate fantasy maps, and shares her love of nostalgia by writing recaps of R.L. Stine's *Fear Street* series on her blog, *Shadyside Snark*.

THE SEABOURNE LEGACY

Port of Lost Souls Three

When Lola Monteux returns to Port Despardoux after a long journey abroad, she brings back more than the fortune she amassed during her vampire past—she carries with her information about an ancient order of demon hunters that has established operations on her island. But home isn't as she left it. Her tight-knit group of friends has unraveled as grudges threaten to tear them apart.

When danger strikes, the group is forced to take refuge in the hidden passageways beneath Walt Seabourne's sprawling estate. What begins as a fascinating exploration of the mansion's secrets soon spirals into a waking nightmare as they uncover dark truths buried within its walls. Old magic stirs, awakening vengeful forces tied to the estate's tragic history.

As the hauntings grow more perilous, Lola must lead her friends in unraveling a sinister mystery. Someone—or something—is targeting them, and with each new discovery, the stakes rise.

The cost of failure isn't just their friendship—it could be one of their lives.

Chapter One

The firelight danced across the polished wood of the Seabourne Estate study, casting restless shadows over walls lined with leather-bound tomes and ancient maps. The room's grandeur might have at some point impressed Lola, but tonight it was stifling, weighted as she was by the unease smoldering inside her since stepping off the boat this afternoon.

With her back to the crackling fire, a stack of papers in her hands, she stood in front of her friends like a professor giving a lecture. Six weeks since she'd left the island, to go digging—both literally and metaphorically. She'd scoured archives, traded favours with old contacts and taken risks she shouldn't have.

But as she faced the three people sitting in front of her, their expressions cast in amber light, she worried her findings weren't enough.

"The Order of Hanta Cythraul." Lola's voice cut through the quiet like the snap of a closing book. "A secret society of demon hunters, centuries old, ruthless and relentless. And now, they're here, and after all my searching I still have no idea what kind of threat they pose."

The faces in front of her reflected varying degrees of tension.

At times like these, the chasm between herself and her friends seemed unfathomable, formed by her years of supernatural experiences and choices they could never fully understand.

She barely understood herself these days, caught between what she used to be and what she was trying to become.

Walt leaned back in his chair, a picture of practiced indifference. His expression, as ever, was unreadable. He could have been planning an escape or simply wondering what was for dinner. Nix, by contrast, bristled with urgency, her brows furrowed as though her thoughts were already sprinting ahead, assembling a thousand theories.

And then there was Gael, arms crossed, eyes dark and defiant, daring her to explain herself. His silence was the loudest.

Lola resisted the urge to flinch under his gaze, a reminder that some wounds couldn't be smoothed over with apologies or time. She swallowed hard and pressed on. "From what I've discovered, the Order of Hanta Cythraul isn't some harmless group of folk-lorists. These people are trained with weapons from childhood, with centuries of blood on their hands."

She took a breath, drawing on the resolve that had carried her through the past six weeks of relentless travel and sleepless nights. Her fingers tightened, the edges of the papers crumpling under her grip. "What I don't understand," she continued, her voice low and taut, "is why I've never heard of them before."

"Six weeks away, and this is what you came up with?" Gael waved a dismissive hand. "Seems like a lot of nothing, after what you put Faye through worrying about you. All of us—" Gael caught himself and looked away.

Despite herself, her stomach twisted. She'd hurt him, and he wasn't ready to let her forget it—not that she deserved to. Still, she wished he could see that leaving wasn't just running away. It was a matter of survival.

"I'm sorry I worried you," Lola said, a healthy wave of guilt crashing over her. Since breaking up they hadn't been in contact;

she'd hopped on a boat a few days after and disappeared for more than a month. She'd messaged him, but he never responded. "I kept Faye up to date with everything I was doing. Well, the parts I could tell her."

"So, you travelled around digging up treasure you set aside for a rainy day?" Nix's sea-blue eyes sparkled at the thought.

"Something like that. I also liquidated some assets, moved some funds around."

"It was dangerous though, right? By doing that you could let your old crew know that you're still alive." Gael's eyes glittered dangerously in the firelight as he watched her.

Lola sighed. It had been a risk she'd had to take. "I only went through bank accounts I'm sure Jacquotte knew nothing about. I've been storing assets for decades, away from the crew's prying eyes. But Nix wasn't far off; I had several caches of treasure actually buried in the ground. I exchanged them and made it seem like it was the inheritance coming from my recently deceased father in Paris. Which is the reason I've been gone for so long, in case anyone asks."

"All of this so you can get a new wardrobe?" Gael gestured at Lola's outfit. True, the clothes she wore were very different from what they were used to seeing her in: hand-me-downs or stolen sweaters. Now, she wore grey wool trousers with a white silk t-shirt and leather loafers. She shivered in delight at the luxe fabrics that brushed gently over her skin.

"Yes, I went shopping. Did you want me to live off Faye forever? Thanks to dearly departed papa, I'm a wealthy girl. And this is money I will use to set myself up as a human, Gael. This is me starting my life. I won't apologize for that."

"Don't apologize for any of it!" Nix clasped her hands together, practically bouncing on her toes. "Do you know how jealous I am, that you got to get off this island? That you went to New York City?" She gave her a mock-serious look. "Next time you have to smuggle me in your suitcase. I won't even need snacks or air holes. Just pack me between your sweaters and I'm good to go."

"I'm sure we could give you a few air holes," Lola said.

Nix grin softened and she tucked a strand of copper hair behind her ear. "Someday, though," she said, almost to herself. "I'll see all of it. The world's too big to stay in one place forever, right?"

Lola couldn't help smiling at her friend's enthusiasm. "I kept this for you. For when you visit." She handed Nix a folded paper from her bag: New York's subway map.

Hands trembling, Nix opened the map, her finger following the criss-crossing coloured lines. "I've always wanted to go," she said, her voice scratchy. "It's just that..."

"You'll go, someday," Lola said. "We'll go together. I can show you...everything."

"That sounds like pure freedom; to just go anywhere you want, nothing holding you back." The longing was tangible in her gaze. "I've never left this island, you know."

"Really? Not even to go to the mainland?"

Nix shook her head, scarlet flushing over her cheeks. "It sounds ridiculous, I know, but between helping out at the shop and taking care of the kids, not to mention my dad needing to run the lighthouse every night, there's just no time for us to get off the island. And it's expensive..."

"It'll happen, I promise you. Oh, I'll show you Paris!"

Nix looked as though she wanted to bottle that promise. "You don't know what it's like, being stuck here. Even Gael has gone places."

"I've been to Halifax. Twice." Gael's gaze softened as he took in his friend. "So I'm not exactly your expert world traveller."

"And I only ever go to posh resorts so my parents can brag about them," Walt added. "Trust me when I say they're not pleasant experiences."

"But Lola, you've seen everything." Nix let her fingers trail over the lines on the map, tracing out her hunger to explore.

"But I've never seen the world during the day."

Gael's gaze never left hers. She could implode from the heat behind them; there was more than anger simmering there. "And leave everyone else behind, right?"

"It's not like that." Lola found she couldn't meet his eyes. Surely wanting to explore the world as a human wasn't a crime? Freedom was supposed to feel lighter than this. It wasn't supposed to feel like she had to cut ties with the people who grounded her. But the thought of staying, of letting the world shrink around her again, was unbearable.

"How did you get back into the country?" Walt asked, oblivious to the tension. "I'm assuming you're carrying more cash than would be considered legal?"

Lola cleared her throat, relieved to be released from Gael's gaze. "You're not wrong. I still have contacts along the coast. I sailed with an old friend from Maine across the Bay of Fundy, missing unfriendly ports that might ask questions. Like who I am, and why I'm carrying tens of thousands of dollars on my person."

Nix let out a choking gasp at the sum, as Gael scowled. "You smuggled money into the country."

Lola let out an impatient huff. "I can't actually operate under the confines of your government here. My very existence is a lie. Yes, I'll have to bend some rules to survive. That's how I've made it this far."

His eyes glinted darkly. "Lola Monteux, morally grey since 1942. You don't think the rules apply to you at all, do you?"

A loaded silence descended between them as Lola and Gael faced off. She raised her chin defiantly, wondering what other accusations he was going to throw at her.

Nix cleared her throat. "Back to the order of the Hanta Cis-whatever," Nix said, tripping over the word. She brushed her red curls out of her face with a brusque hand. "The Order of the HC. Reiko is one of them, a demon hunter? Like, they are a part of the Otherworld?"

Nix had fallen for Reiko over the summer, but the girl hadn't been honest about who she was, or why she was here. She'd used Nix's crush to get closer to Lola and her ties to the Otherworld.

"She's a part of the Order, but I'm not sure of their actual place within the Otherworld. It seems to be influenced by the mythology of many cultures, from Japanese to Scandinavian—a real international mix. They must take secrecy seriously, though. I was a vampire for eighty years and I've never heard of them before."

"Where did you get this information?" Walt stood and began to pace, tracing his finger along the book spines. "If they're so secret."

"I tapped all my old contacts in the Otherworld, at least the ones that were still safe to approach," Lola said. With her fragile human body, she found travelling through the Otherworld took a toll on her. She returned to the island exhausted, dark shadows spreading under her eyes and barely able to put one foot in front of the other.

While she travelled, she felt stretched thin, as though her essence was drifting away from her. She would wake up with her head foggy, full of dreams of the oak forest of Duchesne, the memory of a voice calling out to her already forgotten. These dreams had followed her every night until she resisted falling asleep.

Dreams weren't her biggest fear, though. Far scarier were her demon contacts, now that she was no longer a vampire. Some would have known immediately that she was now human, and she stayed away from them. Others were a decent bet they wouldn't kill her on sight, and she tried her luck with those. Very little had any good information. The Order of Hanta Cythraul was more legend than reality.

"I wish I could have gotten information on what they want, and if they're a threat to us."

"If it helps, Reiko has started at Duchesne High School and is now right in there with the hyenas," Nix said, referring to the pack of popular kids who had bullied her most of her life. "Besties with Sam Lynch, if you can believe it."

"That *is* shocking," Lola said. "Sam is a nightmare. Maybe Reiko thinks *she's* a demon."

"Why are we assuming the Order is bad?" Gael asked. "I mean, isn't killing demons good?"

"But what is their agenda? *Why* are they killing demons?"

"To make the world a better place?" Gael raised his eyebrows as though this was obvious. "Demons are evil, they kill demons. I'm pretty sure I'm on their side."

"Not all demons are evil, Gael." When he snorted, she rolled her eyes. "Not all creatures from the Otherworld deserve to die. Some are very good; some are neutral, just trying to live their lives."

He wouldn't let up with his hard stare. "But do they deserve to live in our world?"

Lola placed her hand over her mouth, hiding the quiver. Gael had changed so much from the innocent boy he was before she'd introduced him to the wicked side of the Otherworld. Before he met her, Gael would have believed in kindness before all; she wouldn't have to convince him that not everyone from the Otherworld deserved to die.

She had done this to him; taken someone wholly good and brought darkness into his life.

Glancing away, she concentrated on the room where her friends huddled around the carved mahogany desk. The Seabourne's study reflected their wealth and status on Duchesne Island: his father a wealthy trader and his mother, the mayor. The study was scented with the faint vanilla aroma of pipe tobacco.

Her gaze caught on a particularly dark and foreboding painting that graced the wall behind the desk, of a dour man in a stiff pose glowering down at them all.

"Walt, this guy looks just like you."

Nix let out a snicker and Walt coughed. "Thanks, Lola."

"I mean, not his expression. But look at the eyes, and the jaw. If you turn out to be a miserable old man who kicks puppies, this would be you."

"I will hug puppies every day from here on out, then." Walt approached the portrait with wary steps. "My illustrious ancestor, the very first Walter Seabourne. He made the family fortune."

"Let me guess, through hard work and good deeds?" Gael asked.

Walt's smile lacked humour. "He was a rumrunner during Prohibition. Duchesne Island was a great place to smuggle contraband booze; the massive network of caves on the island was a perfect hiding place. I've even heard legends that this house was built with tunnels that access the caves. Apparently, the original Walt Seabourne became paranoid as his smuggling business got serious and the whole place is full of secret passageways, hiding places and escape routes."

"Have you ever found anything?" Nix's eyes were round.

"A few." Walt's gaze sought out the darkened shadows of the study. "When my army of nannies grew tired of me, I went exploring the dark nooks of the house. So that's where my family fortune came from. Criminal activity."

He sounded glum, so Lola nudged him. "Don't worry, most of them do."

Gael snorted, but Lola couldn't tell if it was scornful or if he was trying to hold in a laugh.

When she looked at him, he schooled his face into passive indifference. "You start school tomorrow, then," he said. "Two weeks late."

Lola waved her hand. "I'm sure the tragic passing of my father in France will help smooth things over. I'll admit I'm a bit nervous. My education has been...thorough...in many ways, but I've never been to a formal school. That I can remember, anyway."

"How did Faye explain that one?" Walt asked.

"She only repeated what I told her," Lola said of her guardian.

"I attended a boarding school in Europe that focused on life experience."

"Like treasure hunting and jewelry heists?" Nix asked. "But nothing about calculus?"

Lola let out a pent-up breath. "After everything that's happened, I just want things to go smoothly. Keep my head down and get through these next two years."

"I don't really get why you're doing this." Gael's words began to heat up again. "Going to high school. It seems so trivial compared to what you've done. I mean, you have all your money. You have all your *life experiences.* Why bother?"

"Staying on the island for another two years and completing high school gives me an effective backstory. I can go to university and develop an actual normal human life. I want to be free to do whatever I want."

"You'll stay for two years, and then what? See you later? *Sayonara* Faye, I'm done using you, too!" His words spurted out in a jumble, then he reared back, as though he hadn't meant to say that.

"I'm not using Faye; I never meant to use anyone." Her shoulders slumped. Starting over was supposed to be simple: hide in plain sight, finish school, build a life. But the shadows of her past were never far behind. "She's aware that I'm not planning on spending my whole life on Duchesne, and she *wants* that for me. It's a normal thing to want."

"I still don't understand why being normal matters to you."

"You don't have to." Lola swallowed the snap in her voice. "I've never had the chance; my life was taken from me. It's fine if you don't get that."

"I just think you're being unfair to Faye. It's obvious she cares about you and you're already preparing to check out of her life."

"That's not what I'm doing at all!" Lola stormed towards him, getting close enough that she had to crane her neck up to take in the near-foot difference in their height. She was tired of dancing around his hurt feelings. A spark of heat erupted in her chest. The way his eyes lit up, she was certain he felt as well, whether it came from anger or desire. She pointed a finger in his face. "How dare you—"

The door to the study flung open. Standing on the threshold, lit up by the light of the fire with a swath of darkness behind her, stood Walt's mother, pale as a ghost.

"Your father is coming," she said in a strained whisper.

The Seabourne Legacy, coming October 2025

Sign up for the newsletter to stay up to date!

READ THE WELL OF SOULS

Don't miss out on the heart-racing beginning of the Port of Lost Souls series. Find out how Lola found her way to Duchesne Island.

Get The Well of Souls now

Lola Monteux, a treasure-hunting vampire, is betrayed by her crew and sentenced to death. Desperate to evade her fate, she embarks on a daring escape to a haunted island cursed for her kind. Her solitary mission: to unearth the fabled Well of Souls treasure, rumoured to bestow invincibility upon demons like her and grant her the freedom she craves.

But as Lola succumbs to the enchantment of the island, a powerful magic weaves its spell around her. She is inexplicably drawn to Gael, a local boy, and his group of misfit friends. Undercover as a teenager, Lola discovers the joys and vulnerabilities of her long-lost humanity, and begins to lose sight of her original mission —to secure her survival at any cost.

DISCOVER THE SIBYL AND THE THIEF

Invisible, cursed, and running out of time, Sabine Gillesella's only hope lies in the hands of a blind orphan—the only one who can see her.

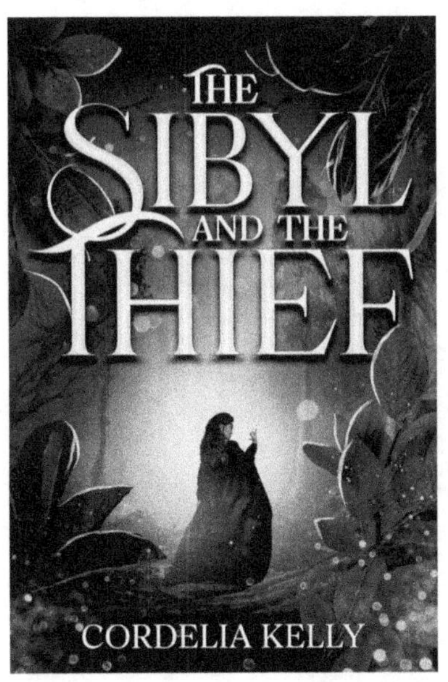

Get The Sibyl and the Thief here

Sabine Gillesella has betrayed her people by working as a spy for Duke Aurich, the most powerful man in Illyamor. But now she has been cursed with invisibility and her time is running out before she fades away completely. When she meets Anora, a blind orphan who swears she knows how to help her, Sabine must follow her through a haunted forest, or risk losing more than her life.

Bound by fate, Sabine and Anora uncover truths that challenge who they are, revealing a destiny greater than they ever believed. As the land crumbles around them, they must summon the courage to weave the fabric of the realm back together and restore balance to a world on the brink of collapse.